getting over

jack wagner

elise juska

doWn tOwn press

New York   London   Toronto   Sydney   Singapore

An *Original* Publication of POCKET BOOKS

A Downtown Press Book published by
POCKET BOOKS, a division of Simon & Schuster, Inc.
1230 Avenue of the Americas, New York, NY 10020

ISBN: 0-7434-6467-2

First Downtown Press printing April 2003

10   9   8   7   6   5

DOWNTOWN PRESS and colophon are trademarks of
Simon & Schuster, Inc.

For information regarding special discounts for bulk purchases,
please contact Simon & Schuster Special Sales at 1-800-456-6798
or business@simonandschuster.com

Designed by Jaime Putorti

Printed in the U.S.A.

acknowledgments

I am very lucky to have had such talented writers and supportive friends help see this book along its way: Kerry Reilly, Clark Knowles, Kevin Bresnahan, Kieran Juska, Diana Kash. Thanks to Margaret-Love Denman, whose workshop gave rise to the original story, and Bob and Peggy Boyers at *Salmagundi* for publishing it. To Whitney Lee, for her constant support and infectious energy, and Lauren McKenna, for her no-frills advice and vast CD collection. To Ben, for the Jams; Amanda and Brian, for the brainstorms; Brian and Therese, for fielding many neurotic questions; and Maureen, for falling for Jack Wagner in 1984 and never completely getting over him.

For my parents

Frisco: *Once upon a time there was a rock star who met a princess . . .*
Robin: *Did they live happily ever after?*
Frisco: *Isn't that how all good stories end?*

—General Hospital

1

bass guitarists

SIDE A

"Welcome to Paradise" —Green Day
"Cool Rock Boy" —Juliana Hatfield
"Summertime Rolls" —Jane's Addiction
"Man in the Box" —Alice in Chains
"Higher Ground" —Red Hot Chili Peppers

As Karl the Bass Guitarist cruises along the Garden State Parkway at 90 mph in a black Saab Turbo 9000 with Rage Against the Machine's *Evil Empire* thumping through the two amp–eight driver audio system, I suspect it will soon be over between us. We are heading into the depths of New Jersey, where I will be meeting Karl's mother for the first time.

"My mom's going to be stoked," Karl pronounces, jerking to a stop at the bottom of the off ramp. He reaches out and flicks the volume down. "I don't usually bring chicks home."

"Oh?"

"She doesn't even know we're coming."

"Wow."

Karl gazes at me from behind his black shades and reaches over to knead my thigh. He has no idea what he's set himself up for. Historically, to meet a rock star's mother is to be exposed to the parts of himself he hides on stage. It's to discover his embarrassing memories and vulnerabilities, every bad haircut, nickname, wet bed, lunch box, moon walk, band uniform and early eighties cassette he's ever tried to deny and leave behind. These are just the kinds of intimate details I try to avoid in a person.

I stare hard at the flapping windshield wipers until the light turns green. "Green," I pounce.

When Karl doesn't react, I point at the window. "The light. It's green."

"Oh." Karl gives my knee a squeeze, turns the Rage back up, and stomps on the gas. "Cool."

Karl is oblivious to our immediate danger as he speeds toward his mother's house. "Oblivious" sums up Karl's role during most of our thirty-three-day stint as a couple. We are your basic girl-meet-rock-star story: met on a Friday night, at The Blue Room, where his band (Electric Hoagie) was making its debut. Most of the rock stars I date these days I meet in The Blue Room, a two-story bar/coffee shop in Philadelphia. Like me, the place is equal parts Philly and arty: the first floor has comfy *Friends*-style couches, giant cups and frothing lattes, while the bar upstairs is presided over by battered dartboards, black light, and a beer-gutted bouncer named Ron who smells like fried steak. By the back wall of the bar squats a scuffed plywood stage.

As the Hoagies tuned up, I studied Karl the Bass Guitarist.

Physically, he was dateable. Mid- to late-twenties, thin but toned, reddish crewcut, sharp blue eyes, two gold hoops in his left lobe, one in his right brow, shadow of scruff from jaw to chin. He was wearing army shorts shredded at the bottoms and a black T-shirt that said TRY ME.

Mid-set, I caught his eye as he screamed lyrics inches from the mic.

Post-set, he found me lingering deliberately near the bar.

"Hey," he said.

"Hey."

From there, it was pretty much textbook: a) I complimented the band, b) he bought me a beer, c) we found a pockmarked booth where we gulped our drinks and talked music and life and suffering-as-art while the blacklight made his teeth and eye whites shine like minnows in a tank, and d) we went back to his pad—even used the term "pad"—a basement apartment with shag rug, lava lamp, surly cactus.

"You're beautiful," he said, voice thick with Bud Light.

"Thanks."

"No. I mean it."

"So do I."

He ran one calloused fingertip down the side of my face. "I could really get into knowing you," he murmured, and looked deep into my eyes.

Deep.

Since making his first move, Karl's role in our relationship has not been too proactive. What we do and when we do it has been left largely up to me. I'm like the Events Coordinator—

dialing movie theaters, reserving concert tickets, cooking my famous tuna casserole—while Karl watches what transpires between us as if it's happening of its own accord. Sometimes, when he looks up from plucking his guitar, he'll squint his eyes and bob his head as if absorbing my tiny apartment for the first time: the table set for two, beanbag chairs, melting candles, VH1's *Rock Across America,* a fat cat. Me.

Karl is thumping the heel of his hand on the steering wheel. It's raining hard now. The car feels like a sauna.

He nods out the window, then says something I can't make out.

"What?" I yell over the music.

"Main"—he mouths exaggeratedly—*"drag."*

It's one of the saddest main drags I've ever seen. The awning above the strip of stores reminds me of a giant dish towel, long, limp, and dripping. Underneath it, the store windows are crowded with merchandise found only in closets and garages, paper products and cleaning products and lawn ornaments shaped like tulips and ducks.

"Quaint," I reply.

I should clarify: this trip to meet Karl's mother does not have any deep significance. It was not planned in advance to further our relationship or symbolize our growth or affirm our commitment or any of the things Hannah (my best friend) and Alan (her "partner") always seem to be doing. It was a plan born of boredom: a rainy Sunday in June, and Karl's sudden recollection that his mother had things for him to pick up at the house.

Which doesn't surprise me. In my experience, rock stars'

mothers are the most coddling mothers around, the type who like to feed and pinch and dress their sons even when they're over thirty. It leads me to suspect that most rock stars were mamas' boys growing up. That their entire musical careers might, in fact, be delayed rebellions for the overprotection they endured as boys.

But look closely, and you'll discover most rock stars are still mamas' boys at heart. Check inside their fridges: tinfoiled frozen lasagnas, homemade chicken soup, crustless egg salad sandwiches. Bathroom cabinets: cartoon Band-Aids, Flintstones vitamins, bottles of cherry-flavored cold medicine. In public, they might use the meds for recreation, swigging them for a preshow buzz. But I've found that, in reality, most rock stars are nothing like they seem.

I imagine it's something like the way other women are drawn to athletic men. Or outdoorsy, spiritual men. Men who make fruit shakes and have firm soccer calves. Men with blond childbearing genes and conservative mutual funds. Mine sounds like a ridiculous preoccupation, I realize, one that any literate, college-educated woman should have outgrown by age twenty-six. And, in most areas of my life, I am open to new experiences. I've tried roller blading and tae bo. I ate hummus, once. I read *The Beauty Myth,* twice. I recycle and vote. I borrowed Hannah's Buddhism books and, for ten days, practiced finding my center on the commuter rail.

Still, there is something about a rock star I want. I use the term "rock star" loosely, of course. They don't have to be actual stars (which is fortunate, since they never are). They don't even have to play rock music (though it's preferred). I've dabbled in classical, jazz, rap, even (briefly) show tunes. The reasons behind my infatuation are not entirely clear, even to me. It's not as simple as looking for a mate who likes white-water rafting or wants to raise the kids Catholic. It's more of a passion I'm looking for. A way of thinking deeply. Feeling deeply. Living against the grain.

Take Karl. His world consists largely of the space between his headphones, but I don't mind this inwardness about him; in fact, I kind of like it. It's intense, mysterious, slightly off the mark. It is nothing like Harv, my mother's second husband, a man who lives life from the smack-dab middle: a straight highway of credit cards and tip cards and Hollywood blockbusters, life as predictable as all-American pink pork cubes skewered along a kabob.

But despite my determination, rock stars invariably disappoint me. If it wasn't the bassist who wore tighty whities, it was the lead vocalist obsessed with Debbie Gibson, or the keyboardist who called me "dude." Still, I remain convinced that the real thing is out there. By now it's evolved into a kind of quest: to find the rock star who doesn't disappoint. The one who fits the image. Who does the trick. Who earns every overused cliché and cheesy song title, who will single-handedly "love me tender" and "love me in an elevator" all night long.

"In other words, the one who probably doesn't exist," Hannah mused. We were eating breakfast in Denny's at the time. This was about three months ago, four in the morning, twenty minutes after I'd leaped from the bed of my latest Blue Room find: a hard-rock drummer who'd asked me to stroke his feet to help him fall asleep.

"I think when you find the right man, his imperfections are the things you'll love about him most," Hannah yawned. Her mind was awake, but the rest of her—pajamas, flip-flops, and curly, pillow-smashed red hair—was not. "They're the things that will surprise you about him. The things you never could have dreamed up."

I'm sure she is right. Hannah is studying psychology. She has a loving family. She has a boyfriend who calls her "sweetheart" without irony. She is my oldest and dearest friend. Still, I didn't believe her for a second.

"Mmm hmm," I murmured, chewing a bacon nub.

"Maybe it's fear," she said, plucking a strawberry off the top of her fruit salad. Even at 4:00 A.M., Hannah is relentlessly healthy. "The way you tend to . . . terminate relationships. A manifestation of your fear of commitment."

Believe it or not, Hannah actually talks like this. In her defense, she didn't always. When Hannah and I became friends in fifth grade, most of what we spoke was "Valley talk," the short-lived lingo of "gnarlys" and "gag mes" that managed to infect even the suburbanest of suburban Philadelphia. That was the same year Hannah's family moved here from Minnesota, the year we discovered boys, demystified lockers, and started changing our clothes before gym. It was also the year my parents fought without stopping and I escaped to Hannah's house as often as I could.

From fifth grade onward, Hannah and I have become progressively more different. In high school, she headed cleanup drives while I memorized Van Halen lyrics. In college, she studied abroad in Africa and I pierced my nose. When she has a bad day, I recommend a Funyun; if I have a headache, she tells me to massage my navel. She's switched from coffee to herbal teas. She's given up meat and TV. She's feng shuied her apartment. She's fallen in love with Alan.

"It's not that I'm afraid of commitment," I argued, chewing harshly. Hannah and I have a deal: she has permission to practice her psychology on me if I'm allowed to get irrationally upset and eat bacon. "I just want what I want. It's like my Nanny used to say, I'm fussy. I like my orange juice with pulp. I like my boyfriends with souls."

I am fond of citing Nanny in moments like this one. My grandmother died about four years ago, and in retrospect has become my biggest fan. "Eliza plays the field," she was fond of saying. And: "Eliza's a tough nut to crack." These were compliments, I'm pretty sure. My mother, on the other hand, has made it her life's work to criticize me about anything and everything: piercing my nose, piercing my navel, wearing torn jeans in public, painting my bedroom black in high school, living in an "edgy" neighborhood of Philly (i.e., Manayunk, where there are boys with tattoos and modern art), and never managing to "stick with" boyfriends long enough.

"Maybe you just need to be a little more realistic," Hannah was saying. She popped a grape in her mouth. "You hold men up to sort of, high, standards."

I felt the familiar beginnings of a caffeine headache creep into my temples. For not the first time in my life, I found myself lamenting the fact that I couldn't have a best friend who gave advice like "screw the bastard," a friend who took me out and bought me Jello shots, a friend who abandoned me in corners of bars with guys named Trey wearing Dockers and CK for Men.

"You mean, I have to settle," I said.

"I mean, not all people will be as perfect as the ones you watch on TV. People have imperfections. They have moles. They have allergies. They have . . . mothers." She paused and sneezed. Hannah is allergic to everything. "It's like when I first met Lily," she said, blowing her nose on a napkin. "I felt this new intimacy with Alan. It was like I got to know him on another level."

I stared her in the eye, trying to deny the pounding in my temples. "What if I don't want to know him on another level?"

The minute Karl's mother spots him on the porch she flings the door open, grabs his face in two hands and squeezes. His hard-lined, sharp-stubbled rock star's cheeks bulge into two prickled dinner rolls.

"Sweetie pie!" she says. Her tone has a nervy edge that reveals, clearly, Karl should have called first. "I didn't know you were coming! If you'd told me, I would have vacuumed! I would have swept! I would have bought cold cuts!" She spots me standing behind him. "And who's this?"

"That's Eliza."

"Eliza!" says Mrs. Karl. Her tone has the kind of cheerful wariness with which all rock stars' mothers assess me at first, wondering which girl I will turn out to be: the one who will haul her son off to Baja in a cloud of funny-smelling smoke or the one who will manage to rein him in and get him mowing lawns and making babies. Mrs. Karl surveys me up and down: flared black jeans, gray T-shirt, nose ring, hair cut shoulder length and tucked behind my ears ("just don't wear it too short," my mother is fond of saying, "men might think you're a lesbian"). I'm sure Karl's mother can tell I'm not wearing a bra.

"Hi, Mrs. Irons," I say.

She nods, looking suddenly uncomfortable. It's as if by giving me the once-over, it's occurred to her how she herself must look. She clutches her flowered housedress over her pillowy breasts, while the other hand flies up to her red-gray hair and flutters there like a nervous moth. "Oh, I'm so embarrassed. I haven't even put on my face," she says, then proceeds to touch her eyes, cheeks, earlobes, as if confirming that, without decoration, they are all still there.

"Mom, chill," Karl says.

Mrs. Karl drops her hands and sighs, emotion gone stale and practical as a cracker. "Well, come on in," she says. "I'll get you kids something to snack on."

Mrs. Karl ushers us into the living room, then disappears. The room is filled with little things, thingy things. Ceramic dogs and blown eggs, commemorative plates and spoons, a revolving brass clock, wooden dolls stacked one inside the other—things that strike me as eccentric and pointless and yet, oddly familiar. Karl and I each sink onto a daisy-patterned ottoman. I pull my knees and elbows in tight to my body, afraid I might send something crashing to the floor.

"It's a good thing you caught me," Mrs. Karl is calling from what I assume is the kitchen, to the tune of crumpling plastic and thumping cabinet doors. "I was just getting ready to go to the store. Your father's out golfing with Larry Harris, even though I told him he'll catch cold in the rain."

"Uh huh," Karl replies. He is watching me without blinking. It's the slightly unnerving expression Karl gets when he's preparing to kiss me. Karl is a hard-core kisser. When he leans in, I take a breath.

"But you know he never listens to me. He's always sneaking potato chips after I'm in bed. Does he think I don't *see* the crumbs in the morning? And the Krimpets in the basement. Does he think I don't know about those? He has a mole on his back he won't get checked, and he stands so close to the microwave it's like he *wants* radiation poisoning."

If there's anything more unnerving than kissing Karl, it's kissing Karl with his mother not ten feet away. In general, kissing Karl is pretty repulsive: too wet and too overt. And yet, there's some strange satisfaction in it. Afterward, I always feel as though I've been through some kind of taxing team sport: a moment's disorientation, a pleasant buzz, then a steady ache and the dim, proud feeling of having "played hard."

When I hear his mother's footsteps, I pull back. My lips are throbbing. Mrs. Karl appears holding a tray topped with two glasses of lemonade, a fan of crackers, squares of bright orange cheese. She's managed to put on lipstick, a bright red that veers in and out of the lip line. I can't help feeling sorry for her.

"It's the best I could do on short notice," she says, placing the tray on the coffee table. "It's those crackers you like so much, Karl. The buttery ones."

He nods and scoops up a handful, dribbling them in his mouth like M & Ms.

"Take a lemonade, Eliza," she instructs me.

I pick up a glass. It's a freebie one, from McDonalds. Under my thumb, the Hamburglar grins at me from behind his mask. "Thank you," I smile.

Mrs. Karl remains standing, waiting for me to sip it, so I take a gulp to prove my sincerity. Then she looks to Karl, who is crunching contentedly on crackers. Satisfied, she can finally sit. She herself doesn't eat or drink anything, I notice. I suspect she is one of those housewives, like my mother, who cook and clean all day but are almost never seen to rest or eat.

Now it is totally quiet. The only sound is the intermittent crunching of Karl's teeth on the buttery crackers he likes so much. Mrs. Karl is watching him with a small red smile, like a squashed cherry.

Finally I say, "I like your house, Mrs. Irons."

She shifts her gaze to me and presses her lips together. I can tell she's not sure if she can trust me or not, whether I am being honest or just kissing up. It's true, however. I do like her house; in a general sense, anyway. After six years of studio apartment living, any place with two floors and a basement feels like a mansion to me.

"Thank you," Mrs. Karl says. Her mouth pinches tighter, two purse strings drawn shut. "So," she says. "Eliza. Do you play music, too?" From the polite but pained look on her face, I can tell that she, like me, is recalling Karl's last girlfriend, who sang lead in an all-girl band and had her name legally changed to Lioness. "Or," she adds hopefully, two fingers starting to fidget at the hem of her dress, "do you do . . . something else?"

I have two options here. I can tell Mrs. Karl about the job I don't get paid for: the book I am trying to write. Or, I can describe the job that actually produces a paycheck. Graciously, I go for the latter.

"I'm a copywriter," I tell her. "For a travel agency. It's called Dreams Come True." When she doesn't react, I add, "Inc."

"Oh really?" Mrs. Karl says. Her face is relaxing. She sits forward and clasps her hands around her knees like a little girl. "What kinds of things do you copywrite?"

"A little bit of everything. Ads. Brochures. Radio spots. Press releases." Karl, I notice, has stopped eating to listen, and I wonder if this is the first he's heard of specifically what I do in the hours we're not together. "Basically, I write about exotic places people can go on vacation. But I don't go on them. I just read about them. Then I advertise them. So other people can go." Spelled out, it is the most depressing job in the world.

Mrs. Karl looks pleasantly confused. Karl's expression does not change. When neither of them makes a move to speak, I keep talking to fill the silence. I describe some of Dreams's vacation spots, then provide a couple of average hotel room rates and amenities. Feeling reckless, I toss out a few of my recent headlines:

Heavenly Hot Spots!
Sexy, Sizzlin' Summer Getaways!
Escaping The Woe-is-Me Winter Blahs!
At one point, I'm speaking entirely in adjectives.

Finally, in a moment that I'm sure feels metaphorical only to me, I inhale and conclude: "I write about fantasies. But here I am, stuck in reality."

An ice cube pops, my cue to get offstage. I think a Hummel actually scowls. Mrs. Karl's smile fades into a look of concern. "Mmm hmm," she murmurs, passing me the crackers like a consolation prize. Karl is nodding appreciatively.

Fixing my eyes on a daisy-shaped throw rug, I sit back and nibble on cheese. So far, I must admit, Mrs. Karl hasn't been that terrible. There have been no childhood stories, no trophies, no bronzed baby shoes. Any minute, though, I am positive she'll feel a bout of nostalgia coming on. First, she'll bring out the photo albums. Or she'll set up the slide projector and start narrating. Or she'll tell me the play-by-play details of the messy, painful, thirty-seven-hour labor that produced baby Karl.

When I finally dare to look up, it is even worse than I imagined. Mrs. Karl has defied all rock star–mother precedent by bypassing the childhood/nostalgia phase and going straight for the jugular: personal hygiene. I watch, horrified, as she plucks and pokes at Karl's rough stubble like it's a pesky weed that's invaded her garden. Before I know it, she's prodding at his gold hoop earrings, scouting his lobes for infection. She's picking up his hand and examining under his fingernails.

Karl's rock star image is fading by the second.

I know I need to act fast. Glancing around the room, I search for someplace secure to rest my eyes. Porcelain dogs. Porcelain saints. A pinecone bunny. A wreath made of shellacked Oreos. Panicked, I alight on the family portraits lined up on the windowsill. They are airbrushed, framed. I feel, momentarily, safe. But in a matter of seconds, I have identified the true origin of Karl's blue-eyed, red-haired rocker brawn: Ireland. Karl descends from a long line of pale, plump Irish people who beam at me from 8 x 11s, pink-cheeked great-uncles and great-great-uncles primped and propped and scrubbed clean by their wives, then filled to the brim with tea and sausages. When I turn back to Karl, I could swear his face has bleached a few shades.

"That sounds like a nice job," Mrs. Karl is saying, hands refolded innocently around her knees. It's a few seconds before I realize she's still referring to me. "I'd love to travel someplace someday. The Bahamas. The Bermuda." The Bermuda? *The Bermuda?* My head starts to pound, a small pickax between my eyes. "Someplace nice and sunny," she says, sighing. She turns back to Karl. "You need to be careful in the sun, you know, honey. Next time I'm out, I'll pick you up some sunscreen."

Back on the road in Karl's black Saab Turbo 9000 with the two amp-eight driver audio system, I am part frightened by what just happened and part dreading what must happen next. Karl is jamming to Korn, hot damp air is blasting through the sunroof, and I am trying to control my headache by recalling Hannah's advice about talking gently to my cranium.

Unfortunately, contrary to the spirit of the exercise, all that comes to mind is *Screw you, cranium!* The only spot of comfort in this fiasco is the anticipation of gloating when I recap the afternoon for Andrew.

If my best friend Hannah tends to be abstract, my best friend Andrew defines concrete. The man is made of calculators and train schedules, Bic pens and neckties, packs of minty fresh gum. He is a law student at Penn, lives in Chestnut Hill, and reads books with words like "Earn," "Win" and "10 Tips" in the titles. I tell him he's going to end up one of those guys who paces on train platforms, barking into his cell phone, crunching on antacids, heart about to leap screaming from his chest.

"That will never be me," Andrew says with mock sincerity. Ever since his dad's bypass surgery, I joke about this because it terrifies me. "I will never have a cell phone."

My two best friends have little in common besides their friendships with me. They try hard at conversation, but everything they say just misses the other. Hannah's words waft past Andrew's ears. Andrew's zing over Hannah's head. I watch their conversations like cartoons, complete with *whap*s and *blam*s and *whoosh*s.

Andrew: So, how's the psych school treating you?

Hannah: Oh, pretty well, I guess. I'm learning a lot. That's the important thing.

Andrew: I thought making money was the important thing.

Hannah (thoughtful): I know what you mean. It's easy to forget why we do what we do . . . to lose our centers. We need to be careful not to neglect our spiritual side.

Andrew (confused): But I love neglecting my spiritual side.

Eventually, my two best friends wind up silent and perplexed in each other's presence. Hannah takes Andrew far too seriously. Andrew can't conceive of someone so lacking in irony. I figure I'm somewhere in between. Part of me views life with Andrew's casual distance, roughhousing with it, boxing it into bad puns, slinging an arm around its shoulders and buying it a martini. Another part of me knows that nothing, absolutely nothing, rolls right off me.

Technically speaking, I have a repartee with Andrew that I'll never have with Hannah; some of this stems from the fact that Hannah doesn't watch TV. Andrew and my conversations are sharp, subtle, almost scriptlike, relying on a shared history of college and pop culture that requires little explication. With Hannah, conversation is more patient. It requires more pauses and thoughts and words. Sometimes I wish I could toss out a reference like "pork chops and applesauce," knowing she'd be right there with me. (She wouldn't. I tried it once and she gave me a brochure about the dangers of fatty acids.) Despite all their differences, however, both my best friends think the rock star/mother curse is in my head.

"No one's mother is that bad," Andrew insists.

"They are."

"They're not."

"Why would I make this stuff up?"

"You're not making it up. You're just exaggerating. Like always."

By "always," Andrew is referring to life since he met me: freshman year of college. Both Andrew and I went to Wissahickon, a small, expensive school made of brick and pine trees in the hills of central Pennsylvania. Technically, we met while passing a Nerf ball between our chins during an awkward freshman icebreaker. But our first real conversation was on a Saturday, one month later, when the rest of our dorm was still out partying and both of us had retreated, half drunk, to the basement "lounge" to watch late-night reruns of *The Brady Bunch.*

"You know," Andrew said. We were sitting side by side on the single puke-green couch that hadn't yet been stolen. "Jan doesn't get the credit she deserves. She's a cute girl."

"Maybe." It was the Grand Canyon episode, part one of the three-parter when Bobby and Cindy get lost in the hills, the gang gets thrown in jail, and Alice rides backward on a mule. "But Greg's the real babe of the show," I said, slurring so "babe of the show" sounded alarmingly, but sort of interestingly, like "Barbarino." "Remember the one where he called himself Johnny Bravo?"

"Almost as good as the one where he made Mike's den into a bachelor pad," Andrew said, earning my instant respect. "That episode is what made me lobby to turn my parents' garage into an apartment."

I snuck a glance at him. He was wearing the Wissahickon uniform: khakis, Tevas, fleece pullover, and a dirty baseball cap swiveled backward. He was cute, in a generic sort of way. "So did you?"

"I tried. It was freezing and full of power tools and giant spiders. The groovy chicks didn't exactly come running."

When the show was over, we lapsed into a few rounds of "Bob-BY! CIN-dy!" mountain-call impressions, then discussed the other kids in our dorm and discovered our opinions were the same about virtually all of them. And finally, because we were drunk, and because it was late, and because there was nothing left to talk about, we kissed. Everyone kissed everyone in college. Sitting alone in a dorm lounge at 3:00 A.M. on a Saturday, there really seemed no other plausible way to get up and say good night.

But even in that first kiss, it was obvious something was missing between us. Our kisses were too kind, too considerate. We paused for Andrew to adjust a contact lens. I sneezed; he drew back and said "gesundheit." We were too unself-conscious around each other too fast. Yet, for the next six weeks, we made a valiant attempt to be a couple. We slept together (but never "slept together," a gut instinct for which I am eternally grateful). We stored things in each other's rooms: his saline solution on my dresser, my tampons in his desk drawer. We went to breakfast in our pajamas. We tried to fight, but they were stupid fights (which is the best episode of *Three's Company?* which is better, Cocoa Krispies or Puffs?) and there were always smiles twitching on our faces, as if we were two actors trying to stay composed during a love scene but ready to dissolve into hysterics, link arms, wander off the set and grab a chili dog.

By December, we admitted—to the chagrin of my mother, who had fallen madly in love with Andrew over Parents Weekend—that we were just good friends, friends who were both lonely and liked bad cereal and sitcoms. Still, many people insist that Andrew and I will one day end up together. Between us, it's become a running gag.

"You're way too blond," I tell him. "You're one of those healthy, happy-go-lucky blond guys who bug the hell out of me."

"You're one of those brooding dark-haired chicks," he replies. "You people make me tense."

"You just don't like me because I'm not a lawyer."

"And you don't like me because I don't play rock 'n roll." Sometimes Andrew accents this line with a few moments of awkward air guitaring. It's one of his habits, like wearing socks with sandals, that I've told him he really should try to break.

"If only you were gay," I sigh. "Then we'd have the perfect '90s friendship."

Now, even though Andrew and I dated for just forty-one days eight years ago, the experience has entitled us to a certain familiarity when it comes to each other's love lives. It gives us the right to chuckle lightly and say things like "oh, *that*" and "I forgot you did that" and (see above) "you're just exaggerating, as usual." Having dated for forty-one days eight years ago also rules out our ever completely approving of anyone the other person dates. This is because you understand, on some subconscious level, they chose that person over you.

For example, Andrew's current girlfriend. Her name is Kimberley. *Kim-ber-ley.* It sounds like an adverb or adjective. I could use it to describe a vacation spa ("where expert masseuses will *kimberley* relieve your sore muscles") or a Mexican villa ("where the *kimberley*, gauze-draped beds will float you to sleep under the stars").

Like all of Andrew's law-school girlfriends, he and Kimberley do a lot of debating. Whether movies are good or bad. How big a tip a waiter deserves. Where to get the best pizza in Center City and the cheapest place to park and/or fastest way to get there. It's a different kind of arguing than the halfhearted pop-culture disagreements Andrew and I had in college. With Kimberley, it's more like legal foreplay: heated, stubborn, packed with legalese, yet groping each other the entire time.

In the end, of course, I want Andrew to be happy. I will support his decisions. I will endure his habits. I will delicately avert my eyes when he debates with his girlfriends. I will be kind to these women and accompany them to ladies' rest rooms in restaurants and talk to them about candid, girlish things as we pee—how our makeup is smearing in the heat, how PMSed we are—topics that are exclusively female and therefore qualify us as having bonded.

And I will take Andrew's advice seriously. Like Hannah, he is often more sensible about my life than I am. Whenever he argues me on the meet-the-mother point, however, I can conveniently remind him of the night I met his mother for the first time. Thanksgiving Day, freshman year, at his parents' house in rural Vermont where his mother, over the peach pie and coffee, made him perform "Over the River and Through the Woods" on his old trombone.

It is silent as Karl parks outside his apartment. We didn't speak much on the ride home, though the tunes were so loud it didn't feel obvious. Now, it feels obvious. The silence is thick, waxy, difficult. The car smells like the lasagna his mother handed him as we were leaving, which now slumbers on the floor of the backseat, heavy with congealing cheese. It has just started to rain again, drops assaulting the windows like thousands of drumming fingernails. I wonder if it feels as symbolic to Karl as it does to me.

"Coming down?" Karl asks.

I stare at my lap, considering the offer. If I go inside Karl's basement apartment, I can predict every detail of what will happen next: the way he'll toss the lasagna on the counter and crank up the Limp Bizkit, followed by the round of sex on his scratchy tiger-print blanket. I have a flash of Karl's Celtic-white arms and legs, scruff picked clean by his mother, breath smelling like buttery crackers. And after, the way he'll pluck at his guitar, shirtless, shoeless, forking cold lasagna straight from the pan. I can already imagine the noise of it, the sweat of it. The noise and sweat of it.

"I don't know," I say, affecting a yawn. "I'm really tired. I think I need to go home and unwind."

Karl frowns. He takes his hand off my knee. "What's going on?"

"What do you mean?" I poke at a hole in the seat cushion, burying my finger to the knuckle.

Karl shrugs, waiting. He is very good at waiting. Maybe it's all the time spent in his head. "Usually, when people say they have to unwind," he says, "there's something that wound them up to begin with. That's what I mean."

It is always, always, in moments like these that rock stars will surprise you. Just when their image has begun to splinter and crack, just when their true self is starting to peek through, they will say something surprising, something insightful, something to catch me off guard.

"It's not that kind of unwind," I try to explain, forcing myself not to look at his biceps or chest-ceps or suddenly attractively earnest blue eyes. "Honestly. It's just . . . I have some stuff to do. Laundry. Bills. Errands. I haven't fed Leroy since, like, Wednesday."

This is not true and Karl knows it. To his credit, he doesn't accuse me of lying. He just watches me, direct and unblinking, while my guilty glance skitters from his denim lap to his AC/DC key ring to the floor mat, littered with empty coffee cups and scratched, sticky guitar picks. "I know," he says, and I can feel his eyes roaming around inside my conscience. "You want to go home so you can work on that book."

The concept for the book is this: it will be a guide to dating rock stars. It will be part fiction, part nonfiction. It will be part humor, part personal health. It will qualify as sociology, how-to, reference, and the performing arts. Each chapter will focus on a different kind of musician—an ambassador from the instrumental genre, if you will—and what to expect (and not expect) if you date them. I consider it a public service, a way of using my collective experience to better the world. Maybe, as a bonus, I'll figure out where my own rock star is hiding.

As of yet, I haven't actually started writing the book. I've taken notes, made lists, scribbled ideas. My latest brainstorm is to begin each chapter with songs from a would-be mix tape readers can play as they read along. It would function like any good mix should: triggering a memory, evoking a mood, recalling an especially regrettable year of the 1980s. Capturing the tone and lyric of your life in a particular moment.

The Book With Mix Tape idea grew out of my original scheme, which was Movies That Smell. I still think this idea has merit. The concept is this: you sit in the movie theater and can actually smell the scenes as you watch them.

Examples:

a) *Mystic Pizza* = Italian sausage and pepperoni.

b) *Beaches* = sunscreen and ocean breeze.

c) *Forrest Gump* =

"But what do you do if it's a war movie?" Andrew had asked, after I called him to relay my plan. "Or are all the scenes going to be ones that would smell good?" I could practically hear his brain working over the phone, a series of popping cash register drawers. "That means you're basically ruling out all movies set in major cities. The Rockys. The Godfathers. *Taxi Driver.* Anything Woody Allen. You're going to have to pick ones set only in places that smell good . . . like the south of Spain. Like Sevilla." He paused. "Did I ever tell you how it smells like oranges in Sevilla?"

I did mention that Andrew was practical-minded. He also has a tendency to get carried away with his own good sense sometimes, questioning and rationalizing until there's nothing left of a great idea but a few conjunctions. Whenever possible, he also likes to flaunt the fact that he studied abroad our junior year—"Sevilla," he calls it, accent and all—and I, because of lead vocalist Win Brewer (see Chapter Eight), did not.

Hannah had a more personal take on Movies That Smell. "That's so you, Eliza," she smiled. "You want to enhance reality. Magnify it, stretch it. You become unsettled when things are too real."

It was then that I decided the world wasn't ready for Movies That Smell (plus, Andrew had started scaring me with legal talk about people with allergies). So I've redirected my focus: a Book With Mix Tape is the way to go. I haven't told either best friend about it. Karl knows there *is* a book, but not what the book's about. Maybe I won't tell anyone until it's finished.

Because, for now, I'm thinking this book is a pretty good idea. A valuable social resource, a clever book + music marketing concept. Or, it's what my elementary school art teacher was trying to warn my mother about after I made Michael Jackson's head out of papier-mâché. "Eliza has so much creative potential," she said, sighing. "I just worry about how she's choosing to harness it."

2

celebrities

My first bout of rock-star love struck when I was ten years old. When you're ten, unlike when you're twenty-six, having a crush on a rock star doesn't make you weird. Everybody's doing it. You're supposed to be doing it. It's the grade-five, peer-pressure equivalent of smoking pot or having sex in high school.

My crush was on Jack Wagner. His rugged blond face coated every inch of my bedroom ceiling, door, and walls. Jack lived a double life: musician by night, soap star by day. At three every afternoon, I watched him as Frisco Jones on *General Hospital*. Later, when my parents started their nightly round of arguing—Mom's needly jabs, Dad's weary dismissals—I locked my bedroom door and plugged my ears with headphones, trying to ignore the word "divorce" that buzzed around me like a gnat.

"Divorce" was the word in garish red letters on pamphlets in the guidance office. "Divorce" was the point of ABC After School Specials and Judy Blume's *It's Not the End of the World*. "Divorce" was what happened to kids whose parents fought too much, like Jenny Sousa's, whose dad moved to Acapulco to sell baseball caps on a beach. Balled in my bed, I closed my eyes and drowned my worries in the sounds of the greatest mix tape ever made: two sides of back-to-back Jack Wagner's "All I Need."

The beauty of '80s music was this: rock stars weren't afraid to speak their feelings. Back then, it wasn't corny. It wasn't suspicious. It wasn't desperate. Men could spill their guts in a flood of synthesizers, cymbals, A-B-A-B rhyme schemes and long notes high as women's. They were genuinely impassioned as they "brought ships into shore," "threw away oars," and "made love out of nothing at all." Even heartbreak was delivered with a bravado that seems almost comical to me now. As a grown-up, I find that kind of openness terrifying. But in 1984, it was acceptable, even desirable, and it was the way I loved Jack Wagner: with confidence, fearlessness, and a T-shirt bearing a steam-ironed decal of his sultry face.

"What's that?" my mother pounced, the first time she saw it.

She was sitting at the kitchen table painting her nails a frosty blue from one of the numerous bottles she kept in the refrigerator door, wedged discreetly among the sweet relish and Italian dressing. *Very Violet. Magic of Magenta.* Her hair was, as usual, sprayed and coiffed into a perfect ball. She was wearing a short-sleeve white sweater with pants and jewelry all in matching teal.

My mother is a woman greatly concerned with appearances.

"It's Jack," I said, cool as a cucumber, heading for the back door.

"Hold it!" She stood up and stuck one leg out, aiming her blue pump at the door. I think the woman was prepared to physically bar me from being seen in public. "Who?"

"Jack Wagner," I said, and sighed upward so my bangs fanned out, my newest and coolest move. "He's a rock star."

Mom's lipsticked mouth pinched shut like an olive, aimed and fired. "You had a rock star's face sewn onto a T-shirt? One of *your* T-shirts? One of the T-shirts I bought you new for summer?"

"It wasn't *sewn*," I pointed out, the only glitch I could find. At age ten, I still possessed some amount of guilty fear around my mother. I didn't lie to her. I rarely disobeyed her. If I was going to blaze a man's face into one of the T-shirts she bought me new for summer, I was at least going to be honest about my methods. "I got it ironed on. At the mall."

She planted one hand on each hip, like a TV mother, her wet nails splayed like sharp wings. Mom was master of the TV-mother moves. TV-mother angry = hands on hips. TV-mother annoyed = arms folded across chest. TV-mother disappointed = arms folded/head shake combo. Her neck and face were flushed deep pink.

I was about to explain the innocent circumstances surrounding the decal—a misguided trip to Everything Ts, the hissing steam, the seductively loud Van Halen on the radio, and the intense peer pressure I was getting from my friend Katie (whom Mom already disapproved of because Katie's mother let her eat pixie sticks)—when she looked in the shadowy direction that was my father.

"Lou," she said. "Are you listening to this?"

My father—then he was Dad, later I would remember him as Lou—was seated in the darkest corner of the living room, ensconced in his old green recliner. If the man wasn't at work (a job I knew nothing about except that it required him to wear dark suits, come home late, and be perpetually sullen) chances were he was in it. The chair was like his own mini-universe, where he lived alone in his drab corduroys and wrinkled, untucked Oxford shirts, with a dark foamy beer and a messy newspaper, playing slow jazz albums that dipped and sighed and seeped like a moat around his feet.

The chair was an ugly, threadbare monstrosity. A memento, my father said, from back when he was a "bachelor" (a distinction he liked to make, and often, as if he once belonged to a completely different species). He and the chair were starting to age together, even resemble each other, like the elderly and their pets. As the chair sagged, so did my dad, drooping at the shoulders and softening at the gut. Cushion foam was falling out in tufts, like middle-aged hair.

Needless to say, Mom hated the chair. She hated the ugliness of it, the greenness of it, the music and memory that separated us from it. But most of all, she hated the cat scratches. At some point during Dad's crazy bachelor days, the chair had been ravaged by a cat that belonged to one of his ex-girlfriends. It was weird, as a kid, to imagine Dad with any woman other than my mother. But the reality of that woman and her cat sat in our living room every day.

What kind of woman lets an animal rip up her furniture? Mom would mutter, as she jabbed around the chair with the nose of the vacuum cleaner, though I'm sure the answer terrified her: the kind of woman who was carefree and spontaneous, the kind of woman who took in strays and fed them fish sticks, the kind of woman who, after sex, left scratches on men's backs.

Once, after school, I caught my mother trying to stitch up the cat scratches. Dad was at work, my sister Camilla was at one of her alpha-child extracurricular activities, and Mom was hunkered like a burglar on the living room floor: intense, sweaty, and brandishing a mini-sewing kit in her hand.

From the kitchen doorway, I watched her. It was the most disheveled she had ever looked. Her hair was pinned up sloppily in a couple of my ribboned barrettes and her shoes were kicked off, revealing the dirty soles of her nylons. Straight pins were lined up between her lips and she was mumbling through them as she poked and prodded at the stuffing leaking from the chair. My instinct was to crack a joke, to startle her, but I didn't. I couldn't. I felt too embarrassed for us both. Instead, I crept up to my room and drowned in "All I Need," over and over, until Dad got home.

As it turned out, my subtlety didn't matter. Mom's covert operation failed, the damaged chair proving to be a) too old, b) too soft, and c) too sentimental to be done away with. In the end, the scratches stayed, the chair stayed, and so did daily proof of the fact that my father would never be as committed to my mother as she wanted him to be.

"What," Dad replied to her. His tone was flat as an ink stamp. Living with Mom had drained the man of his energy, until his speech began losing punctuation. Question marks had been missing for at least a year. He hadn't managed an exclamation point since 1979.

"Look at her," Mom snapped. I cringed, as I did every time she got angry with my father, wishing she would be nicer so he wouldn't take off for Acapulco to team up with Mr. Sousa. "Her shirt. It's a decal. From a mall. One of those shack-type places." This was delivered as if the Everything Ts and Sunglass Shed were of a lower caste than the Gap and Crabtree & Evelyn.

Dad sipped his beer, not even glancing at me. This was not unusual. He didn't interact much with any of us, unless it involved passing food at the dinner table or changing channels on the TV. As a seven- and eight-year-old, this didn't strike me as strange. For all I knew, this was how all fathers behaved. It wasn't until I met Hannah's family, and saw *The Cosby Show* for the first time, that I realized not all dads were as distant and disinterested as mine.

"For God's sake, Linda," he sighed, running a hand through his thinning, rumpled hair. A hiss of a sigh, like a tire sagging. Every day, a little more sagging. His chair, his shoulders, his tone of voice. "Leave the kid alone."

I was triumphant. At that moment, it didn't matter that Dad never tucked me in at night. That he never taught me to ride a two-wheeler. That he never took me on secret Dairy Queen runs like Hannah's dad. Sitting in his embattled armchair, he was my ally against my mother. When he disappeared less than a year later, it was for California, not Acapulco, and it seemed only appropriate that the chair was the first thing to hit the curb.

*   *   *

The June after fifth grade, exactly two months before Dad/Lou would leave us, my love for Jack Wagner grew more organized. My friends and I created a fan club for our rock stars named, brilliantly, Official Rock Star Fan Club. We convened on Saturday afternoons. We carried handmade club membership cards. We tossed around the phrases "old business," "new business" and, for reasons unknown, "order in the court."

The ORSFC consisted of me, Hannah, Katie Brennan, and Cecilia Kim. Cecilia was the shyest among us. Her father sold home security systems and, maybe as a result, her life was airtight. She wore her hair caught back in long braids, pinched at the ends with rubber bands (not hair elastics, but actual rubber bands, the brown ones that came wrapped around broccoli and newspapers) and was not allowed to stay out past five or drink anything carbonated. Cecilia's house was rigged with an elaborate security system, epitomized by the pulsing red dot in a corner of the living room ceiling that we tried to outsmart by squirming around the floor on our bellies. If the system got accidentally set off, we all knew the password—BABA, after Cecilia's teddy bear—which Mr. Kim had chosen and which seemed, to me, the ultimate act of paternal love.

Katie Brennan, on the other hand, was the renegade. Blond-haired and blue-eyed, she was a girl just killing time until she got old enough to date. She straightened her teeth with braces, curled her hair with Party Perms, experimented with adhesive earrings—all of it preparation and practice. As if through sheer will, she was the only girl in the fifth grade who'd managed to grow any semblance of a chest yet. She already wore a bra, and had perfected a high-pitched giggle that Hannah and I agreed was annoying but that boys inexplicably seemed to like.

Katie had two sisters, both in high school, so naturally she was our CI (Club Informer). She explained the mechanics of blow jobs. She gave us a detailed report on the night Mr. Brennan found a naked boy in her sister's bed and chased him out of the house with a five-iron. She smuggled a tampon into our OCM (Official Club Meeting), where we watched it expand in a bowl of water, eyes popping, until it was the size of a small raft.

Hannah and I had resigned ourselves to the fact that Katie would grow up faster than we would. Between the two of us, it was still a dead heat: neither wore a bra, had her period, or had kissed a boy yet. But unfortunately for me, that was where the happy similarities ended. In fifth grade, I had begun to sprawl until my legs comprised roughly eighty percent of my body, while Hannah remained cute and small—one of only about a million things I envied about her. Like her canopy bed. Her guinea pig. Her station wagon. Her red hair. Her mom, because she said "shit" and knew how to French braid. Her dad, because he wasn't mine. Her older brothers, which I'd always wanted so I could meet their friends and borrow their clothes. Her Minnesota accent, which I filed in the same exotic category as braces, glasses, and broken bones (for the signable casts). But the thing I envied most of all was her sunporch, where the ORSFC convened.

The sunporch at the Devines's was—is—my favorite place in the world. It's casually messy, scattered with sunlight and shadow, torn phone messages and Monopoly money, stray sneakers and drained lemonade glasses. This was the kind of overspill I knew existed in the houses of happy families, and the kind that was missing from my own house, scoured bright and tense as a griddle. From the ceiling hung Mrs. Devine's curly plants, each one carefully christened—Otis, Clarissa, Marguerite—and cradled in a sac of beaded macrame. In one corner, Mr. Devine's Victrola stood like a holy relic, battered albums splayed in reverence at its feet.

I, of course, felt a special sense of entitlement to the porch at the Devines's because a) I was Hannah's best friend, and had the clot of rainbowed friendship pins on my Tretorns to prove it, b) I was the one she was going to overnight camp with in July, and c) I was the only one invited to stay after the Club for dinner.

Dinner at the Devines's was like no meal I had ever known. Because it was summer, they ate on the porch around a wooden table crowded with citronella candles and messy, juicy seafood. My mother, had I been naive enough to tell her, would never have allowed me to eat food involving guts or bibs. But the Devines didn't care. Before digging in, they all held hands and volunteered what they were thankful for—a litany of things from Bob Marley to thunderstorms to super-crunchy peanut butter. Afterward, in the quiet that clung to us like a held breath, Mr. Devine would make his nightly pilgrimage to the Victrola.

He referred to the albums like close friends—Janis, Carly, Bruce—similar to Mrs. Devine and her hanging plants. We waited at the table while he paged through them, considering each one, then carefully slipped one out of its jacket. He placed it gingerly on the turntable, pulling on his beard. Both Hannah's parents had signature hair—Mr. Devine a wild gray puff sprouting from his chin, Mrs. Devine an explosive mop of brown corkscrews—the combined genetic effect of which was Hannah's orange curls. Between their plants and albums and prayers and hair, I had a suspicion that the Devines were "hippies"—a word I'd heard Nanny utter in the same hushed, fearful breath as "cancer" and "Chaka Khan."

Only after needle touched vinyl could the family dinner truly begin. Hannah's two brothers ate mountains of shellfish, cracking backs and sucking bones and dunking crab legs in butter like balls into hoops. They teased Hannah and me relentlessly, stepping on our toes, stealing our food, and pulling our hair, all of which I enjoyed immensely (naturally I had crushes on both of them). Mr. and Mrs. Devine never got angry about the noise or the mess. After dinner, they curled up together among the wine and wicker, singing along to staticky Cat or Van.

During ORSFC meetings, however, the sunporch was official business only. Hannah, Katie, Cecilia, and I sat in a cross-legged circle, armed with Fruit Roll-Ups and stacks of music mags. ORSFC protocol was this: each of us adopted one rock star who was exclusively ours to fall in love with. We fell in love with John Waite. We fell in love with George Michael. We fell in love with every member of Human League, Duran Duran, and Cutting Crew. Some of these are the same stars I catch these days on VH1's *Where Are They Now?* But back then, if one began losing popularity, we simply replaced him with another, like the members of Menudo when they got too old.

The allotment of crushes happened pretty peaceably. Cecilia liked the guys with the nice smiles, the Howard Joneses and the

Andrew Ridgeleys, the ones who looked the least like burglars. Her crushes were usually brief, halfhearted. (She did manage a two-week commitment to Huey, of the News.) Katie went for the more rebellious, the Van Halens and Princes, the ones who sang risqué lyrics about hot sex and Corvettes. Even then, Hannah saw the men as studies in human behavior, examining Rick Springfield's leap from tube to song with the curiosity of a social historian. I, of course, remained faithful to Jack.

The motivation behind our having separate crushes was more economical than emotional. Basically, it allowed us to rip apart our mags and divvy up the pix among us, which bought more rocker for our dollar. The pix were glossy 8 ½ x 11s, seductive shots of rock stars with oily, half-bared chests, rock stars reclining against Mustangs or pine trees, rock stars sitting in their kitchens or bedrooms in "Just Like the Boy Next Door!" montages. We didn't just read for the pictures, though. We read for the articles, too. The mini-bios. The up-close-and-personals. The could-you-be-the-girl-he's-looking-for's? In answer to the all-important question "Does (insert rock star here) have a special someone?" the answer was invariably, encouragingly, "Not yet!"

Most of our ORSFC meeting time was spent trading bits of insider info about various rock stars: hidden quirks, ideal girl-friends, random likes and dislikes. A pet kitten. A passion for cornflakes. A red Saab. Endless amounts of smooth-spun, prepackaged, third-person details that had us convinced we knew these men inside and out.

"New business!" I would announce, stomping my foot in lieu of a gavel. "Hannah?"

getting over jack wagner

"He always eats all his vegetables," Hannah loyally reported, reading from an up-close-and-personal.

"Awwww," supplied Cecilia. She was good at making these kinds of sounds. She had two rabbits.

"Avocados are his favorite," Hannah added. Even then, she was a vegetarian at heart. "Sometimes he eats avocado sandwiches."

"Grody to the max!" Katie sang, knowing she'd scored points for talking Valley.

"Listen to this," I jumped in. "Looking for a girl who is honest, likes to take long walks, curl up by the fire"—I chomped my Roll-Up, skipping over "ride horses" and "be spontaneous," and concluded—"a girl who will take the time to get to know the real him."

Another "awwww" from Cecilia.

"That's nothing," Katie said, and stood up on her wicker chair. Katie was known for stunts like this. With elaborate care, she took a picture of George Michael and licked it up and down, whispering, "Wake me up before you go-go."

Needless to say, Katie Brennan would never be without a prom date. In high school, in the gym locker room, she would fascinate and terrify us with stories of boys climbing in her bedroom window, and offer as proof the purplish hickeys spotting her neck like some kind of rare disease.

Katie withdrew her tongue, dropped back into her seat and collapsed into giggles while the three of us laughed or squirmed or both. Then we looked to Cecilia.

"Ummm . . ." she stalled, scanning her article, twisting the tip of one braid around her finger. "He has a sister . . . and her name's . . . ummm . . . Roberta?"

I suspect Cecilia Kim just wasn't cut out for following trends. She was starting to go a little bit fashion-haywire, once brandishing not one but two sparkly gloves during the *Thriller* era. Years later, she would startle the junior high school with a psychotic combination of neon scrunchies and leg warmers. I'm not saying we all weren't out on fashion limbs in the '80s, but Cecilia seemed to misfire a little more than average, like a person who learned slang from a textbook. Eventually she'd give up on trends altogether, burrow away in the honors track, and resurface years later as our valedictorian to deliver a speech entitled "Facing the Future: Life Without a Net."

My father left that August. He did it while my sister and I were away for a month at an all-girls overnight camp. I've since wondered if my mother sensed Lou was preparing to leave, and sent us away to spare us the pain. To protect our innocence. To prevent emotional scarring. Not that it worked. My memories of Camp Mohawk now seem like a bad joke, a trick, an elaborately loud, colorfully bad musical staged to distract me from what was really going on in my life.

Looking back, it's the stress and rigor of it all that seems most ironic. At the time, surviving Camp Mohawk was a matter of life and death: the greatest physical and mental challenge I would ever endure. Just the basics of daily living required speed and strength and fortitude. Cramming pizza bagels in your mouth before they were gone, getting showers before they were cold, swimming fast, running fast, rowing fast, holding your own in late-night sex talks and never, ever falling asleep early to guard against being TPed. I don't think I completed an REM cycle once in twenty-eight days. I lay in my cot, Jack Wagner swelling in my ears, alert and awake to the point of pain, hoping Victoria Moore wouldn't choose that night for one of her notorious one-acts.

Victoria—a.k.a. Big Vicki—had been a "Hawker" since she was six and already wore a D-cup. It was obvious to me, if no one else, that there was a connection between overnight camp and premature development. For Vicki, the chest was a source of pride. She was bigger than any other campers, bigger than our counselors, bigger than our camp directors. Some nights, if we were lucky, she'd aim a flashlight at herself and make a shadow of her torso on the bunk wall, chest flopping and bouncing like a deranged shadow puppet.

Hannah didn't get as rattled as I did by showering, racing, or Big Vicki. She was a camper straight out of the brochure: the freckled face you pay to see grinning above promises like *Learn Sportsmanship!* and *Make Friends for Life!* In reality, Hannah wasn't great at any sport or art or craft, but she did them all with gusto. She scurried fearlessly along the ropes course. She patiently knotted daisies into chains. When a bat got loose in our bunk and the counselor on duty screamed "Kill it! Smush it!" Hannah calmly trapped it under a plastic shower caddy and set it free.

Even Hannah's enthusiasm couldn't convince me to like Camp Mohawk. This wasn't necessarily Mohawk's fault; I just wasn't all-girls camp material. I despised team sports. I preferred

39

walking to running. I'd always been suspicious of marshmallows (what *are* they, exactly?). I missed boys and TV. I was
painfully aware of the fact that Jack Wagner could have a hit
single and I would have no idea. Perhaps it was only fitting that
the single part of Mohawk to pique my interest was Dave: head
swim instructor/rock star.

Dave was the son of the Camp Directors: Flo, and a man who
went by the name of Buzzy. Flo and Buzzy looked approximately
alike: short, round, and pudgy, with matching visors and peeling
noses. Somehow, they had managed to produce a son who was
blond, tan, and rock hard, with hair that hung a little long and
curled at the back of his neck like something dangerously pubic.
Dave wore a tangle of rope and bead around his neck, nestling in
the hollow of his brown throat. In general he, like me, exuded
utter disinterest in and disdain for all things Mohawk, which only
reinforced my growing conviction that we were totally in synch.

The exception to my anti-Mohawk rule was the Saturday
night bonfires. Each week, the entire camp gathered in a giant
circle on the soccer field to eat s'mores and sing folk. The song
list was carefully chosen to evoke premature nostalgia, a sadness
that would mount over the weeks and come to a crazed, crying
head in the last few days of camp. "Leaving on a Jet Plane."
"You've Got a Friend." "Desperado" (for the mood, not the
lyrics). The singing was led by none other than Dave, who
played a mean six-string. When he sang he closed his eyes and,
occasionally, bit his lip.

Though most of my Rest Hours were spent scribbling madly in
my diary about Dave, chances were slim he would have been able

to pick me out of a lineup. It was difficult to single yourself out at a camp where everyone moved in herds and wore regulation orange T-shirts. It wasn't until the last week—Day 23, to be exact—at Bunk Cherokee's daily swim lesson, that I saw my chance.

"Listen up," Dave said, with no emotion in his voice whatsoever. He was wearing his signature black shades, so it was impossible to tell if he was looking at us, through us, or was even awake. "Today we're doing lifesaving."

This was the final phase of our month-long swim course, the culmination of three weeks of doggy-paddling and freestyling and listless dead man's floating (a sport for which I'd discovered I had real talent).

Then Dave yawned the magic words: "I need a volunteer to play the drowning victim."

Let me be clear: under normal circumstances, the word "volunteer" would have sent me running in the opposite direction, especially if it meant being on flat-chested, half-naked display in front of all my fellow Cherokees. But I knew this was a golden opportunity. I was pretty sure even fake drowning would involve some sort of fear and concern. Definitely, there would be physical contact.

Casually, I offered my services: "Me! Dave! Over here! Pick me!"

"Fine." He jerked a blond thumb in my general direction. "You."

Within seconds, I found myself plunged into the deep end of the Mohawk pool while the rest of the Cherokees ringed the edge to watch. I looked to Dave for instruction.

"Act like you're drowning," Dave said.

For several minutes, I splashed and flailed to the best of my ability, even croaked "Help! Help!" a few times for added effect. I was working on rolling my eyes back into my head when I saw the end of the metal lifesaving pole heading swiftly in my direction. I grabbed onto it with both hands, then went limp, flopping from the end as Dave towed me in toward shore. When I felt the lip of the pool collide with my elbow, I opened my eyes and there it was: Dave's tan, gorgeous face mere inches away from mine.

"I'm counting to three," Dave said, taking my hands in his. "Then I'm dunking you."

"Okay" was barely out of my mouth before I was choking down a mouthful of chlorine, and found myself heaved onto the side of the pool where I lay dramatically coughing and spluttering. It was no act this time, but my bunk couldn't tell. They gave me a polite dribbling of applause.

After twenty-eight days, I was ambivalent about leaving camp. I was ambivalent about going home. The only thing I felt with any conviction was exhausted. Aside from the occasional Rest Hour or strategic trip to the infirmary during *General Hospital,* life in the woods had a relentless quality of motion: getting from sport to sport, meal to meal, one end of the sack race to the other. With all this activity, my parents rarely crossed my mind. Overnight camp was a small life, an island of a life, something like being away at college. The western hemisphere could have been on fire and we'd go on rotating the work wheel and eating marshmallows off sticks.

I received a total of three notes from my mother (none of

which I answered) written on "A Note from Linda" stationery. Each felt like a mini-scolding, a tidy list of thinly veiled reprimands like *Are you eating? Are you sleeping?* and *Are you cleaning your ears?*, punctuated with a *P.S. Be good.*

From my father, I received just one. It was written on the back of a yellow sales receipt from Rydal Auto Service. The letter, for him, was oddly sentimental. He wrote about how hot it was getting, then segued artfully into how old I was getting, how "life is short" and I shouldn't "mess around." That's all I remember. I read it twice, thought it was weird, threw it away and rushed off to claim my share of pizza bagels. Now, of course, I wish I'd kept it. Now, of course, it seems prophetic. I was holding the evidence of my father's preparation to leave us: a receipt for a new muffler and parting advice to his daughter. The last of the loose ends.

On our final morning, I waited with Hannah and my duffel on the grassy, buggy hill by the dance shack, listening for our names to be called through a bullhorn when our parents arrived. Most Hawkers were milling around, hushed and weepy, like graduating seniors. My sister was one of these. I watched her swapping phone numbers, addresses, and long, shuddering group hugs with girls she barely knew. Camilla always had this innate girlishness about her, a keen ability to hug and chat and gossip for hours on the phone. Years later, it would translate into a talent for baking the perfect pineapple ring and fitting into a wedding dress with no alterations.

Hannah's name was called before mine. "Hannah Devine, come on down!" yelled the not-at-all-funny Flo.

43

Hannah stood and shouldered her duffel, as our bunk gathered around to say good-bye. I watched her circle the crowd, returning the hugs people gave her. When she stopped in front of me, we didn't hug. We didn't have to.

"Call me tonight." She flashed me the peace sign, and came on down the hill.

It was nearly three hours later that my mother arrived. By that time, all the other Hawkers were long gone. Flo had retired the bullhorn and sat on the porch of the camp office, fanning herself with a *Cosmo,* and glancing at us now and then with irritation. Camilla sat next to me, subdued. Gnats circled our heads. Mosquitoes sucked our ankles. Our proximity required that we fight, but we were too hot and too tired to manage more than a few handfuls of burnt grass tossed in the other's direction.

When Mom appeared at the bottom of the hill, she was alone. And I don't just mean alone in the literal sense. She had a quality of aloneness about her, the look of a woman cut off and wafting, lacking a point of reference. She wore a big, untucked T-shirt and old khaki shorts that made her look wide and bloated. Her blond hair looked flat, dull, its natural brown beginning to creep in at the roots.

My heart thudded in my chest, in the hollow of my throat. Our mother never looked like this. She was always in place, always presentable, always kempt. Her outside never revealed any traces of what was going on underneath. As she got closer, I saw her eyes were red and swollen.

"Where's Dad?" I asked, scrambling to my feet. I needed to locate him, to pin him down in the world, to know that he was in the ugly green chair sagging prophetically in the corner of our living room. But I already knew that he wasn't. "Is he at home? In the car? Where is he, Mom?"

Mom focused at a spot somewhere over our heads, the dance shack or the tennis court or the thin, hot, drifting clouds. It didn't matter. Camp Mohawk was another world, a place we'd left behind us years ago.

"Mom?" Camilla said, and I heard fear in her voice, too.

"Come on, girls. Let's go."

Looking back, I believe it was on the ride home from Camp Mohawk, while my mother told us how our father hadn't come home from work on Friday, how he'd left no forwarding address, and how all of his jazz albums had disappeared with him, that the three of us began to solidify into the women we have become. My mother seemed to shrink inward, voice fading, knuckles whitening on the wheel. My sister appeared to grow a head taller, shoulders squaring, chin rising, voice taking on the crisp, purposeful ring of a business memo. I huddled in the backseat, knees drawn to my chin, watching the world from the other side of the window.

Within a week, my sister had found her Dad-substitute: her new boyfriend, Ivan. Ivan was long and shy, dressed in button-down browns and greens. He was running for student council president. Really, Ivan wasn't presidential material. He was a little too gangly, a little too bucktoothed, a little too eager to please. He never seemed convinced of anything, even the easy things—whether to sit or to stand, whether to kiss Camilla on the cheek or the lips (I was spying, natu-rally)—much less the issues plaguing the student body of York High.

But for Camilla, Ivan's campaign was a project she could throw herself into. It was something to occupy her hands and her mind, like a patchwork quilt or a suffering vegetable gar-den. Camilla and Ivan spent long hours making posters at our kitchen table:

Who Can? Ivan Can!

I've An Idea: How 'Bout Ivan?

They penned slogans on four hundred oversize buttons with permanent Magic Marker. If Ivan was being sloppy, Camilla grabbed the marker from his hand as he fumbled: "Is there any-thing *I* can do? Is there *anything* I can do?" Sometimes I could tell she was downstairs in the middle of the night by the squeak of a dying marker.

Ivan was a good person, which is probably why, had he won, he would have made a bad president. Every night when he arrived at our house, he came into the living room first to say hello to Mom.

"Good to see you, Mrs. Simon," said Ivan, tall and awkward as a hat rack.

Invariably, Mom was glued to her own Dad-substitute: prime-time television. She peered up at Ivan for a long, slow moment, squinting under her matted bangs as if trying to fig-ure out where she knew him from. It was at moments like these when I worried, briefly, that we would soon end up either pan-handlers or circus freaks.

Then Mom's face would crack a tentative smile. "Good to see you, too," she would say, and turn back to the screen.

In general, Mom didn't have much contact with the public in the year after Dad/Lou left. But she hadn't completely lost her senses. Camilla and I were still fed and heated and laundered and bought the occasional pair of underwear or socks. Mom upped her hours to full-time at the doctor's office where she typed and filed and made pots of coffee. As soon as she got home the sweatpants and tube came on, a spasm of light and sound in the dim living room.

I have to admit, I understood Mom's TV attraction. The burst of energy, the endless menu of channels, the sensation that your life is not empty or lonely or repetitious when in fact it is all of those things. Mom favored the shows with happy endings: happy couples disembarking cruise ships, happy families frolicking in prairies. Preprime time, she was partial to the game shows, with their promise of sudden fortune or, at the very least, parting gifts.

In the afternoons, before she got home, I still watched *General Hospital*. Naturally, since my father disappeared my crush on Jack Wagner had grown only more intense. At the supermarket, I grabbed up every soap opera mag that had his face on the cover. I wrote out every lyric to "All I Need" in varying fonts and sizes. And on Saturday afternoons, as always, I headed to Hannah's.

"Going to Hannah's," I informed Mom. "For the Club."

No response.

"Probably staying for dinner."

Still nothing.

"Might even sleep over."

Finally, Mom looked at me. "Are you sure you're not impos-ing?" she would say, forehead knotting up. After all those years of criticizing us, her hard shell had collapsed like a tarp, expos-ing a mush of nerves underneath. Both parts of her personality derived from the same impulse—the need to look right, to act right, to not stray too far from the norm—but after my father left, what was once snapping and nitpicking was reduced to its embryonic state: worry.

I, however, had no patience for whatever my mother was going through. As far as I was concerned, my dad had gone away because she'd driven him away. "Yes, I'm sure. They *like* having me there," I said, with an emphasis that seemed to miss her completely.

"Well, okay . . ." she drifted, hands restless in her lap. "When will you . . ." she began, but didn't finish, distracted by something on the TV screen. It appeared that, caught between husbands, my mother was unable to finish anything.

At Hannah's, interest in the ORSFC was rapidly fading. The others were getting more and more interested in real boys, less and less enthusiastic about the intimate details of Wang Chung. Cecilia stopped attending, giving us some bull-crap story about piano lessons. Katie came but brought her own agendas, which included teaching us how to give hickeys to our forearms. Even Hannah was getting preoccupied. She officially "like-liked" Eric Sommes, her partner in science lab, who had staged a one-man sit-in to protest dissecting earthworms ("Hell, no, they won't regrow!").

Some weeks, I would get stubborn and try to keep our meetings focused, like they used to be. I reported the most revealing rock-star details I could dig up. Hannah and Katie waited politely until I was finished, but I could tell neither of them was really listening. They knew my father was gone, my mom was getting weird, my sister was dating that Ivan guy, and they should be really nice to me.

At night, when I couldn't sleep, I wrote letters to Jack. I propped a flashlight against my pillow (an unnecessary move, since Mom had stopped checking lights-out) but which made the letters feel more illicit, impassioned:

Dearest Jack,
  Me again. I had another bad day.
  Only you would understand.

I scribbled until the pen hurt my hand, then drifted off to sleep with the flashlight glowing under my Garfield blanket, dreaming of my life at eighteen: a life of "careless whispers," "first real six-strings," and a boyfriend who would immortalize me in song—"Oh Sherrie" or "Sister Christian" or "Jessie's Girl"—then bust out of town with me on the back of his "broken wings."

In retrospect, that Thursday night had a quality of doom about it. Maybe it was the fact that Halloween was in two weeks and I didn't have even a costume idea. Maybe it was the fact that Hannah had officially kissed Eric Sommes (who she described only as "kind of mushy") and I officially had not. Maybe it was the fact that the student council election was the next day and Ivan was in our kitchen fumbling through his campaign speech while Camilla yelled things like "Enunciate!" and "Where's the eye contact?" and "Convince me, Ivan! Convince me!"

Whatever the reason, that night Mom agreed to let me watch *Entertainment Tonight.* It wasn't her first choice—she would have preferred *Wheel of Fortune,* with bubbly Vanna and good-natured Pat and ceramic wildlife for three hundred dollars—but tell me, what was not to love? *ET* had mansions. Fashions. Tropical vacations. California stars with California cars. It was a different world from the one we lived in, and that was why I liked it. Maybe it was something like the world my dad lived in, which I pictured revolving around a new chair, a better chair, maybe a bright chaise longue complete with a) umbrellas, b) tequilas, c) mystery women with d) mystery cats, or e) all of the above.

EXCLUSIVE BEHIND THE SCENES PHOTOS! the headline flashed. Out of the corner of my eye, I saw his face appear, then disappear, next to a smiling, pretty blond woman. My heart started pumping wildly. A NEW BEAUTY IN PORT CHARLES! NEXT . . . ON ET!

Cut to a coffee commercial. My stomach dipped and spun as coffee plinked happily from an automatic drip. Had it been him? Definitely not. It couldn't have been. It was another headline, a different headline, an exclusive-behind-the-scenes-something-else. I didn't breathe until *ET* was back on screen.

"On TV's hit daytime soap *General Hospital,* some guys can have *any* woman they want," said the female voice-over, smooth as whipped cream. "And hunky Frisco Jones—played by *real-life* hunk Jack Wagner—is no exception. But when a blond beauty joins the gang in Port Charles this season, Frisco will see that one special lady is *all he needs . . .*"

It was the kiss of death: the lyrical reference.

The next sixty seconds of my life felt like someone banging my head against a wall. A painful, mocking burst of a photo montage: blond hair, sparkling blue eyes, big white smiles, a quick pan of the *GH* set. And then—poof!—it all disappeared.

It happened so fast I wasn't sure it had happened at all.

But it had, of course. Jack Wagner had a new woman in his life. She was blond and pretty and perfect, of course. She would one day become his wife, of course. Of course, of course. It was a moment of raw, bare truth, the first in a lifetime of raw, bare truths about rock stars I'd wish I had never known. And for every one of them, from that moment on, there would be that same "of course" at the end of the sentence: a mixture of shock and expectation, disappointment and inevitability.

Within minutes, I was sobbing so hard I couldn't catch my breath. I felt Camilla hold a glass of juice to my lips, but I was crying too hard to drink it. Ivan kept repeating, "Is there anything I can do? Is there *anything* I can do?" When I felt my mother touch my shoulder, I shook her hand away. I ran upstairs, locked my door, ripped the posters from my walls, threw myself facedown on my bed and cried because I'd lost him.

3

best friends

"Running to Stand Still" — U2
"Dreams" — Fleetwood Mac
"Driving Sideways" — Aimee Mann
"Girlfriend in a Coma" — The Smiths
"Everyday I Write the Book" — Elvis Costello

After deserting Karl and his lasagna, I feel too bad about what happened between us to sit down and start writing about it. Instead, I wander the one-room heat trap I call my apartment. I read CD titles. I pick through old mail and coupon flyers. I stare at the mess of magnetic words on the fridge: "Sublime dawn." "Chocolate feather." "Hard anarchy" (from Karl). I skim the scrawled lists I've hung beside them—"Movies to Rent," "CDs to Buy," "People to Get Back in Touch With"— and inventory my cabinets: boxes of carbohydrates, jar of tartar-control cat treats.

For a moment, I see the apartment the way an outsider would: lonely, neurotic, vitamin deficient. A litany of beige foods. A cat substituting for a child. A kitchen that stays clean (but not too clean) in fear of becoming its mother.

My apartment is on the second floor of a gray three-story row house in the Manayunk neighborhood of Philadelphia. Most of Manayunk is made up of old skinny row houses squashed together on steep, winding, one-way, dead-end streets. Drink too much, then walk too fast, and the neighborhood can make you dizzy. The residents are a mix of big, thick-skinned families who haven't moved for ten generations sitting on their front stoops, chewing on cheesesteaks and cigarettes, and a new wave of twenty-somethings who rent group houses and flood the bars, coffee shops and art galleries on the newly revived Main Street.

My downstairs neighbor is your classic old-time Yunker: a sixtyish chain-smoker named Margaret with a raspy voice and a chihuahua who yaps at the sound of a light breeze. Her windows are crowded with garish suncatchers, angel statuettes, and this ominous pair of stickers: WELCOME JESUS and BEWARE OF DOG. By now, I've grown immune to the sounds and smells of Salem Ultras and *Who Wants To Be a Millionaire* seeping through my floorboards.

Until recently, my upstairs neighbors were a young couple: Chloe, a vegetarian sculptor, and Mark, an investment banker. Shockingly, they broke up. ("Fundamental differences," Chloe spat, when I ran into her outside by the trash cans throwing away pottery shards.) My new neighbor I haven't met or even seen yet. I've heard him, though: pianist. Typical, new-wave Manayunk. Probably a closet case with no phone or friends or overhead lights.

I open a cabinet, rip open a pouch of chicken-flavored ramen and wander to the east corner/living room, crunching it raw. Outside it's drizzly and depressing, but that doesn't stop some neighborhood kids from playing stickball in the street. For bases, they've grabbed up some of the arrogant orange cones and frayed lawn chairs people line by the sidewalk to hold their parking spots.

I flick on the plastic fan in the window, pick up the phone, and dial Hannah. "I'm here," I tell her machine. "Karl isn't. Call me." To Andrew's machine I say only, "Hey, call me back," trying to distill any desperation from my voice in case Kimberley happens to hear it. I wonder where my two best friends could possibly be on a rainy Sunday afternoon at 4:27. Everyone is home on Sunday afternoons at 4:27. That's the time when people watch sports and eat roast beef. The streets are empty, except for kids and orange cones, on Sunday afternoons at 4:27.

I put down the phone and roam my bookshelves, open *Ulysses* for the hundredth time, read one line, close it. I consider paying a few bills, just so I haven't completely lied to Karl about my plans for the afternoon (since it's pretty clear I'm not unwinding) but in the end, I don't pay or do anything. In the end, I reach for Leroy, my mean gray ball of a cat who on the rare occasion will sense my distress and show me affection, and flop down on my bed. Ramen and Leroy. Love's last resort.

I hate this part. The part between the middle and the end, between the conversation where you need to "unwind" (i.e., get him out of your sight for a while) and the conversation where you need to "take time" (i.e., probably never speak to him again). Between the moment when you know you will break up with him and the moment when you finally do break up with him. Because there is always that initial moment—the instant when your rock star does that one small but critical, spontaneous, no-going-back, split-second-of-a-thing that reveals, instantly but definitely, that you will not be spending the rest of your life with him. For example:

a) the moment in bed when he asks you to "stroke his feet" (a direct quote)
b) the moment on the beach when he's wearing a bikini bathing suit and/or tossing one of those obnoxious whistling beach toys
c) the moment over dinner when he utters the phrase "crazy-ass chick" and
d) is referring to you when he says it.

These are not big things, not like political preferences or religious beliefs or really bad haircuts. They are not as premeditated as all that. These are the moments that happen by instinct, not designed to score or convince or impress, and that's what makes them more alarming.

In my current situation, Karl's mother ferreting all over his face was "the moment," although it's not really about what *she* did. It's the way *he* just accepted her doing it—didn't even seem to notice, in fact—as if being ferreted over by your mother is any twenty-seven-year-old male's natural state. My mind spirals into the future until I am suddenly a wife/mother and Karl is a husband/father and has a lapful of kids yanking at his big red beard while I remind them all to wash behind their ears. And, oh yeah, we have Hummels.

Now that "the moment" has occurred, of course, the question that poses itself next is: why keep dating him? Hannah would say these are the moments you have to talk about, to work through, to peel back the layers and take your relationship to the "next level." (Wherever that is. South Jersey?) I say, once you've had "the moment," there is no going back. The moment has been said, yelled, eaten, spit, stroked, whatever. It's out there.

Suddenly, from the apartment above, the thump of a piano chord reverbs through the ceiling. Leroy panics, gouges my thighs with his claws, hurls himself from my lap, and hunches on the floor like a lion on the alert.

"Leroy, chill."

I sometimes talk to my animal. So?

"It's just our neighbor. Stay cool."

Leroy doesn't unclench. His eyes dart around, paranoid, as if the music might manifest itself into a giant mouse at any moment. Unfortunately, my cat has inherited some of my lesser qualities: edginess and intimacy issues and a reluctance to exercise. I myself was jumping at The Piano Man the day he moved in, when Leroy and I sat clutching at each other on the couch, listening to the clumps and bangs and stricken tinkles as the movers hauled his piano through the narrow stairwell to the apartment upstairs.

Thankfully, The Piano Man isn't a bad musician. Today I recognize Chopin's "Minute Waltz" from my brief career as a music major at Wissahickon. I close my eyes and listen, trying to relax, trying to let the music put me to sleep and wash away my cares. I wonder briefly (and not for the first time) what The

Piano Man looks like, then decide (not for the first time either) that he has ragged fingernails and hair growing out his ears.

When I've tried so hard to relax I've induced a headache, it's time to admit there's only one option left. I pick up the remote. I press the bright orange ON button. I let myself succumb to *Beverly Hills, 90210.*

Ah, yes. Everything is as expected in Beverly Hills. Steve is cheating on a test. Valerie is cheating on a boyfriend. Dylan is brooding and Brandon is saving the world and Donna is touting her virginity while wearing skirts as big as Post-it notes. As if picking up the vibe of mass media that's swallowing me whole, Hannah returns my call.

"You're upset."

"Yes."

"It's Karl."

"Yes."

"You're watching TV."

"So?"

"Stand up. Grab an umbrella. Meet me at the Garden."

Generous Garden is an herbal tea shop in Center City. Hannah loves the Garden because it is serene and quiet and herbal. The Garden makes me self-conscious and tense, for the same reasons. I agree to meet her there because I am the needy and she is the needed. Only at 4 A.M. can the needy choose the meeting place because a) few things are open at that hour besides Denny's, and b) the needed is too tired to care.

I take a near-empty train to 15th Street, then walk the last few blocks to the Garden. The streets of Philadelphia are pretty deserted on a drizzly summer Sunday; basically, it's me and the handful of other poor bastards who aren't at the Jersey Shore for the weekend. A guy and girl with pierced lips are arguing in front of Lo's Oriental Rugs. A grizzled guy in a Phillies cap is sitting on the curb, chomping a meatball sandwich that probably came from the cart on the corner: one of those mysterious metal boxes no bigger than my closet, yet capable of producing anything from scrambled eggs to pork roll within seconds from its suspicious, sizzling depths.

I pass the meatball guy, not caring how I look. Philly is a good city for people like me. People who like to feel inconspicuous. Who eat red meat. Who prefer to wear sweatpants with no makeup when they run to the drugstore. It's not a place that's overly fashion-conscious, health-conscious, PC-conscious, or even polite. It's a city where food is unabashedly bad for you. A city where people are what they are. If you don't like what they are, at least you're not kept guessing.

"Hey, sexy," says the Meatball Man.

And another thing: compliments are not hard to come by. Granted, they don't come from the kind of men you want to meet, date, or even make direct eye contact with, but when your love life is a mess it's sometimes nice to get that moment (however quick and sort of creepy) of affirmation.

I veer gingerly away from Meatball, and two blocks later, arrive at Generous Garden. Hannah is waiting under the dripping awning. She's wearing a gauzy purple dress and an old-fashioned yellow slicker, even has the hood pulled up with no trace of embarrassment whatsoever. Hannah is fearless like that.

I am wearing my standard comfort outfit: battered baseball cap, battered jeans, battered back-of-the-package "I Love Fig Newtons" T-shirt complete with Leroy's claw marks, and battered, thick-soled clogs. Clogs, I've found, are good for sadness; they are loud, heavy, sure of themselves. Clogs give sadness the impression of being anchored down.

Hannah gives me a hug and we duck inside out of the rain.

Like I said, the Garden is serene. Hidden behind the tapestries and African violets, the speakers tinkle Indian music or Arabian music or Enya or those simulation-rainforest tapes. Today, it's Gregorian chant (Music Theory again). At the front of the store, a glass counter is filled with what appear to be fatty pastries, but are actually lumps of honey, carob, and various grains and seeds and wheats. It's a rare bastion of health in a city whose claims to fame include cheesesteaks, cream cheese, and scrapple, a meat product that is literally gray. "Our food is non-violent," smiles a cartoon cow by the register.

"A raspberry hibiscus tea," Hannah says to the cashier. "Please."

The cashier smiles. She is a waif. Pale, fat-free, lost in some kind of waistless frock. She's probably very in-touch-with-her-body. I've noticed that people who are in-touch-with-their-bodies often look like she does. Maybe they're so in-touch that they can't ever be fully well, always honing in on some ache or cramp or ailment. Maybe all the herbs are depriving them of some essential junk, and they'll soon discover Tastykakes's Krimpets really are the forgotten food group.

"Coffee," I tell the waif, then add "black" for dramatic

effect. She looks at me as if I've just asked her to go out back and slaughter a deer.

Hannah and I pay and make our way to a tiny, glass-topped table in a corner. Everyone in here is steeping tea leaves or reading books or writing in journals. No one speaks above a whisper. My clogs sound like gunshots.

Hannah sits down and spreads her equipment before her: pot, pump, cup, spoon, mash of tea leaves. She shrugs off the hood of her raincoat and her orange hair explodes, damper and frizzier than usual. I notice people notice her. This is not unusual. Hannah is the kind of person people stop to look at: thin, bright as a flag, with hair that flies out in all directions, pale skin with a smattering of freckles, cheeks in a perpetual blush. She is beautiful, but unaware that she's beautiful, which makes her all the more beautiful. In her presence, my rock-star boyfriends tend to clam up; they get rattled just being near someone so unrehearsed.

Hannah takes off her raincoat and drops her bag on the floor, a giant tapestry sack covered with patches of quilt and tiny mirrors. Then she begins the process of steeping her tea. She's not speaking, but I know her silence isn't lack of attention. She is waiting for me to start.

"God. I don't know," I begin. This is my standard beginning. I take a gulp of coffee, scalding the roof of my mouth. It tastes awful. I hate black coffee. "It's just not working out, I guess."

"Why?" Hannah says. "What did he do?"

"He didn't *do* anything." This is my standard initially defensive response. Then I fall silent, brooding while Hannah pours her tea. It's childish, I know, but at this point it's not about maturity. It's about tradition.

"Fine," I give in. "Here it is."

She looks up, takes a sip.

"We went to Karl's mother's house today, to pick up some stuff, and while we were there she started, like, ferreting through his facial hair."

"Ferreting through his facial hair?"

"She was kind of picking at him. Preening him. It reminded me of a ferret."

"Ferrets are very underrated pets."

"Well, this one wasn't. This was a mother ferret attaching herself to a twenty-seven-year-old man ferret. It was not okay." I take another gulp of coffee, feeling emboldened. "But the ferreting wasn't the worst of it."

"What was?"

"Just . . . Karl. The way he just sat there while she did it, like it was totally and completely normal. The thing is, for him, it probably is." I take another burning swallow. "God. I don't know."

Hannah laces her fingers around her teacup. Then she closes her eyes to think. Never in my life would I be caught in public closing my eyes to think; I feel vulnerable when I sneeze while driving. But Hannah is less worried about the external world, more attuned to her inner rhythms. It's the reason she doesn't eat meat, isn't afraid to talk about her feelings, always knows exactly when her period is coming. It's the reason she dates men who call her "sweetheart" while I run from men because of their taste in swimwear, the reason she finds herself in long-term relationships and my longest commitment to date was to Jack Wagner. The reason she will one day make a wonderful counselor, and I an efficient bean counter or bricklayer.

"So," she says, opening her eyes. "You're breaking up with him, I guess."

At this stage, my reputation precedes me. "I don't know. Yeah. Probably." I stare at the top of my coffee: flat, black, sinister as a poker chip. "I think he might already see it coming."

Hannah nods, but I know she isn't close to finished. She swallows and lowers her cup, spilling some pinkish tea onto the saucer. When she speaks again, it's her therapist voice: a long, slow string of ellipses. "I know I'm repeating myself, Eliza, but . . . have you given any more thought to the possibility that . . . you're attracted to guys who won't stick . . . because of your father?"

And there you have it. Exactly the kind of insight I crave but hate. The advice I want but don't. It doesn't take a genius to make the distant father/elusive rock star connection, but for some reason I need Hannah to keep reasserting it. It's times like these when having a best friend studying to be a psychiatrist is both handy and terrifying. Obviously, I'm looking for feedback when I call her, especially when I'm fresh from a "moment," especially when I agree to meet her at the Generous Garden. Because, deep down, I really do want to understand myself. I'm just not crazy about the process of doing it. It's kind of like eating vegetables. Balancing my checkbook. Going to the gym. Going to college. Probably, in the end, it will have been worth it.

Hannah blows on her tea, sending tiny ripples across the

surface. "I mean, on some level, you might be worried you'll end up like your mother did . . . when your father left."

I nod, sort of. It's tough to argue these points with Hannah, considering she was there. She witnessed my parents fighting and my mother numbing over. It was her sunporch that became my surrogate bedroom, her family that I adopted as my own. It was she who was watching TV with me the night I burst into tears over the injustice of *My Two Dads*.

"Maybe you're taking steps to prevent what happened to your mother from happening to you. Like avoiding relationships that involve any risk . . . or depth. True depth." She says this kindly, but the extra emphasis is not lost on me: that the kind of "deep" I date is actually shallow as a puddle.

I feel myself growing defensive again.

"I mean, by looking for this perfect musician," Hannah goes on, "you can pretty much guarantee you're not going to find him. So relationships will never get that serious . . . or require a real commitment." She pushes a damp curl off her forehead. "After all, commitment is scary."

I know, on some level, Hannah is making sense here. Still, I lurch back with a clumsy, "So you're saying my mother is scary? Is that it?" which isn't relevant and isn't even believable, since my mother is the last person I would rush to defend. It also isn't spoken at the required whisper, which prompts the woman at the next table to look up, frowning, from *Feeding the Inner You*. Even the Gregorians sound annoyed.

"Sorry," I say.

Hannah nods, understanding. Too much self-assessment at

once is like drinking a can of soda too fast; it can make you feel oversaturated. Overmemoried. I find myself recalling what my house felt like in the weeks after my father left: the blaze of light from the TV, the black rotary phone I begged to ring, the ragged green recliner hulking by the curb. In truth, it wasn't my dad I really missed; he'd been so distant, there wasn't much *to* miss. What I missed was me—the kid I used to be. A normal kid. A kid with two parents and a sibling. A kid whose biggest worries were figuring out her locker combination and convincing her mother to buy her Guess jeans. A kid with every piece of her family, if not happy or healthy, at least intact.

"Maybe we could talk about something else?" I say. Of course, by shifting the conversation to Hannah's court, I know what I'm setting myself up for. There is only one topic that could present itself next.

"Well, Alan and I are planning a trip to the Amish country."

Bingo.

According to the textbooks, Hannah's relationship with Alan Pinkerton is the picture of mental health. Unlike the rock star wannabes I date, Alan Pinkerton is a grown-up. He has a full beard. He wears bedroom slippers. He is a psychology student, like Hannah, though he's been at Penn a year longer than she has. They met when Hannah entered the program two falls ago, after she got back from London. For Alan, either the proximity of academia or the proximity of Hannah's year in London seems to have entitled him to be part British. He says "post" instead of mail, "cheers" instead of see ya. He calls me "e-LI-za," with a mournful note on the second syllable, like some trying-to-be brogue.

On the outside, I smile at Alan politely. On the inside, I am screaming: *You're from Newark, for fuck's sake!*

The funny thing is, I think Alan recalls Hannah's London experience more fondly than she does. For her, it was the "transitional year," the "growing year," the year when all the inclinations she'd been born with—an obsession with animals, a talent for listening—hardened into diets and stances and careers. She worked at a food co-op, where she fell in love with a lad named Reuben and, soon after, moved into his flat, which had a great view and a sturdy teakettle and a window ledge where pigeons came for muesli in the mornings.

I learned all about Hannah's life via postcards—"On my way to Spain!" or "Recipe for Pudding (easy)" or "Think I'm falling in love!"—while I moped around post-college Philly, dating the bassist from Roller Toaster and plastering my freezer door with stoic Royal Guards and Big Bens. I resented Hannah, though I didn't like to admit it. I resented her willingness to take risks. To travel abroad, to give up chicken, even to fall in love. To do all the things I didn't dare. Although I told myself frequenting The Blue Room was living on the edge, all the risk in my life truly began and ended with the nipple ring on my Roller Toaster.

But in December, the Big Bens stopped coming. Reuben had left Hannah. Reuben had left London. And for three weeks, Hannah didn't get out of bed. In March, Mrs. Devine flew to London and came back with Hannah, who started applying to med school for psychiatry.

"I want to go horseback riding," Hannah is saying now. "And Alan will insist on trying all the native Amish foods."

"What are native Amish foods?"

"Oh, you know. Apple dumplings. Shoo fly pie."

"Shoo fly pie?" I say, feigning shock. The *Inner You* woman lifts her head and sighs. "That sounds violent. Isn't killing flies required?"

Hannah flashes me a sly smile. "I guess you'll never be stopping by the Amish country, Eliza. No rock stars allowed."

I grin. She grins back. Any dry wit Hannah has acquired over the years I take partial credit for. Likewise, any emotional maturity I've achieved I owe in part to her. We are more different now than we were as kids, but that's the way old friends work, I think. With new friends, what you have in common is more circumstantial: colleges, jobs, hobbies, acquaintances-of-the-hour. What old friends share goes deeper than that. Your lives can branch off in completely different directions, but always, you share that knot of a past—heartbreaks and sleepovers and screened-in porches—and the raw, peculiar memory of yourself which, in part, belongs to them.

Phone message from Andrew: "What up, G? What going down?"

This is unfortunate. Andrew's attempts at hip lingo fall into the same embarrassing category as his attempts at air guitaring. I've noticed that he seems to be practicing both more frequently lately, especially when something grown-up happens in his life—investing in a new stock, trying a new vegetable—in an effort to convince himself he's still carefree and childlike.

"Anyway, it's me," he says. "Got your message. Give me a buzz." Andrew's message clicks off and the automated answering

machine man comes on: "No. More. Messages." Like I need this
guy rubbing it in. Sometimes I have visions of the automated
answering machine man trying his best to maintain a monotone,
while laughing into his sleeve between messages and stuffing his
mouth with pork rinds. One day he'll just come out and bark
something like: "Same. Old. Messages. Loser. Get. New. Friends."

I go into the west corner/bedroom and crawl into my PJs.
It's almost a quarter past nine. It's too quiet. No phone ringing.
No TV rambling. The Piano Man seems to have packed it in.
Karl didn't call, obviously. Should I feel disappointed? No. Do
I? Not really. Not specifically. Not justly, anyway. After all, I'm
the one who said I needed to unwind. I return to the living
room, turn on VH1—an intimate *Behind the Music;* tonight,
the Fleetwood Mac story—and dial Andrew.

"Hey, Eliza," he answers, before I can speak.

Andrew's ability to identify my phone calls freaked me out
for exactly two days last October. I went through the phases of
a) Andrew as impressive, b) Andrew as spooky, c) Andrew as
genuinely clairvoyant, and d) Andrew and I as psychically con-
nected and possibly destined to be soulmates after all, before I
realized he'd just gotten Caller ID.

"I know you can ID me, Andrew. You don't have to keep
proving it."

"But it's fun."

"You're right. It's a ball." I settle deeper into the couch,
pulling an afghan over my knees. "What are you watching?"
This is our standard greeting, and a quick test of the other's
state of mind.

"X-Files. You?"

"Behind the Music." Both of these sound fairly healthy.

"What's the musical story tonight?" Andrew says. "Drugs? Divorce? Bankruptcy?"

"I don't know yet. I just turned it on."

"Right." I hear him pop something in his mouth and crunch. Probably Cracker Jacks. "So, did you go out with Bon Jovi today?"

"Actually, I might have almost finished with Bon Jovi today."

"Oh yeah? How come?" I can hear him smiling as he waits for my reason. "Does he have a pet bug? Sing badly in the shower? Say 'idear' instead of 'idea'?"

This is one of the downsides to having best friends. You become too obvious.

"We went to his mother's house."

"Oooohhh!" Andrew says, sucking in his breath like a crowd watching a goal graze the net and just miss. "The fatal Eliza-mother move. Which did she break out first? Photos or live action film?"

"Neither. It was worse. She was kind of, ferreting in his facial hair."

"Ferreting in his facial hair?" The smile audibly disappears. "What the hell does ferreting mean? That's not a word."

"It is a word. I should know. I do words for a living."

"It is not."

"It is."

"Hold on. I have a dictionary right here." It's true, he does. I can see it lined up next to his phone along with his thesaurus, phone book, zip code directory, and eighty-dollar art history textbook he bought in college, never opened, but refused to sell back because (his story) he might want to refresh himself on the material in the future or (my story) he wanted to keep the pictures of naked women.

"Here it is." I hear him flipping pages, mumbling to himself. This is hitting Andrew where he lives: the practical, provable world. "F. Ferret. Noun. Mammal. Fur. Feet." I hear him pause, then snap, "Fuck."

"Told you," I say. "Ferreting." As if sensing the presence of foreign animals, Leroy saunters by with his tail in the air. I start patting my lap like a maniac. He glances at me with disdain. "Anyway. Like I was saying . . ."

"No, wait. Are you kidding me?" Andrew says. "Ferreting? Since when?"

I can sympathize with this. I am familiar with the surreal, disjointed feeling of having discovered a word that's common to the rest of the world but which you've never heard before. It's like the first time I encountered "mirage" at the age of eighteen. It can be truly disconcerting. You start to wonder what other common words—the equivalent of table, chair, cake— have been narrowly missing your life for twenty-six years.

"Let it go, Andrew. You get the idea," I say, settling deeper into the cushions. "She was picking in his goatee. Then she was looking in his ears. Then she was checking out his nails . . ."

"You mean grooming," he interjects. "She was grooming him."

"Fine. She was grooming him. Whatever. It was disgusting."

He yawns, returning to my orbit. "Yeah, that sounds pretty

gross." I hear the thump of the dictionary closing, then another Cracker Jack crunch over the line. "So you pulled the plug?"

"I guess. Almost." I glance at the screen, where Fleetwood appears to be starting the 9:30 P.M. decline.

"How did you break it to him?"

"I didn't, really. It was a weird moment. We were in his car. It smelled like lasagna." The thing is, Andrew will understand the gross, insignificant significance of the lasagna detail without my having to explain it. It's good to have friends like this. "I told him I needed to go home and unwind."

"Ooohhh!" He makes the annoying, missed-goal crowd noise again. "The fatal Eliza-unwind move. So have you?"

"What?"

"Unwound."

"Not exactly. I went with Hannah to that herbal tea place that stresses me out." I consider asking his opinion on what Hannah said about me dating guys I know I'll never get close to, but decide against it. There are certain places Andrew and I just don't go. It's one of the main differences between male and female bonding, I think: with men, all you have to do is joke around, watch *Seinfeld,* and toss a Frisbee to affirm the strength of your friendship; with women (after the initial PMS confessional in the ladies' rest room) it gets harder, quieter, denser, until emotions are required of almost every conversation.

"So where'd you go this afternoon?" I ask, opting out.

"Nowhere," Andrew says, crunching. "Who goes out on rainy Sunday afternoons?"

"Where were you then?"

"Here."

"Then where were you when I called?"

"Oh." His chewing pauses, as if caught in the act of something. "I was here. I mean, for the most part I was here."

"You suck at lying. You were home when I called you. Why didn't you pick up?"

He's quiet for a long moment. Too long. "Well, Kimberley was over."

I start to get a queasy feeling.

"We were kind of . . ."

The picture is suddenly, painfully clear: Andrew and Kimberley in the throes of passion and/or legal debating, the phone ringing, Andrew hesitating, Kimberley whispering something like, "If you let it ring, I'll make it worth your while," and then the two of them falling on the bed half dressed as my message plays naively in the background, sounding more desperate, I'm sure, than I remember it.

"Andrew, I think I gotta go. Fleetwood's not looking so good."

Dreams Come True, Inc. is the last place I feel like being on Monday morning but there I am, riding the elevator, bright and early. "Bright and early" is actually a popular inter-office phrase, along with "How are *we* today?" and "Happy Monday!" (or Tuesday, Wednesday, etc.) and, occasionally, "Howdy-do!"

Dreams is a happy workplace, a family of a workplace, a workplace that exists in the plural "we." On birthdays, we all crowd around the desk of the VIP and sing like those chipper, bebuttoned waiters and waitresses at franchise restaurants. Then there's card opening, cake eating, sometimes candle blowing and wish making. It's a wonder we get any work done.

I step off the elevator at Floor #12 and slouch unhappily down the posh hall to Dreams. It's hard to miss: the door is plastered with a poster of a tan, blond couple sitting in a heart-shaped hot tub. The tub is filled with rose petals, and the blondes are gazing at each other over the rims of their garish pink drinks. Across the dusky sky are the words: *Ever feel like your life is . . . missing something?* Like every morning for the past almost-two years, I bitterly shove open the door, resolve to find a new job tomorrow, then force a smile on my face when I'm confronted by Dreams's front receptionist: Beryl.

Beryl is about sixty years old and looks exactly as a Beryl should: round, pink-cheeked, twinkly. Beryl is of an age when people called boyfriends "fellows," an age when people were named, well, Beryl. She's also of an age when people had warm, patient telephone manners; problem is, she has no modern-day telephone savvy. This combination makes for a lot of cheerful "Good mornings!" and good-natured "Oops! What the dickens?" while staring, perplexed, at the blinking lights of her phone pad. I would be willing to bet that Beryl's children gave her a VCR one Christmas and it's never left the box.

"Happy Monday, Eliza!" Beryl sings. I check out her pin. Beryl has an endless supply of pins that appear, one each morning, at the top of her collar. Today: a sterling silver bunch of grapes with smiley faces.

"Happy Monday," I return. "Cool pin."

"Well, thank you!" Beryl smiles, then her smile heightens to a beam. "Guess who got a promotion this weekend?"

I don't have to guess, but I do, for her sake. "Donny?"

Donny is Beryl's twenty-eight-year-old, unmarried grandson that she has been trying to set me up with for almost two years. I don't think it's any special credit to me; all the other twenty-somethings in the office just happen to have long-term boyfriends, boyfriends who call the office and come to staff parties and even send flowers, which creates a major buzz of inter-office gushing and sniffing. My boyfriends are a different brand. They're not long-term. They don't make phone calls in the daytime. They surely don't send flowers. Beryl probably doesn't even know they exist, which makes me an eligible bach-elorette for the Donster.

I have been avoiding the Donny date for a couple of reasons:

a) He's twenty-eight, and apparently has been single for almost two years. Not necessarily bad but, you know. Pause for caution.

b) He's not a musician—which I know sounds simplistic and lame—but, to make matters worse, he is a busi-nessman. It's not so much the simple fact of his being a businessman that makes me wary. It's everything that I assume must have preceded this: every ironed sock and slick interview and childhood dream (i.e., did Donny have an actual passion to become a busi-nessman? or just no passion to become anything else? and which is worse?).

c) The issue of Donny's automatic PCT: pop culture translation.

A person's PCT is the first celebrity—from movies, music, TV—who comes to mind when you hear their name.

Elton = John.

Clint = Eastwood.

Of course, a PCT can vary based on a person's age and experience. In some circles, Johnny = Depp. In others, Cash or Carson. But no matter who you are, there's no getting around Donny's PCT: Osmond. One might argue that he's probably presenting himself to the public as Don rather than Donny by now. But really, Don isn't much better. (PCT = Ho.)

Personally, I don't want a boyfriend with a PCT too obvious. In that way, Karl was nice. Jung, yeah. Sagan, maybe. But Karl's name didn't make anyone leap to mind the way Donny's does. In fact, I think Karl was the first and only Karl I've ever known. Karl was a good name, a clean slate of a name, a name free of any glaring associations—pop culture or otherwise—and therefore one I can eventually file away with Zach and Jordan and Travis and every other male name I dated once and am therefore unable to ever date again.

"That's great," I tell Beryl. "Tell him congratulations for me."

"You could tell him yourself," she says, giving me a great big wink. "He's a real catch, our Donny. He has so much drive!"

"Drive?" I know, for sure, that Beryl did not come up with "drive" on her own. I have to wonder, then, who she picked

"drive" up from. Donny's mother? Donny's father? Donny himself? This possibility is too horrific to dwell on.

I stare at the smiling grapes, mumble, "Maybe someday, Beryl"
for the umpteenth time, and scurry in the direction of my desk.

On the way, I peer into the posh, monstrous office of our
boss who, not surprisingly, isn't in it. Our boss is rarely on the
premises. Her real name is Marian, but I have secretly renamed
her the Queen Mother. The QM is sleek, single, has fingernails
long as clothespins, and is always traveling—which I suppose, if
you run a travel agency, is the main perk. She calls in at least
once every day from wherever in the world she happens to be
partying (runways, beaches, tiki bars) and when she returns,
brings us little presents of chocolates and key chains bought in
international airports, like a surrogate mom.

I arrive at my desk, drop my bookbag, and stare down at the
mess of travel brochures. It is strange, being poor and working
in this business. On the one hand, I am immersed in a lifestyle
that feels unreal to me: expensive hotels, exotic resorts, luxury
cruises. At the same time, all that unreal stuff intensifies what *is*
real: my brown-bottomed coffee cup, my bitten-down nails, my
"Joke a Day" calendar (an office birthday gift, "because you're
the funny one!") and worst of all, the poster of a tanned,
perfect-bodied woman lounging on a St. Barth beach that
hangs, unfortunately, just above my desk.

I wave to Maggie, the Travel Agent in the cubicle next to
mine. She flutters her fingers at me and points exaggeratedly to
the receiver, confirming what I already see: she's on the phone.

"I have that information on Paris right here, Mr. Warner,"

Maggie chirps. "Could you hold for a second while I put my finger on it?" She puts Mr. Warner on hold and breezy, tropical "hold music" seeps from her handset. "Happy Monday, Eliza," she smiles at me.

"Happy Monday, Maggie," I intone. It's easy to feel a little like a cult member at Dreams.

Maggie starts riffling through a file cabinet, humming to herself. Maggie is pretty and nice. All the Travel Agents are pretty and nice. They are the kinds of women all girls were supposed to grow up and become, women with pressed blouses and painted fingernails. They grew up on the Main Line, went to prep schools, and can spend hours discussing the latest innovations in strapless bras and fat-free yogurts. They all have boyfriends, of course, and eventually engagements, office showers and weddings and honeymoons. (Aha! *That's* why so many pretty, nice women with boyfriends end up working at Dreams: easy access to honeymoons!) Anytime one of the Agents gets married, I include a tidbit in our company newsletter. Usually it's a photo of Agent and "hubby" on a tropical beach with the caption: "Dreams's own travel agent gets dreamy!" or something like that. We call it PR.

Maggie resurfaces with folder in hand, sips from the can of Diet Coke that is forever on her desktop, and reconnects with Mr. Warner. "Thanks for holding, Mr. Warner! We have hotel rates starting at two hundred and thirty—that's U.S. dollars— for a standard double . . ."

I locate my laptop in the midst of the mess that is my desk—old files, stray photos, vacation guide books and videos, a paperweight shaped like a pineapple, a book called *Words That*

Pay!—and turn the computer on. The screen glows a greenish gray. It's not like a TV screen, sucking you in instantly with brightness and happiness and volume. A computer screen starts slow, blank, a gradual scattering of icons in the emptiness.

Today's task is to finish the article I started on Friday: "Passion on Puerto Vallarta!" But first, coffee. I head to the "kitchen," really just a strip of Formica in the back of the office with a coffeemaker, sink filled with empty cups, and mini-fridge stocked with cases of Diet Coke and hunks of leftover birthday cake. When I walk up, Tracy the Travel Agent and Aileen the Travel Agent are nibbling from last week's chocolate frosted, while Aileen describes the dinner her boyfriend Leonardo (PCT so obvious it's not worth mentioning) cooked her Saturday night.

"Hey, Eliza!" they greet me, then look down at the cake and blush. "Never too early for cake, right?"

"Definitely not."

"Want some?" Tracy asks prettily.

"Thanks. I think I'll start with coffee."

"Do anything interesting this weekend?" Aileen asks nicely.

The Agents are always interested in my weekends. I think, because I have a nose ring, they suspect I have a really wild weekend lifestyle involving raves and cops and VW buses. They'd be disappointed to know I usually log several reruns of *Alf.* I do, however, frequent The Blue Room. Ever since I told them about the band I saw there wearing nothing but thongs, they've regarded me and my life with a mixture of fear and fascination.

"Any good stories?" Tracy asks, with hope in her voice.

I consider my options here: the herbal shop with Hannah,

the almost-break-up with Karl, the sex-prompt phone message to Andrew, the now infamous ferreting story. For a minute, I consider the possibility that Tracy and Aileen the Travel Agents might actually be the ideal audience for this ferreting business; they will be appropriately grossed out by the gesture itself, but will not care what it reveals about my relationship patterns or whether the verb form of "ferret" exists or not.

In the end, I resort to a little in-house humor. "Oh, not much. Flew to Puerto Vallarta and back. Can't you tell?" I say, and hold out my forearm, pale as a raw crescent roll.

They laugh and fork up another bite of cake. They think I'm funny, even when I'm not being funny. I suspect they wouldn't be caught dead being funny.

"So anyway," Aileen says, picking up where she left off. "Then he served this flounder, with a kind of béarnaise . . ."

I sugar and milk a cup of coffee 'til it's practically a Yoo-hoo, then wave to Tracy and Aileen and return to my desk. Between sips of caffeine, I float to a few music Web sites, check my E-mail (one reminder about Dreams's vacation policy which I delete, one chain letter from an old college friend that begins: "If you stop reading now, you will be unlucky in love for . . ." which I delete) and then, finally, open "Passion on Puerto Vallarta!" and pick up where I left off.

4

drummers

SIDE B

"Welcome to the Jungle" — Guns N' Roses
"I Love Rock-n-Roll" — Joan Jett & the Blackhearts
"Looks That Kill" — Mötley Crüe
"Jamie's Cryin'" — Van Halen
"Hit Me With Your Best Shot" — Pat Benatar

The first rock star I knew in real life was Z Tedesco. I'd gone to school with Z (then known as Zachary) since we were in Mrs. Blakey's kindergarten class. Back then, he was far from rock star material. He was a small, bony, oily kid who brought pastrami sandwiches for lunch in paper bags, a kid who scowled in every school picture, a kid no one envied because he had to learn the cursive "Z" while the rest of us were still plodding through "E"s and "F"s.

Z had no apparent musical inclination back in Glendale Elementary, though it's tough to detect that kind of raw talent while clapping along to "ta-ta-ti-ti-ta" or singing the PC-before-its-time holiday medley of dreidels, Santa Clauses, and

Hispanic reindeer named Pablo. Z had no interest in girls, either (not that any eight-year-old boy really does) but I don't remember him ever even talking to a female, not once. Not even to borrow paste or bum a Tastykake in a kind of genderless camaraderie. He was a boy's boy: slick and Italian, with a lock of black hair that fell across his forehead like a mini-Fonz.

Though Z was intense as a kid, he hadn't yet channeled it into his future calling: rock music. In grades one through five the focus of his intensity was kickball. He was fiercely good at it and fiercely competitive about it, diving around the field and scurrying around the bases with his gold cross bouncing in the tan hollow of his throat. God help the weak kicker who took the plate when Z was playing. If you were on his team, he would groan and curse and kick up clouds of dust in a general show of support; if you were on the other team, he would yell something sensitive like "Easy out!" and wave his team in close. I prayed not to be on the same team as Z Tedesco, but not because I couldn't handle his disgust. If I was on the opposing team, I could at least concentrate on practicing cartwheels with my friends in the outfield without any undue pressure.

Fast forward to the beginning of tenth grade: September, a Saturday night, the York High School Talent Show. Me, Hannah-and-Eric-Sommes, Katie Brennan, and Jessica Walkins (she'd replaced Cecilia, had an in-ground pool and a doomed obsession with Milli Vanilli) are sitting side by side on a gym bleacher dressed in head-to-toe fluorescent (it was cool then, really). I am more or less recovered from the Jack Wagner blow of 1984 and have dedicated my love life to real musicians.

Noncelebrities. Musicians I could evaluate myself, without the interference of *TV Guide* or *People* magazine. Musicians I could actually see and touch and talk to and hopefully start kissing— fast—since Hannah-and-Eric had already made the ominous leap from second base to third.

In the front of the gym, under the scoreboard, a stagelike surface had been erected where the talent show's "talent" would be performing. The setup was kind of like a younger, larger, and more sober version of The Blue Room. The show would consist of a variety of acts—song, dance, circus, and other—and a win- ner who was determined by the "applause meter" (i.e., Mr. Farley the gym teacher, who shouted things like "Is that the best you can do, Panthers?!" and terrified us into clapping harder).

The talent show lineup that year was typically lame: a trio of girls perched on the edge of the stage with guitars and prairie skirts, gazing off over our heads and singing "Where Have All the Flowers Gone?" twenty years too late; a sophomore juggler whose balls started rolling around the stage, prompting the entire crowd to dissolve into hysterics; Billy Crow doing skate- board tricks; the blond, pigtailed Henry twins tapdancing to "I Get a Kick Out of You"; a surprise entry by Cecilia Kim, plunk- ing out "My Bologna Has a First Name" and "You Deserve A Break Today" from *The Big Book of Commercial Jingles;* a chubby, earnest tuba player; and a frightened freshman wafting around on stilts.

Then, just when the crowd was starting to get restless, out came Z. Or, I should say, Z appeared. He seemed to simply materialize on the stage, a stoic Italian god behind a drum set, encircled in a single pool of blue electric light that beamed down from the ceiling of a gym that was suddenly sunk in darkness. Z's hair was still jet black, but longer, with a bandanna wound around his forehead. His look: loose jeans, a tie-dyed T-shirt ripped off at the sleeves, a hoop in his left ear, a rose tattoo on his right bicep, and the old gold cross still glinting in the core of his throat.

Z raised his drumsticks in the air. He tapped them four times slowly, paused, closed his eyes, then let loose on that drum set like an uncaged beast. The gym seemed to draw a collective breath as Z slammed on the cymbal, banged on the bass, jammed and slashed and sweated in the center of a mash of disorganized noise (he would later call it "free form") with arms flying, hair flipping, feet bare on the pedals. He closed his eyes and bit his lower lip, tendons leaping from his arms.

Naturally, the crowd went wild. Mr. Farley started blowing maniacally on his gym whistle, but the clamor quickly swallowed him up. Within minutes the whole gym was on its feet, stomping, moshing, dancing, chicken fighting. An invisible tech guy started blinking the blue light on and off. A sprinkling of lighters appeared in the upper reaches of the risers.

Z was a rock star.

I'm starting to think that everyone must have had one person they dated, early on—probably in the impressionable mush of adolescence—who was critical in forming their "look." Defining their "image." Cementing their "type." After I saw Z Tedesco bring the house down, I went home and banished all fluorescent from my closet. I boxed up all two-toned jeans, and hid any shoe that involved jellied plastic. The next day I pooled my babysitting money, went to the mall, and invested in a wardrobe of blacks and grays, a splash of tie-dye, dark eye makeup, and a tube of gel to make my hair go flat, flatter, as flat as possible—the beginnings of the new me.

I wasn't the only girl at York High who was profoundly affected by Z's performance. On Monday, you could spot us a mile away. We were all wearing new T-shirts: solid black (for the tentative), tie-dye (riskier, but still pretty safe) or the tie-dye/band name combo (only for the truly brave). To wear a T-shirt with a specific band's name on it was a major commitment at this early stage, and I spotted a few misfires in the hallways—nice, nervous girls looking panicked and lost in too-big T-shirts with knives and roses and Megadeths sprawled across their chests.

I opted for the basic tie-dye-T-shirt-with-blue-jeans ensemble. This is not because I was afraid to commit to a band—I had worn a giant decal of Jack Wagner's face, for God's sake, had carried around an Official Rock Star Fan Club membership card; I was not a kid afraid of band commitment—I just wanted to bide my time. I was feeling fairly confident about my chances with Z, and didn't want to announce too much too fast. I was pretty sure I didn't look as nervous and conspicuous as the other Z-converts.

"Eliza!" Hannah exclaimed at lunch, when she took in the new me.

I'd arrived at our usual table, located securely in the center of the soph section of the caf, between the soccer/cheerleader table and the choir/drama table. To our left, soccer players and cheerleaders flirted en masse, the girls giggling and whispering, the boys cracking jokes and slapping low fives. To our right, the drama kids frequently burst into song— "Memories" or "Too Darn Hot!"—like some wannabe *Fame*. Once, they had attempted a choreographed number that culminated in lunch aides pulling Henrietta Meara off their table shouting, "I want to live forever!" Fortunately, with that kind of commotion, my friends and I usually attracted little notice.

"You look . . . different," Hannah said, as I dropped my orange tray. She had her usual healthy brown bag of homemade lunch and I my Philly-fried cheesesteak bought with the three dollars Mom had handed me that morning.

I shrugged, scraping back a chair.

"I don't mean bad," she amended. "Just, different." She picked up a celery stick and gnawed it like a toothpick.

Eric Sommes, who had been sitting beside her scrawling in a notebook full of sigmas and pis, raised his head and surveyed my new look. "Wow," he said, but it was an innocuous "wow." Not like *"wow, she's hot"* or like "wow, you're *nuts!*" I could tell nothing from Eric's bland, nasal "wow" and unfortunately, he was the only male opinion at my disposal.

"Thanks, Eric," I said, unfoiling my sandwich.

Then Katie Brennan arrived on the scene, decked out in striped leg warmers and a shirt with a rainbow spilling across the chest and arms. She plunked down her daily soft pretzel and

Diet Coke (did Katie turn out to be a travel agent?) then looked at me and squealed: "Oh. My. God!"

Unlike Eric, Katie was not too cryptic. She was plainly horrified by the new me, but this was to be expected. One could argue this was actually a point in my favor. Katie was a slave to '80s fashions, a girl born ready for '80s fashions, bold and loud and leg warmed to the core.

"What happened to you?" she said, and started laughing so determinedly that soda spurted out her nose. Katie could make even the gross come off as cute and pink. "Eliza, what did you *do?*"

I shrugged again, the picture of nonchalance. "It was time for a change," was all I said, and took a cool bite of my heat-lamped cheesesteak.

"I *guess!*" Katie said, glancing at the soccer players/cheerleaders beside us. It had long been obvious to Hannah and me that Katie was just sitting with us until our proximity to the soccer players enabled her to merge, unnoticed, into their table. In the meantime, she certainly didn't want any of us hurting her chances at getting there. "You look like Pat Benatar!" she laughed, loud enough for every soph in the caf to hear.

I felt my cheeks burn. Coming from Katie, being compared to Pat was the gravest of insults and everyone in earshot knew it. Thankfully, before she could say anything else, the choir/drama gang, probably resentful the spotlight wasn't on them, launched into a full-table rendition of *Phantom*.

Katie tossed her blond ponytail in the general direction of the soccer players. Then, satisfied she'd saved her reputation from near disaster, she launched into an overly loud recap of her latest conquest: a senior on the swim team. "I know he's like three years older than me, but it's perfect because he's really immature . . ."

Left alone, I fumed with my sandwich. To be honest, I wasn't too concerned about my friends' opinions. Now that the heat was off, I didn't mind being compared to Pat Benatar; in fact, I was secretly pleased. I'd already begun to realize that I wasn't like my friends, or my sister, or my mother, or most of my classmates for that matter. I "danced to the beat of my own drummer," as Nanny would say. There was only one person whose opinion I cared about, and I knew where to find him.

The Quad: a square, stark fish tank of a place comprised of ashtray/trashcans, picnic tables, pockmarked benches and scraggly, unmowed patches of grass. The Quad was the physical hub of the high school, visible via window from the caf, the main lobby, the math wing, and the music hall. I guess "Quad" originally derived from "quadrangle," though over the years the two words had lost all association. "Quad" had taken on an identity all its own, connoting all kinds of ominous, mysterious, and possibly illegal things.

The Quad's distinguishing characteristic was this: it was the only place in school where kids were allowed to smoke. As a result, the four-walled space was filled with crushed cigarettes, tie-dyes, tattoos, and miles of denim brewed together in a haze of gray. If they'd only had beer out there, it would have passed for a keg party. There was even a speaker system (from back in the day when the Quad was for general socializing, not just smoking) that played music audible only from outside. When the door to the Quad opened, the entire caf caught a scary, trippy snatch of Led Zeppelin or Pink Floyd or one of the other bands the Quad would pick apart for their yearbook quotes.

The kids who hung out there were officially called the Quadders: revered, and slightly feared. The Quadders were cool, but not the cheerleading, class-officiating, paint-your-face-blue-at-football-games kind of cool. They were *truly* cool, the kind of cool that defied school spirit. It wasn't that they actively protested things like Pajama Day and Backward Day and all the other self-conscious "days" designed to psych us up for Homecoming Weekend. They never scoffed outright at the Christmas Dance or the soft pretzel drive. Quadders seemed genuinely oblivious to these things, gliding through the hallways sleek as panthers (as opposed to Panthers, which covered the rest of us). They walked with poise, cigarettes behind their ears. They never tripped. They hardly ate. They rarely carried backpacks. They always cut gym.

I didn't know many Quadders in specific. None, actually. A handful of them always appeared in the final pages of the yearbook under "Other Graduating Seniors," as if even the fact of graduation had escaped their notice. But I knew, for sure, Z would be out there. From the safety of our table, I scanned the Quad and found him: one foot on a bench, one foot on the ground, hair in ponytail, cigarette in hand, girlfriend-free, and—God help me—actually drumming on his thigh with his left hand. He was probably mentally composing as he stood there. In that moment, the phrase "dancing to the beat of my own drummer" reached new heights of symbolism as I stared at the boy who I knew was, without a doubt, my soulmate.

Of course, even something as staggering as discovering someone was your soulmate wasn't enough to drive me out into the Quad to meet the guy, not in plain view of anybody in the caf, lobby, math wing or music hall, not to mention every Other Graduating Senior. The entire social structure of York High would probably have gone haywire, jocks dating geeks, brains cutting classes, prom queens playing softball, Led Zeppelin disappearing in a pop of static and airwaves in distress. I was in love, not insane.

If my one-critical-person-forming-your-image theory is correct, then probably I should credit Z Tedesco not only with my black-and-tie-dye wardrobe, but my entire career as a college English major. Probably he's the reason I became word obsessed in the first place, the reason I know "ferret" is a transitive verb, the reason I write catchy headlines for a living, the reason I'm always mentally editing spelling and grammar mistakes on billboards, storefronts, and Chinese menus, and probably, ultimately, the reason I'm writing a book. I trace all of this back to the fact that Z was on the staff of the school literary magazine: *Transformations.*

I discovered this by no act of fate, but through the very goal-oriented, time-consuming scouring of the previous year's yearbook, looking for Z's face. My methods sound a little pathetic, I know, but in situations like these you need to capitalize on your strengths. Behind-the-scenes is where I work best—not on the stage, on the phone, on the kickball field. I prefer to be tucked behind televisions, laptops, magazines. If my search was pathetic, at least it was privately pathetic, unlike the wan, fearful girls draped in XXL Mötley Crüe sweatshirts who looked as if they'd been spooked by their own shadows.

Locating Z in the yearbook wasn't as simple as I thought. As it turns out, Quadders don't go out for too many extracurriculars, and the pretalent-show Z kept a low profile. No wonder I'd barely noticed him since kickball games at Glendale Elementary. He appeared only twice in the two hundred and fifty pages of the York Yodel: once among the generic rows of the freshman class (still scowling) and once in the staff shot of the literary magazine, slumped low in a desk chair, looking intensely thoughtful, the white nub of a cigarette pinched between forefinger and thumb.

My mission: to track down the first *Transformations* staff meeting. In what turned out to be a brilliant move on my part, I asked my English teacher, Ms. Horn. "I certainly ought to know when it is," she beamed. "I'm only the faculty adviser!" Then she went on to tell me how glad she was that I was "finally embracing my potential as a writer" (this based on one bullshit-filled bluebook on *Ethan Frome).*

The following Monday, after school, I prepared myself for the meeting. In the bathroom, I applied black mascara and eyeliner. That morning, I'd picked out my favorite new tie-dye and a pair of jeans I'd managed to bust up a little—some stray white threads at the cuff, a hole at the knee—but not too much, preserving the illusion that the damage had happened organically.

In the mirror, I arranged an expression on my face that I thought was dreamy, thoughtful, deeply preoccupied, and held it tight, barely breathing, as I headed for Room 117.

It was your basic gray-green classroom. It also happened to double as a chem lab, which explained the periodic table hanging incongruously among the scattering of tortured artists. Ms. Horn beamed at me as I entered. I couldn't beam back, for fear of wrecking the expression on my face, so I flicked her a low wave. There were about ten kids sitting in chairs: a clump of giggling, fluorescent-clad upperclass girls, a few pale, skinny, bespectacled boys (layout, I guessed), and one morose chubby girl with a pierced nose. Then I spotted Z. He was sitting alone in the back of the room, legs sprawled under the desk, dressed all in black and wearing a half-lidded squint I would later realize was probably boredom or rudeness or marijuana—but I took then to be, you know, deep.

I chose a desk two seats from Z's: not so far that we couldn't talk if we wanted to, not so close that I was being obvious. I felt a touch of pride about the fact that none of the other Z-lovers had had the same idea I did. The pack of upperclass girls was oblivious to anyone but each other, the glasses guys were talking Dungeons and Dragons, and the morose chubby girl had her head bent over a book (she was probably the only one of the lot who actually wanted to read and write, not just accumulate activities for college applications or score a date with a rock star).

As I was inwardly congratulating myself on my ingenuity, four kids—two girls, two guys—floated through the door and sat in a row on the long table at the front of the room. They carried themselves with such ease that I knew immediately they were seniors. All of them were dressed vaguely, genderlessly alike, in loose, flowing pants or willowy skirts, wide-sleeve shirts, long hair and sandals, and a variety of homemade jewelry. They were sucking on lollipops and sitting so close their shoulders touched. I think I fell in love with them all on the spot.

"Hello, everyone," said one of the girls, giving us a big wave. The room hushed. Her voice was smooth, slow, melodic, kind of like Mr. Devine's folk albums. "Welcome to the first meeting of *Transformations.*" School literary magazines always have titles like this—*Reflections* or *Connections* or *Inspirations*—one abstract plural noun in italics. "These are the editors for 1988," the girl said, and wafted an arm toward the three beside her, who introduced themselves.

"I'm Skye. Fiction editor. Peace."

"Maya. Poetry editor. Hello."

"Avery. Art and layout."

The first girl pointed at herself. "And I'm your editor-in-chief. Karma."

How is it that people born with names like these always end up becoming people like them? You'd never find someone named Skye or Karma working in an insurance agency or an investment firm. As Karma kept talking, poetry-editor Maya slid off the table and began circulating the room, handing each of us a lollipop.

"It's really awesome to see new faces out there," Karma said.

"And for those of you who are new, this"—she reached behind her and produced a large, rainbowed box with a slot on top— "is our submissions box. It lives in the main office, so students can drop their contributions in at any time. Our job, during these meetings, will be to read the pieces in the box, comment on them, discuss them, and decide if they reflect the essence and the purpose of *Transformations.*"

It was at this point that it began to dawn on me how under-qualified I was to be there. I had no business assessing other people's writing, not with a reading background that consisted mainly of *Bop* and *Teen Beat,* with a sprinkling of *Ethan Frome* and *Horton Hears a Who.* It hadn't occurred to me yet that I would be called upon to work—and worse, speak!—at this meeting. Maybe I could just be the group secretary or some-thing, writing down what others said and occasionally shouting out old catchphrases from the ORSFC: "New business!" and "Order in the court!"

"Okay," Skye took over, crossing his legs at the knee. I'd never seen a man cross his legs at the knee before. "What we want is for you guys to come up here, grab a piece from the box, and read it . . . in pairs," he added, as if an afterthought, or an act of divine intervention.

I felt a shiver down my spine. This was it. My biggest break ever, bigger even than playing the drowning victim for Dave the Camp Mohawk lifeguard. I felt myself stand, barely touching down on the gray-green tile, float to the peace-and-love box, and pluck from it a single sheet of pink paper. Heading back to my seat, I could see Z hadn't moved. I looked at him. He looked at me. I raised my eyebrows. He shrugged. With that, we were partners, and it was as I always knew it would be: my soulmate and I could communicate without words.

As Z and I dragged our desks together, I began to worry about our pending reintroduction. At the high school level, students were the combined product of five different elementary schools. Would Z remember me from Glendale? Probably not. If I reminded him, would it be a smooth conversation starter, or a disastrous reminder of my listless kicking and cartwheeling during those kickball games? I decided to play it safe.

"I don't think we've met," I said. "Have we?"

He shrugged again. "Don't think so."

"Me neither."

He drummed his knuckles on the desk. He wore a ring. I was infatuated.

"My name's Eliza, by the way," I offered.

He nodded. "Z."

I knew shaking hands would be too weird, but I was dying for some skin. I considered sitting shoulder to shoulder, like the editors had, but decided we weren't quite ready for that. Instead, I put down the pink paper I'd grabbed from the box, though I couldn't have cared less what was on it: a poem, apparently, called "dying again," by someone named Michelle Klein. I didn't know her. I glanced at Z as he looked at the page—did he know Michelle Klein? did he love Michelle Klein?—but he registered no recognition. He read the poem through, then leaned back in his chair.

Oh, right. The poem.

dying inside
  by: michelle klein
everytime i see you
i'm dying inside
everytime i dream you
i'm dying inside
remembering your skin on mine
i'm dying inside
remembering your kisses fine
i'm dying inside

so next time you see me
remember, jake:
i'm dying inside.

When I got to the end (a single tear Michelle had actually hand drawn weeping from the final period) I glanced at Z, who still appeared to be absorbed in thought. I scanned the poem again, to make sure I hadn't missed something. Unfortunately, I was still at the age when the all-lowercase thing seemed arty and cool, and I didn't know yet that poems don't have to rhyme. Still, I wasn't fooled by the artistry of Michelle Klein. My gut told me her poem was bad, really bad, and that this Jake guy should run and keep running.

"Hmmm," Z said, catching me off guard. He breathed through his nose, as if expelling a stream of invisible smoke. "I like the music in this. It's got a cool beat."

Another good point. I guess it was only appropriate that Z would be listening for the music in the poem. I hadn't considered the music. The concept of beat had never occurred to me.

"Yeah," I said, a careful blend of enthusiasm and nonchalance. I skimmed the poem once more; this time, it sounded like a virtual rock ballad. "It's definitely got a beat to it."

Z didn't reply to that. I figured it was now my turn to volunteer something new, something fresh and insightful. Before I had time to consider the consequences, I heard these words tumble recklessly from my mouth: "I like the part about 'your skin on mine.' "

I hadn't meant to say it. It was simply the first concrete noun I laid eyes on, one of the few concrete nouns in the whole goddamn "piece." Regardless, I had unwittingly entered the presence of sex into this, my first-ever conversation with Z Tedesco, and while I had been prepared to wear tie-dye and black makeup, to seek out Z in the yearbook, even to be his poetry partner in the staff meeting of the school literary magazine, I was nowhere near so bold as to say the words "your skin on mine" to Z Tedesco out loud and on purpose.

But, strangely enough, the boldness appeared to be working. I felt Z's stare on the side of my face, creeping along the curve of my ear, my cheekbone, lingering on my mouth. He leaned forward, smelling like cigarette smoke, and whispered, "My favorite part is 'your kisses.' "

To "swoon," according to Ms. Horn's vocab list, was to "fall into a state of ungovernable ecstasy." It's as good a definition as any to describe what happened to me on the afternoon of September 30, 1988. After the meeting, I followed Z outside to the grassy fields behind the gym where I hoped the true *transforming* was about to happen. We sat. We mutilated dandelion heads. Z drummed a twig against his knee. Both of us sucked lollipops. Neither of us spoke.

Finally, I ventured: "You were really good."

Z turned to face me, his eyes unreadable behind the mirrored shades.

"In the talent show, I mean." It was the first of many conversations in my life that would begin with a musical compliment and end with me getting it on with the complimentee.

"Yeah," Z agreed, nodding. "It felt good up there. Really good." He looked up at the sky, as if remembering the glory days, then surprised me by flopping backward on the grass and sighing, "Man, check out those clouds."

This, too, would soon become textbook: the dreamy, moody astral reference (stars, moon, clouds, etc.) that would occur between the musical compliment and the getting it on. But back then, it sounded new and amazing.

"Aren't they amazing?" Z said, echoing my thoughts.

Dutifully, I looked up at the sky: a far-out panorama of wisps and puffs and residual Philly smog. "Yeah," I said, and was momentarily blinded by the sun as I felt Z's warm hand engulf mine.

Before I knew it, I had materialized on the grass beside him, kind of like Z had behind his drums at the talent show. I snuck my lollipop from my mouth and flung it behind me as far as I could. I tried to concentrate on my palm not sweating. I tried to recall Katie Brennan's old ORSFC lectures on the mechanics of French kissing, but could remember nothing except a few bio bits about Duran Duran.

The embarrassing truth was, I had never kissed a boy before. In my defense, it's not that I hadn't had the chance; it's just that the options weren't all that appealing. There was Danny Farley, a pasty boy who I landed on in a game of Spin the Bottle, then had to feign puking to avoid; Ivan's little brother, Isaiah, who Camilla occupied herself with trying to set me up with for the month after Ivan lost the student council election; and shy, sweaty Brett Kimco from algebra, who tried to grope me at the ninth-grade picnic after he downed a jug of spiked Gatorade and hadn't been able to look me in the eye since.

It wasn't an impressive showing, I realize. And yes, Z was the first kiss to take place under circumstances that weren't artificially manufactured by either alcohol, my sister, or an empty Sprite bottle. But the way I see it, another girl would have kissed pasty Danny Farley just for the sake of having kissed pasty Danny Farley. I was being selective.

As Z leaned toward me, I tried not to let my total lack of experience show. I watched my twin image approaching, terrified, in the lenses of his shades. At the last second, I closed my eyes and tilted my head to the side, like couples always did on *General Hospital*. Z's lips, when I felt them land, were softer than I'd expected. They were actually kind of nice. They tasted like green apple lollipop.

But then, just as I was starting to get the hang of things, Z's tongue came on the scene and came on strong: small, hard, concentrated spirals, like a mini-electric mixer. I panicked. I felt my throat begin to close. I considered a) running for my life or b) spiraling in return, but didn't feel courageous and/or coordinated enough to do either.

Someday I would look back and realize Z's kisses were sloppy, slobbery, overly aggressive—the whole phallic nine yards. But in that moment, I had no frame of reference. I figured Z had to be an experienced kisser (he was a rock star, after all) and it was probably just my naivete that made the experience so revolting. In the presence of his expertise, I told myself to relax, make no sudden moves, and wait for the magic to happen.

I dread formal dances. This was true then, it is true now, it will probably be true always. No more formal dances is the main reason I was relieved to graduate high school (that, and no more presidential physical fitness testing). When and if I ever get married I'm going to barter for elopement, just so I can avoid the ritual Chicken Dance, Dollar Dance, and—God help us—bride-and-groom Spotlight Dance. But in the fall of my tenth-grade year, I had a radical attitude about the upcoming Soph Hop.

I had officially been with Z for almost two months, and (after adjusting to his kissing technique) dating a rock star was everything I'd dreamed it would be. In the first week, he made me a mix tape of spooky, echoey Pink Floyd and Led Zeppelin that lived inside my Walkman. We each got an ear pierced at the Blue Horn Mall (my second hole, his fourth). He walked me through my first cigarette: a Marlboro Red, the first of many smoking habits I would temporarily adopt based on a rock star's brand of choice. During lunch, we'd leave school to have prolonged makeout sessions in my living room (this avoided me having to be seen entering the Quad, or him leaving it) fumbling along to Guns N' Roses's painfully loud but surprisingly sexy *Appetite for Destruction*.

On weekends, we usually went out either Friday or Saturday night, though there weren't many places our worlds could comfortably overlap. The thought of our friends mingling was too weird ("Quadders, meet Katie Brennan; Katie, meet Quadders") and our families were off limits, too (mine for obvious maternal reasons). Z's house, according to him, was a "cell block," which struck me as angstfully, musically perfect. In my mind, it was a row house, blunt and gray, tight with tension, with a cast including a witchy, one-eyed stepmother, a father with a grizzly chin who called Z a "good-for-nothin'," a mean black dog who ate metal.

As a result, we wound up spending most of our time together alone. Since we had no cars (or driver's licenses, for that matter) we did a lot of restless smoking and pacing around the highways and byways, playgrounds and Wawas of suburban Philadelphia, the way any suffering young artists should. Z muttered about how a) "All I want is to take my music on the road" and b) "My mother is totally screwing me over." I pitched in how my mother drove my father off to California, blood tingling, blowing smoke streams at my feet.

"Does he ever call you?"

"Nah," I said, trying to sound blasé. The fact that I'd spent most of sixth, seventh, and eighth grades thinking Lou might still appear in my living room after school one day was something I was trying to deny and forget. "I don't need him. I hardly knew him."

Z stomped out his Marlboro and lit a new one. "That's harsh," he said, giving me a slow squint. Then he started muttering again about how a) "All I want is to take my music on the road" and b) "My mother is totally screwing me over."

Normally, I was Z's devoted audience. But in late January, I had bigger things on my mind: the Soph Hop. I admit, I felt a little disloyal to my new tie-dyed self since, according to the rules, I shouldn't have wanted anything to do with something as cheesy and mainstream as a school dance. But I was still a hot-blooded teenage girl. I'd never had a boyfriend, much less a boyfriend coinciding with a school dance, and I planned to take full advantage.

I just had to mention it to Z. As I saw it, the key was in the tone.

Dismissive: "So what do you think of the Soph Hop? Pretty dumb, huh?"

Oblivious: "What's that dance at school called? God, I can't even re*mem*ber . . ."

Unfortunately, I waited until we were hanging up the phone on the Thursday before the Friday of the Hop to make my move. At that point, I'd blown any shot at subtlety. Just as Z was exhaling "Catch you later," it was all I could manage to blurt out, "Can we go to the Soph Hop?" before he hung up the phone.

There was a horrific, endless pause, during which I felt my

entire social existence crashing down around me. Then Z asked: "What's a Soph Hop?" sounding as genuinely clueless as if it were a word on his English vocab list.

I should have known. Such were the perils of dating Quadders: they lived in their own worlds. They were oblivious to grades, top 40 hits, and school-sponsored events. Z probably didn't even know where the gym was.

"It's a dance," I explained, my mouth so dry I could barely move my tongue. "For sophomores."

Z was silent for another beat, while I steeled myself for rejection. Then he said, "Free tunes? Why not."

It was such a brilliant approach, I don't know why I didn't think of it myself. For girls, music is the last thing they are worried about at school dances. Dances are about flowers and dresses and pride and relief and sheets of wallet-size photos you can cut up and distribute among your eighty closest friends. They're about the fat corsage you preserve forever in a box in your freezer among the ice cube trays and cans of frozen juices. But with Z, the music worked to my advantage. I pretended it was all I cared about, too.

The theme of the dance was Candyland, held in the cafeteria-turned-board game. The moment we walked in, I instantly and deeply regretted bringing Z. Pieces of wrapped candy and Bazooka gum were Scotch-taped to the walls. Lollipops hung from tinfoiled trees. In one corner, a plastic kiddie pool was filled with something suggestive of the Molasses Pit. Not even the music could save us, a potpourri of Billy Ocean, Cheap Trick, and Rick Astley.

Naturally, there was not a Quadder in sight. There were, however, tons of parent-chaperons and corsaged teachers and streamers and strobe lights. Hannah and Eric were already there, lingering near the Candy Cane Forest when we approached.

Hannah to Z: "Hi."

Z to Hannah: "Hey."

In one of the stranger cross sections of high school clique-dom, Z and Eric shook hands.

Then we all just stood there, staring blankly at each other. Hannah and Z had talked before, basically to the extent they already had. But for some reason, maybe the fact that we were in formal wear, we felt compelled to take a stab at adult conversation.

"You guys look nice," Hannah offered.

Z and I were both subdued and flowerless. He was in black jeans, a black Izod, and an alarmingly tweedy jacket that stopped an inch short of his wrists. I was wearing a shapeless gray dress that my sister had kindly informed me looked like a giant vacuum bag. That afternoon, Z and I had had an edgy talk about the stupidity of boutonnieres and corsages. ("It's all a scam, man!" Z spat at one point, going on to cite Mother's Day, Father's Day and Valentine's Day as other prime offenders.)

Hannah and Eric obviously had not had such a talk. Despite the fact that Eric was four inches shorter than she was, they looked perfect together. Their outfits were pinned with identical pink carnations; Eric's navy-and-red striped tie complemented Hannah's pale blue dress. Standing there, the four of us could have been an after-school special about not falling in with the wrong crowd.

"So do you guys," I said. "You look great, too."

Silence again. Silence made worse by the suddenly dimmed lights and the opening strains of Phil Collins's "Groovy Kind of Love." Z tugged at his collar, shifting uncomfortably from foot to foot. Hannah's eyes moved from my face to Z's, waiting 'til she caught his eye. Then she ventured, "So, Z, I guess you might not remember me."

All our eyes turned to her. Eric looked concerned.

"From elementary school . . . ?"

Panic tightened my chest so fast it hurt. All at once, I a) imagined all the memories of cartwheels and handsprings and wimpy bunt kicks that might come flooding back to Z at any moment, b) resolved not to let Z mingle with my friends again, *ever,* and c) gave Hannah a sharp, throat-cutting gesture which made her stop midsentence.

Eric turned to her, rightly anxious. "What were you saying, honey?" Meet the only tenth grader in the history of the world to call his girlfriend "honey." "He might not remember you from where?"

But just as all my careful scamming might have been exposed for good, I was saved—or rather, outdone—by a terrifyingly large Italian woman who descended on us out of nowhere wearing a tarplike purple dress and barking: "ZACHIE!"

Zachie?

Z rolled his eyes at this huge woman. "Get outta here, Ma."

Ma?

In one swift, shocking move, the woman's hands were on my shoulders like two canned hams. "Zachie wouldn't bring the girl to the house," she bellowed, "so I had to bring the *house* to the *girl!*" Then she laughed a large, wide, fleshy laugh that made her chest, chins, and upper arms wobble.

Hannah and Eric clutched hands.

"Ma, I told you not to come!" Z protested. He scowled, but it wasn't a scowl of musical angst anymore. It was a third-grade scowl, a pouty scowl, a scowl accustomed to getting Coke with breakfast.

But it was enough to silence Ma Tedesco, who sobered up and stopped her insane laughter. She gazed down at me, her eyes suddenly and alarmingly swimming with tears. My heart started to pound inside the vacuum bag.

"Come visit us sometime, Eliza," she said, sweetly. "We've heard so much about you. We'd love to get to know you better." Then she bent down, engulfing me in a giant purple hug, and thundered off through the Chocolate Marsh and out the door.

I couldn't move. Hannah and Eric glanced at each other, then slipped into the mass of kids rotating in tight circles to Phil. When I looked at Z, he shrugged, squinting at something over my shoulder, trying to look unaffected and resume his cool. But the damage was done. Z's mother wasn't the loveless witch he'd made her out to be. Suddenly his home life flashed before me: a life with a mother who fed him breakfast meats and rumpled his oily hair and badgered him about his girl-friend, a life filled with coddling and big-breasted aunts and superhero bedsheets, a life exposed as horribly, irrevocably, normal.

Z started his absentminded leg drumming, but it wasn't absentminded anymore. It was insecure, self-conscious. A freaking nervous tic. "Sorry about that," Z said, and his breath smelled like—was I imagining this?—pastrami sandwiches from paper bags. As the music bumped awkwardly from slow Phil Collins to Paula Abdul's "Straight Up," Z tilted his head to one side. "Man, this beat isn't bad."

I smiled faintly, and yanked a piece of Bazooka off the wall. As I unwrapped it, I knew that it wouldn't last with Z much longer. I knew he wasn't really my soulmate. I was also reasonably sure Michelle Klein's poem really had been as terrible as I'd thought. What I couldn't have known yet was that Z would go on to date Michelle Klein, or that I would dabble next in the stage band, or that I would eventually pierce my navel and Z his left nipple and by senior year, we would be too estranged to even sign each other's Yodels.

5

sisters

There are few things in my life right now I know I can count on: happily-ever-after on *Love Boat* reruns, moral lessons on *Brady Bunch* reruns, angst on *The Real World,* annual birthday checks from my Great-Aunt Leona with "Burger" written beside the word "Memo," leftover cake and Diet Cokes in the fridge at Dreams Come True and, on the first Sunday of every month, dinner at Mom's.

Sunday dinners are a tradition that began after Camilla got married. The players: Camilla and Scott, Mom and Harv, Sue the cat, and me. Each month, Mom will call to suggest I bring my "friend" (i.e., the supposedly asexual person I'm currently dating and not sleeping with). I laugh—sometimes even throw in "ha!" for emphasis—and refuse. Then she suggests I bring Andrew. I shrug into the phone.

"I don't *understand*, Eliza. Andrew's a good-looking boy. You're a good-looking girl."

For my mother, this is where the equation begins and ends.

Normally I won't bring Andrew, to prove to Mom he's my friend and not my "friend." Besides, Andrew has never understood why she and I don't get along. "She tries hard," he says. "She's so friendly." At which point I remind him that my mother a) has had a crush on him since our freshman year at Wissahickon and b) is nicer to virtually everyone in the world than she is to me.

This Sunday, however, I don't have the strength to face my family alone. They'll ask about my love life. I'll tell them Karl and I broke up. They'll ask why, I'll mention ferreting, there will be frowns, furrowed brows, nervous looks exchanged over the charred meat. Dictionaries might come into play. From there on in, it can only get uglier. I'm still drained enough from the breakup conversation last night at The Blue Room.

Me: Hey.

Karl: Hey.

We were sitting at a table toward the back of the dance floor. I'd called Karl, asking him to meet me there; a subtle way, I thought, of indicating we'd need separate cars to leave in. But he seemed unfazed when he showed up at the table carrying two rum and Cokes, giving me an exhausting kiss and giving a short nod to the guys in the band (Crazy Ape) who were tuning up onstage. Objectively, Karl was looking pretty good, black-clad and stubbly around the edges. But I was now incapable of looking at him without thinking: hygiene.

Me: It's been a while since we talked, huh?

Karl: Yeah. I guess.

M: So what have you been up to this week?

K: The usual. Kickin' back.* Washin'.** Jammin' with the guys.***

M: (deep breath) Listen, Karl, this probably won't come as much of a shock but . . . I guess it doesn't really seem to be working out with us.

K: (incredulous) It doesn't?

M: (incredulous) Didn't you sort of get that impression?

K: When?

M: Last week?

K: When?

M: In the car? With the lasagna?

K: What lasagna?

M: Things felt, I don't know, weird between us. Didn't you think?

K: You mean that stuff you said about wanting to unwind?

---

* Kickin' back: a popular term in Karl's world, used in reference to any act performed motionless and alone, i.e., listening to CDs, smoking a bowl, or watching TV (usually music videos or *Real Stories of Canadian Mounties*).
** Washin': a reference to washing windows for his uncle's company, a job which Karl sometimes rouses himself to do when he's out of cash.
*** Jammin' with the guys: any activity involving the fellow Hoagies. I used to imagine these as hard-core sessions of strumming and composing and arguing band aesthetics; now, I envision "the guys" shaving each other's neck hair.

Up to this point, our breakup had been fairly run-of-the-mill. But now I was beginning to realize that "unwind" might not have the same fatal undertones for Karl as it did for me. He obviously hadn't seen this coming. As I pondered my next move, the lights went down abruptly. The stage pooled electric red. A guy with dreadlocks and no shoes stepped up to the mike. "WE ARE CRAZY APE!" he screamed, followed by the violently loud opening bars of the Ape's first number, a loose approximation of Live's "I Alone." When I spoke again, I was shouting.

M: I thought you knew what I meant!

K: What *did* you mean!

M: What?

K: What did you mean!

M: What did I mean when?

K: What?

I had a flash of those horrible telephone games from junior high slumber parties, the ones where a phrase begins as one thing ("Mindy likes to eat earthworms!") and ends up something completely different ("Minibikes look like George Burns!") and this strikes everyone as very funny.

M: What did I mean when?

K: When you said you wanted to unwind!

M: I guess I just wanted to be apart for a while! To see how things felt!

K: Why!

M: What?

K: Why!

M: Why?

Though not an unprecedented move in my rock star experience, this was definitely rare. Breaking up doesn't usually require too much in the way of explanation. Rock stars are familiar with breaking up. As the songs say, it "hurts." It "stinks." It's "hard to do." It prompts the musical question: "where do broken hearts go?" It's like an occupational hazard, the stuff good lyrics are made of.

But Karl just sat there, waiting for my fumbled response.

M: There wasn't any one reason, I guess! It was lots of little reasons! It wasn't one specific reason at all!

It's difficult to be nonchalant when you're shouting. It's even more difficult to lie well. If this had been a movie, there would be a moment when the music stopped and I was caught screaming something about wanting sex or being gay in front of a roomful of dropped jaws. But it wasn't a movie, and my vocal cords—and conscience—were starting to ache.

M: I mean, don't you think it's weird we haven't talked for almost a week!

K: (shrug).

Right. Probably he wouldn't have. Most of his life was, after all, spent inside his head. I gazed toward the stage, an attempt to end the conversation, to shift the focus somewhere else, but all I managed to do was emphasize the difference between what was happening in our corner of the room versus the rest of the room, a thick, sweaty pit of gyrating arms and heads and hips, one of which knocked unapologetically into our table and sent my drink sloshing over the lip of my glass.

The Ape's first song ended with a whine of feedback and a big cheer of approval from The Blue Room. I stared at the brown, rummy rivulet sidling across the table, heading straight for my lap.

M: I'm sorry, Karl. I'll return your . . .

But as I was about to catalogue all the CDs Karl had left scattered around my car and apartment, he stood up so angrily his chair tipped over backward. His face had turned deep red. "Forget it," he said, fumbling to right the chair. To my amazement, his hands were shaking. "Keep them."

Sunday morning, I called Andrew.

He answered, "Eliza Simon, I presume?"

But I was too tired to mock the Caller ID trick. "I really need you this month," I said, staring into the sugary dregs of my cereal. "I can't handle this dinner. I can't handle my mother. I need someone there who's on my side. Kimberley's a lawyer. She'll understand."

Andrew and I arrive late. Arriving late to Sunday dinners is essential strategy if you want to avoid the predinner chatting. The mid-dinner and post-dinner chatting are painful enough, but at least there are props available (meat to chew, ice to crunch, drinks to refill, damp vegetables to spell things with on your plate). If you're ambitious, you can be drunk by dessert. But during predinner chatting, everyone is on their own. Sober. Propless. A lot of flat jokes and flesh and elbows and miles of empty lap.

When Mom opens the door, her mouth is already open to criticize my lateness. Then she looks over my shoulder and I am instantly absolved. "Andrew!" she screeches, reaching past me to molest him. "Eliza finally brought you along!"

"Good to see you, Mrs. Mackey." Andrew returns her hug.

"Everybody!" Mom shouts, tugging him by the elbow into the foyer, which is air-conditioned down to about fifteen degrees. "Look who's here!"

"Everybody" encompasses all of two people: my sister's husband, Scott, and my mother's husband, Harv. They are standing in the living room, neither one willing to be the first man to buckle and sit down. Both are gripping beer bottles by the neck with one hand, the other hand thrust deep in a pants pocket. A Rod Stewart CD, probably *Greatest Hits* (more than half of Harv's CDs are *Greatest Hits*) rasps on the stereo.

Scott covers the entire room in one crisp, loafered step. He rattles when he moves, as if he's actually made of money. "Andy! Good to see you, bud!" he says, and leans in to give me a kiss on the cheek. "Hi there, Eliza."

"Hey, Scott." I'm engulfed in a wave of tangy aftershave as Scott reaches around me to clap "Andy" on the back. It has always puzzled me what my sister sees in this guy. He has a sycophantic quality not unlike Eddie Haskell's from *Leave It to Beaver*. His blond hair sits on his head in stiff waves and looks perpetually wet. Strange how you can find yourself suddenly, helplessly, related to people like this.

"Hey! Andy!" Harv jumps in, a little too energetically. Harv is not as smooth as Scott, which I guess is something to be thankful for. He's a thick, hairy, heavy specimen of a man who hides behind his body: a sturdy gut that strains at his shirt buttons, a bristly gray beard that totally conceals his mouth. Harv avoids the backslap and goes in for the handshake, then raises his beer as exuberantly as a pack of Mentos. "What can I get you there? Beer? Wine?" He pauses. "Shot of JD?"

This provokes a snort of laughter from all three males, as if they are all remembering some long-ago, drunken escapade that never took place.

"A beer sounds great, Harv," Andrew says. "Thanks."

Harv gives him a salute and charges off, happy to have a job to do. Mom promptly appears at Andrew's left elbow, hooks his arm in hers, and guides him toward the fireplace. "It's so nice having you here, Andrew," she bubbles. She is wearing an annoying yellow sundress that ties in the back, the kind I wore as a little girl. "I always tell Eliza, 'why don't you bring Andrew along?' But you know her, she usually comes alone . . ."

Andrew listens to her go, nodding and smiling in all the right places, while my mother asks delighted questions about his mother and father and promising legal future. He is the one spot of hope my family clings to: the possibility that if I can be good friends with a nice, L.L. Bean-clad boy like Andrew Callahan, there is still a chance I might one day settle down, have babies, wear pastels, and live a normal life.

Having seen enough, I head to the dining room, where I deposit my tuna casserole on the table. Sunday dinners are a potluck, kind of. Mom cooks most of it; Camilla and I each bring a dish. Actually, Camilla brings a dish and I bring a tuna casserole. For the record, there is nothing lame about bringing a tuna casserole. Tuna is familiar, reliable, comfort food. Soft under the teeth. Easy on the heart.

Camilla, on the other hand, would never bring the same

dish twice. Her creation this month appears to be made of glaze only: brown and thick, swimming with pineapples and cashews and celery, with no apparent foundation underneath. I am not a fan of glazes. Or condiments, salad dressings, sauces on pasta. I like to see what's in front of me. I like to know exactly what I'm getting.

"Someone needs to set a place for Andrew!" Mom yelps.

"I'll do it," Camilla says, appearing in the kitchen doorway as if by magic, dinner plate in hand. My sister has been a wife for almost three years, and still excels in her first-bornedness. She is always responsible, always helpful, always meticulous in the details. I think she was born knowing how to iron a pleated skirt. Naturally, her wedding day was perfect: sunny 75-degree weather, a clean cake exchange, a flawless bride-and-groom Spotlight Dance.

I follow Camilla into the kitchen, where she's plucking silverware out of a drawer and humming something I know but can't place, something with a perky Broadway quality. In her wraparound lavender skirt and matching sleeveless sweater, she is as impeccably dressed as Mom.

"Hey, Liza." I hate this nickname but allow it, from my sister. It's one of the concessions of having shared a childhood; we let each other get away with these things. "Good idea bringing Andrew. I haven't seen Mom this happy since they put *Dr. Quinn, Medicine Woman* back on the air."

"It's a ploy," I confide, leaning against the dishwasher. "With him here, she might stay off my back."

"What do you mean?" Camilla says. She is serious.

"Sorry, but are you *present* at these dinners? Do you *hear* our conversations? This whole tradition is just a front for grilling me about my life."

"You're exaggerating," she says, quoting Andrew. She fishes in the drawer for a dessert spoon, still humming what I now realize is "You're Never Fully Dressed Without a Smile" from *Annie.* "They're not that bad."

I roll my eyes elaborately, a move I perfected when I was ten, gave up when I was fourteen, but somehow find myself reverting to whenever I'm back inside this house. Camilla's positivity amazes me sometimes. She has always been determinedly happy, selective in what she notices, particular about what she remembers. She and Scott are constantly commemorating something: first phone call, first date, first kiss (first "you know," she whispered once, blushing furiously), and now, of course, the engagement and wedding. With Camilla, though, it always seems the commemoration matters more than the thing it is commemorating. More important is the hard fact of it, the check-mark-in-the-box of it. If her life with Scott wasn't perfect, I doubt we'd ever know.

"Well, tonight is bound to be especially fun," I inform her, as she shuts the drawer with a practiced flick of the hip. "Karl and I broke up last night."

Camilla stops, midway across the kitchen. She squints at the shiny linoleum, trying to remember which one Karl is. Mom would say this is what I get for not bringing my "friends" to Sunday dinners. "Guitarist?" she guesses.

"Bass."

"String bass?"

"No. Bass *guitarist.*" For the sake of clarity, I add, "He's in a band."

"Which one?"

"Electric Hoagie." She had to ask.

"Oh, right, right," Camilla nods, several times. A fan of little wrinkles has appeared between her eyes, a combination of being worried and being thirty. "Liza. What happened?"

I shrug. I'm not getting into the ferreting details with Camilla. "It just didn't work out. It's not a big deal. We'd only been dating a little while anyway."

"Well, I'm sorry," she says. "I really am." And she really is. Camilla's "sorry" works on different levels, though. Part of it is genuinely sympathetic, but listen hard and you'll hear another "sorry" underneath: one that is profoundly worried. Although my sister is a reasonably modern woman—reads *Ms.* magazine, uses unisex bathrooms—she is old-fashioned at the core. She is acutely aware of things like ticking biological clocks, thinning herds, and other awful metaphors for being unmarried and approaching thirty. Naturally, neither of us can forget the way Mom dissolved after Lou left. Sometimes I think Camilla married young to avoid becoming like Mom was, and I avoid settling down for the exact same reason.

"Don't worry," Camilla says, and surprises me by reaching out to smooth my bangs off my face. "You'll find someone. Just be patient." I feel a strange surge of comfort as she says this, at the same time I feel suddenly fifteen again. Maybe this is why Camilla always had so many friends calling her for advice.

She glances toward the living room and leans in close to my

ear. "You never know," she whispers, a singsong whisper, thick with innuendo. It's the same voice I hear in my head when I read advice columns in women's magazines. "It could be Mr. Right is right under your nose!"

Oh how disappointing. To make matters worse, she then raises one eyebrow in a shrewd, waxed, upside-down U and all I can see and hear is Nanny yelling *"Get your claws in him! Deeper! Deeper!"* until the eyebrow relaxes again, I duck out from under her hand, and Camilla turns to the pantry.

I glance over at Andrew. He is doing the predinner chat with Scott, who is gesturing widely with two hands as if to show something growing bigger. Probably his bank account. Or ego. Or mythical penis. For Scott, asserting his manhood is of primary importance. Ask him where he works and he'll not only tell you the bank's name and location, but launch into a defensive litany of facts and figures and net gains. He's the kind of guy who grunts as he swings a golf club, the kind of guy who mentions his college fraternity in almost every conversation.

If I listen hard, I can make out scraps of sports talk and stocks talk and one conspiratorial "So a Democrat walks into a bar . . ." It's frightening how easily Andrew slips into this manly mode. Rocking on the balls of his feet, throwing his beer back in aggressive swallows. His khakis look identical to Scott's and his voice, when I locate it, sounds as if it's dropped about three octaves.

Just as I am beginning to worry, Scott steps away to play with the stereo knobs and Andrew looks in my direction. He flashes me a grin that is totally zany, and instantly reassuring. He even succumbs to a few seconds of air guitaring which, for once, I do not mind. When Scott rejoins him—"Maggie May" suddenly leaping in volume, as if to announce that now the party is *really* getting going—I know Andrew is laughing as hard inside as I am.

Camilla reappears behind my shoulder. She's still humming (since when is she a hummer?) only now it's something more regal. It sounds like my eighth-grade graduation song about walking through the woods holding my head up high. She's fished a spare linen napkin from the pantry and even managed to fold it in the shape of something vaguely birdlike. Good God.

"Well, Liza," she says, putting the final touches on the linen beak. Her voice sounds funny, as if she's amused herself. "If you want my opinion, I have a feeling you won't have to worry about getting grilled by Mom tonight."

I'm about to inform her that of *course* I will, that I *always* do, and that she might be overestimating the power of Andrew Callahan *just* a little, but before I can get the words out she's cupped the bird, gripped the utensils, given me a wink, and headed for the dining room.

"Everybody!" my mother shouts. I hear a spatter of clapping, like an ineffectual teacher trying to get her students' attention. Any minute now the overhead lights might start flicking on and off. "Everybody! Time to sit down!"

I grab a beer from the fridge and head for the table.

Sometimes, like tonight, I regret giving Harv the silent treatment in high school. He arrived in Mom's life during my senior year, a time when I was capable of resenting practically anyone—crossing guards, bakers, grocers, nuns—so a stepfather didn't stand a chance. Honestly, I don't remember ever having a full, one-on-one conversation with Harv in high school, not even once. Mostly I remember the physical details that began appearing with him. The puddles on the bathroom floor. Whiskers in the sink. Thick, beige slippers with soles worn shiny as cue balls. *Sports Illustrateds* with pages crinkled from getting wet. The smells of foods my mother started cooking: liver and onions, beef and barley soup, stringy hunks of meat with knobs of bone.

But tonight, as Harv fumbles his way through sawing the roast beast, I have to like the guy a little. He tries hard. He adores my mother. He helped pay for my college education and, at graduation, gave me this dorky card with a ladybug on it wearing a mortarboard. He even walked Camilla down the aisle. And his name is Harv, after all, which provokes some automatic sympathy in me. I'm not sure exactly what going through childhood and adolescence named Harvey Mackey does to a person, but it can't be easy.

Harv sits at one head of the table, Mom at the other. "Camilla . . ." she begins to fuss. "Eliza . . ." This woman has no specific objective. Just general fretfulness leaking out, like yolk from an egg. "Eliza . . . Camilla . . ."

Since remarrying, my mother is no longer as nervous as she was alone. Nor is she as strict as she was with Lou. But both qualities still exist inside her and sometimes manifest themselves in strange ways, like the obsessive spritzing of her ferns or the pointless echoing of her daughters' names. Our names are close enough that Mom has always interchanged them, though they are actually as different as names come. Camilla is roman-tic, heroic, a girl who rides ponies and has suitors lining up at her chateau door. Eliza is a name with a sigh inside it; you can exhale it (go ahead, try it) without moving the lips at all.

In my more lucid moments, I understand that Camilla and I are the products of the same difficult childhood: we just reacted to it in different ways. She sought attention by over-achieving. I opted for underachieving. Her life was defined by Girl Scout badges, ribbons, trophies, boyfriends headed to Ivy Leagues, girlfriends with names ending in "i" or "ie." My life was defined, first and foremost, by being none of the things my sister's was. After Lou left and Mom numbed over, Camilla matured into the responsible mother-substitute. I went in a slightly different direction.

If you think about it, though, there really isn't room for two in the responsible mother-substitute department. Once Camilla claimed the job, I had to explore other options. Given enough time, I could argue my entire adult life is, in fact, Camilla's fault (with the same logic I claim Z Tedesco's presence on the *Transformations* staff is responsible for my current, poverty-line copywriting job). When you have an older sibling who's already excelled in academics, sports, scouts, and socializing in general, it takes creativity to carve out your own niche, to discover your own special talents—in my case, piercing, breaking curfew, and blazing through flawed rock stars like a tornado.

"Girls, start passing," Mom manages to articulate, fluttering her hands in the direction of the food. As usual, her nails are freshly painted and her face carefully made up. I notice, though, that her makeup doesn't look as natural as it used to; it seems more conspicuous, as if resting brightly on top of her true face instead of blending in. "The food's getting cold."

Camilla, ever the dutiful daughter, picks up her pan of glaze and turns to her husband. "Honey? Want some?"

"You bet," Scott says.

I shoulder my tuna and pass it to Andrew. "Want some, honey?"

Andrew scoops some casserole onto his plate. "Trying out a new recipe, huh, Eliza?" he says, which my mother finds positively hysterical. The rest of the food starts rotating fast and steamy as an assembly line. Roast beef slabs, mashed potatoes, string beans wading in butter, Camilla's brown glaze.

"It's Thai," she explains, in answer to my grimace.

"She's on a Thai kick," Scott adds.

"Is Schezuan the same as Thai?" Harv mumbles. "I know I've had Schezuan. I don't know if I've had Thai."

"There was this guy in my fraternity," Scott says, chuckling, "name was Billy Fenster. We called him The Fen. This guy was obsessed with Thai food, I'm telling you, I think the guy ate Thai for breakfast."

Sometimes I really miss our doomed presidential candidate, Ivan.

"The Fen." Scott gazes into his glaze. "I wonder what happened to that guy."

"Maybe he runs a Thai restaurant," Harv says without expression.

No one knows how to respond to this.

Andrew pitches in, "Why not?"

Then, from the other end of the table, Mom starts shrieking again, peering down at her napkin bird. "Ooh! I hate to ruin this little guy!"

Camilla squares her shoulders. This is the moment she has been waiting for. "They're swans," she reports. "I learned how to make them in my night class, 'Origami for the Home.'" You'd think by now my sister would stop bringing art projects home from school, but apparently not. "We make all kinds of things," she continues. "Doilies in the shapes of little hats. Guest washcloths in the shapes of ducks."

Who in their right mind would want such things in their houses (with the possible exception of Karl's mother) I have no idea. But the crowd is enthusiastic. There follows a burst of "ooh"ing, "aah"ing, quacking (from Andrew), and general unswanning of swans. Mom's gazing at hers like it's a dying swallow, whimpering as she unfolds each wing.

"It's better than that weaving class," Scott puts in. "Remember that one, honey? We have enough potholders in our house to . . ." It should be a punchline, but falls flat on its face.

"Hold pots?" Harv offers.

Scott looks stricken. I almost laugh out loud. Andrew kicks me under the table, a preemptive strike.

In an effort to divert attention, Scott brushes imaginary lint off his shoulder, then starts kissing ass. "These mashed potatoes look delicious, Mrs. Mackey."

"Well, thank you, Scott."

"Everything does, Mom," Camilla chimes in.

I concentrate on counting exactly three string beans onto my plate as Sue the cat comes whoring around my left leg. Being with Sue always reinforces my respect for Leroy. Sue's the kind of cat who constantly needs you, begs you, mauls you without invitation. I don't trust her kind of love.

"Get away, Sue," I whisper, stomping my foot.

Sue scampers to Harv's leg instead. To my horror, he takes a forkful of my tuna and feeds it to her under the table. This is complete casserole sacrilege, though it does cause me to wonder if, had I been nicer to Harv in high school, he would have slipped me cash behind Mom's back.

Then Mom says: "Well!" and surveys the table. She's checking to make sure all plates are full, all drinks filled, all dishes safely landed. Satisfied, she gives us all a big smile. "Let's eat, everybody!"

This is the part my mother lives for. As everybody starts sampling everything, they make a lot of mmm-ing noises and compliment her up and down.

"This meat is just right, dear."

"Did you use a different seasoning, Mom? Some kind of herb?"

"Everything tastes fabulous, Mrs. Mackey."

There follows a long, noisy silence of clinking and chewing and swallowing. Mom is beaming as she lifts a spoonful of Thai soup to her mouth. I stare at my plate, trying to make myself invisible, but when I glance at Mom she's looking right at me. "So," she says. "Eliza."

And so it begins. The following are the only topics that could possibly come next:

a) my love life ("why don't you bring this musician around to meet us?")

b) my job ("when are they going to send you someplace sunny?")

c) my nose ring ("won't that get infected?")

d) my hair ("why don't you just *try* growing it longer?")

e) and tonight, as a bonus, some coy, suggestive comments about me and Andrew being "just friends."

I am about to explain that it's just this kind of guilt-inducing harassment that is the reason I can't bring the musicians to Sunday dinners (not to mention the reason I can't bring myself to narrate a sex scene in my book) when Camilla cuts in.

"Mom?"

This is an unprecedented move. My sister has put her utensils down and wiped her mouth carefully with her unswanned napkin. She looks at Scott, who gives her a smile of encouragement. What the hell is going on?

Camilla lifts her chin. When she speaks, her voice is trembling. "We were going to wait for dessert," she says, eyes on her plate, "but I might burst by then." A short yelp escapes her, and she squeezes her eyes shut and grips Scott's hand. Her knuckles are pointy and pink. "Scott and I have an announcement."

My sister is pregnant, of course. There is nothing else that could follow the words "Scott and I" and "announcement" and require marital yelping and hand grabbing. She has heard the ticking of her biological clock and everyone at this table knows it. Harv knows it. Even Sue knows it. Mom, of all people, must know it, but manages to keep her expression carefully confused.

The room holds still for one whole minute, silent except for the incongruous background noise of Rod Stewart belting out "Da Ya Think I'm Sexy?" as Camilla's face turns about three shades pinker. Finally, she explodes: "We're pregnant!"

Mom clutches her heart and bursts into tears, a moment she's probably been rehearsing her entire life. Harv raises his beer in an awkward salute. Andrew says appropriate things like "Congrats!" and "Great news!" and reaches across the table to pump Scott's hand. Everyone is on their feet, hugging, back-slapping, wiping tears from their eyes.

Except for me. I can't move. Staring at the belly of my sister's lavender wraparound skirt, I am overwhelmed by a strange, sudden wave of shyness. I can't stand. I can't speak. I can't take my eyes off my sister. I am in awe of her—even intimidated by her—by the reality of what is happening under her skin.

If anyone notices my temporary paralysis, they don't let on. They are clinking glasses and Mom is saying that of *course*, now she sees Camilla is showing! and asking what was she doing, *cooking* in her condition? and posing all the usual questions: "How far are you?" (seven weeks), "Boy or girl?" (we want it to be a surprise), and "How are you feeling?" (fine, fine, just fine).

"Come on, honey," Scott says. "You don't have to be a martyr in front of them." He confides, "There have been a couple of rough mornings already."

Everyone inexplicably laughs. I stare down at the Thai soup running across my plate, staining the rim of the mashed potatoes. Sue reappears, rubbing my leg, and this time I toss her a piece of tuna.

*　　　*　　　*

Parked by the curb in front of my mother's, in roughly the same spot Lou's cat-scratched armchair was dumped after he left us, Andrew and I sit in silence. The car windows are down. Crickets chirp sluggishly on the night air. I'm buzzed from the news and the beers and I don't want to go home yet to my closet/apartment. Camilla and Scott are still inside, rooting through old boxes of baby clothes and toys my mother has already dislodged from the attic.

Andrew is surfing the radio—typical, cheesy Sunday night call-in fare—and stops when he stumbles upon a long-distance dedication. It has all the usual components: thwarted love, miscommunication, a tragic accident in the Midwest. In this one, Sam from Wyoming had his hand sawed off in a tangle with a tractor, and when his letters stopped coming, Melanie from Idaho thought he'd forgotten all about her. Well, Melanie, even though Sam can't write those letters anymore, he *can* send this long-distance love song . . .

"That was touching," Andrew says, as the Backstreet Boys's "Show Me the Meaning of Being Lonely" comes oozing out of the speakers. It's the first we've spoken since Andrew was forbidden to start the car. "Speaking of love," he ventures, "and stop me if you don't feel like talking about it, but how did things go with Karl last night?"

"Fine." I shrug. "You know. The usual."

You'd think I was discussing having a corn removed. Breaking up with boyfriends has become this routine, this mechanical, every one of them the final scene in the same movie:

the predictable meeting, the excitement, "the moment," the disillusionment, the ending. It scares me how familiar I've become with the endings. How accustomed to cutting people loose.

"Are you sad about it?" Andrew asks.

"The weird thing is, yes. And no." I pull my knees up under my chin. "I'm sad, but I don't think it's Karl I'm sad about. I think I'm sad about *not* being sad about Karl."

Andrew doesn't respond. When I glance at him, his profile is dark against the streetlamps. He looks much older than he did in college.

"What if," I say, "my life is actually stuck inside this never-ending cliché where everything keeps happening predictably. It's the same story, over and over and over. Every guy I date is disappointing. Every relationship ends the exact same way." I wrap my arms tight around my knees. "Basically, Andrew, I'm twenty-six and I feel like there's nothing in my life that could take me by surprise. Am I warped?"

"You're not warped."

"Be honest."

"I am being honest. I'm always honest. I'm a lawyer, remember?"

But I'm in no mood for jokes now, lawyer or otherwise. "What if I never find anyone?"

"Oh God, not this."

"Andrew, I'm serious. I need this."

"Okay, okay. You will. You will find anyone. I promise."

"But how do you know? What if I'm just not capable of it? What if it's like a biological thing, like people who can't curl their tongues or wiggle their noses?" I lean my head back against the seat. Outside, the street is getting tipsy, telephone poles and trees and rooftops blurring into one another. "Maybe I can't be any other way."

"Eliza, you can be anything you want," Andrew says. "An astronaut. A ballerina. A firefighter." He reaches over and gives me an exaggerated chin-chuck. "You can even make movies that smell."

I feel the impulse to defend my idea—Movies That Smell was a *great idea*—but I decide to let it go. I am too tired. Something about me feels off kilter, but I can't put my finger on it. I don't feel up to being cynical, not about Karl, not about my mother or my sister and her Thai food and napkin origami. Under normal circumstances, I would have volumes to say about those stupid swans. I would have a field day analyzing the way Camilla announced: "We're pregnant!" Under normal circumstances, I could go off for hours on the use of the pronoun "we" alone.

The thing is, cynical can be exhausting after a while. Without it, though, I feel unprotected. Vulnerable to my own eye.

I turn away from the window. "What if I never have a baby?"

Andrew drops his head in his hands and moans. "Where is this coming from? Scott and Camilla?"

"Who cares." I feel a wave of desperation, feel myself being sucked up in one of those estrogen clouds I've read about in women's magazines. "Don't go getting all practical about it. Just reassure me."

"Yeah," he says, his voice softening. He removes his head from his hands and looks at me. "I mean, of course you'll have a baby."

"You don't think Karl was my last chance at reproduction?"

"You'll find a better dad than Karl, I promise."

"Where?"

"What do you mean, where? There are tons of other bands at The Blue Room."

I know he's trying to lighten the mood, but the last thing I want right now is to be reminded of the sad reality that is my dating pool. I don't want to think about The Blue Room, or the rock star wannabes who play there, or having to potentially make a baby with a Crazy Ape.

"Maybe I need a list."

"What kind of list? Movies to Rent? Words to Outlaw If I Were President?"

"I'm serious. My sister used to have this list. I saw it once, when I was snooping in her room." My voice is starting to quicken. "It was called, 'Things I Need in a Husband.' And look. She got them. Every one of them."

"Okay, okay. Hang on." Andrew flips open his impeccable glove compartment. A light inside pops on. He fishes out a mini-golf pencil and Marriott notepad, saying, "All right. Let's make you a list. What kinds of things were on it?"

"You know," I say, taking a deep breath, "must make blankety-blank salary a year. Must want children. One boy, one girl. Must like golden retrievers. Must want to settle in the sub-urbs. Must celebrate Christmas and Easter." I pause, exhale, and jab at the hole in the knee of my jeans. "Must have good insurance. With dental."

"So what are yours?"

I try to think. Andrew rests the notepad on the steering wheel, poised under the stubby pencil. *Putt-Putt at the Golf Caboose!* the pencil says. It's probably a keepsake from a date with Kimberley. I'll bet Kimberley is a really good golfer. I'll bet the two of them golf neck and neck, and by the time they hit the bonus hole, the combined competition and sexual tension is so intense they're almost nude.

I close my eyes, trying again to focus on my criteria for the perfect man. But anything I come up with sounds childish. Must play music? Must wear black? Must not produce earwax? Must not have mother? Must be passionate? Intense? Deep? I've been looking for these qualities for so long I can't remember what they were supposed to mean, or why I wanted them in the first place.

I open my eyes. Andrew is watching me, waiting for an answer. When I open my mouth, what comes out takes me by surprise: "Maybe I should try dating a nonmusician for a change."

Andrew puts the pad and pencil back inside the glove compartment and flicks the door shut. The light disappears. It is quiet between us, the air dense with crickets and Backstreet and heat. Lightning bugs speckle the darkness. The music sounds as if it's coming from someplace faraway. I wonder if we're about to start kissing. It feels like something is supposed to happen, at the very least one of those "if-we're-forty-and-still-unmarried" pacts. Then something chirps in Andrew's pocket.

"What the hell is that?" I ask.

His face grows long with guilt. The pocket chirps again.

"Oh my God, Andrew. You didn't."

As he slips the cell phone from his khakis, he can't even meet my eyes. He unfolds it and tucks it against his ear. "Hey," he says, in a whisper. He doesn't have to ask who's calling. Not because he's looking at a Caller ID box, but because it's Kimberley. It has to be. "How was your night?"

I fix my eyes outside the window, trying hard not to listen. I focus on the mailbox beside the car window, topped with a humorless bluebird and the words *The Mackeys* in curly, rusting wrought iron. It used to say *The Simons*. Now it says *The Mackeys*. Across the yard Mom's front door opens and Camilla and Scott emerge, laden with plates of leftovers and boxes of hand-me-downs. "Thanks for everything, Mom," I can hear Camilla saying. I watch as they cross the yard to the Saab parked in the driveway. Watch as Scott unlocks Camilla's door. Watch as he places a hand on the small of her back as she slides inside. This is what happens, I think, when you carry a baby: people treat you carefully.

Andrew is keeping his voice low, a lot of "mmm"s, "yeah"s, "me too"s, and a "soon." The Backstreet Boys come to a dramatic finish and the deejay returns, sending us smoothly into a commercial.

"Okay," Andrew murmurs. "Love you, too."

After he hangs up—a smug bleep—he refolds the phone and slips it back into his pocket. Now, of course, everything feels different between us. I watch as Scott and Camilla's red taillights disappear down the street. Mom's porch light snaps off.

"We should go." I say it, so Andrew doesn't have to.

"That was Kimberley."

"Yeah, I figured."

"The phone was her idea."

"Uh huh."

"It's just so we can reach each other, you know, in emergencies." He's trying to apologize or rationalize or some other kind of -ize, but it's only making me feel worse. We both know we're not talking about the cell phone, though what we are talking about I'm not really sure.

Andrew coughs and starts the car. He turns the headlights on. "She was just wondering where I was," he concludes, then nods, as if satisfied with his defense. He starts to pull away from the curb.

"Well, did you explain to her that there's no threat?" I ask him. "That I'm not a lawyer? That you're not a rock star?" It's our oldest and most well-worn joke, but for some reason it sounds bitter, and makes me feel like crying.

Monday morning, bright and early, I march to the front desk of Dreams Come True, Inc.

"Beryl?" I say. "Set me up."

6

saxophonists

SIDE B

"Slave to Love" — Bryan Ferry
"I Melt With You" — Modern English
"Lips Like Sugar" — Echo & The Bunnymen
"Love My Way" — The Psychedelic Furs
"Just Like Heaven" — The Cure

The hierarchy of high school band is one of subtle, but critical, distinctions.

Marching band is the most exposed of the bands. Required uniform consists of polyester shirts and pants, yellow Velcro cummerbunds, plumed hats, epaulettes, and chin straps. Members strut and sweat and blow before crowds of hundreds at pep rallies and football games, assembling the lopsided words YORK, WIN, GO, TEAM and, on occasion, the approximate shape of a panther.

Concert band is a middle ground. Not cool, but at least

understated. They are heard only indoors, at night, at shows attended only by parents, grandparents, and girl-friends/boyfriends of c-band members. Required uniform consists of subtle dark skirts/pants, subtle dark shoes, subtle white tops. Unless you are a woodwind, you're likely to be buried so far in the back you won't be seen at all.

Stage band is the coolest in the band hierarchy. Required uniform consists of dark pants and maroon polo shirts. They are a small group, highly selective, only the best saxes, trumpets, trombones, and horns the concert band has to offer. And if you are sixteen, craving musicians, and have recently sworn off the drummer genre, the brass players of the stage band are the men to watch.

Unlike going to the *Transformations* meeting, I had no specific goals in mind when I attended the York High Spring Band Gala. I hadn't scoured yearbooks. I wasn't looking for love in any way. I was only there because Hannah had asked me to go with her. Eric Sommes was being featured in the "1812 Overture," hitting the BOOM sound effect on the synthesizer to simulate a cannon at key moments.

Eric wasn't officially in the band. He had no musical train-ing. He was only there because the band conductor, Mr. Franklin, had campaigned seriously in the teacher's lounge to find a kid reliable enough to nab those BOOMs, claiming his percussion was "short-handed" (i.e., unreliable and stoned). Eric's computer teacher, Mr. Will, a four-foot eleven-inch, pointy-bearded elf of a man who was regularly stuffed into lockers, recommended Eric for the job. Mr. Will adored Eric because a) he was the only kid oblivious to Mr. Will's height, b) he was a wiz with a Texas Instrument, and c) he was a boy you could truly count on to strike that BOOM when cued.

Not that the entire audience didn't know it when Eric got the cue. Mr. Franklin was not a subtle man. He approached his job as band conductor as seriously as a fighter pilot or a secret service agent. His car—green Volvo, "Band is Life" bumper sticker—never seemed to leave the parking lot, ever. He often carried a walkie-talkie for no apparent reason. He was obese and sweated profusely as he charged around the school, walkie-talkie tucked under his chin, sweat beading on his upper lip, glasses slipping down his nose, sweat circles widening under his arms until they verged on his pocket protector. (The proximity of Mr. Franklin's excessive sweat to the electronic device hugging his neck didn't seem to worry anyone but me.)

The night of the Gala, Mr. Franklin moved with military precision: 7:00 to 7:20: he paced the stage, moving folding chairs, adjusting music stands, pushing his slippery glasses up his nose and inexplicably speaking into a headset; 7:21: he flew into the wings; 7:25: the concert band filled the folding chairs; 7:28: the house lights went down. At 7:30, Mr. Franklin reappeared, having a) added an unnervingly bright red blazer and b) subtracted his eyeglasses. Without the glasses, his face looked small, shocked.

When the concert band finally started playing, they sounded miserable. They were totally out of synch, totally out of tune. To his credit, Mr. Franklin conducted them bravely, as intense as if he were coaching a varsity sport. He sweated so much his reddish buzz cut sparkled under the stage lights. The armpits of his red blazer soaked all the way through. He tossed his arms around with vigor, jabbing his little white wand in the air, moving so much he nearly toppled off the stand when reaching to cue Eric on the BOOMs.

I was prepared for the band's poor playing, but what I wasn't prepared for were the songs themselves. If only they'd stuck to the traditional, the patriotic, it might have been bearable. Instead, most selections after "1812" made the mistake of trying to be hip, the musical equivalent of guidance counselors "rapping." Each song was more humiliating than the last: "Sailor's Hornpipe," a jaunty sea shanty performed by a cluster of red-faced woodwinds wearing straw hats; the choppy "Eye of the Tiger/Chariots of Fire/Nadia's Theme" medley; and, worst of all, the band's final number, a scary approximation of Falco's "Rock Me Amadeus" complete with verbal call and response— hearty "R-r-r-rock me"s from the trumpets and tubas, squeaky "Rock me! Rock me!"s from the flutes and clarinets.

When the concert band stood to bow, looking damp and stunned, I wanted to run. The Spring Band Gala was a substratum of York High School I simply wished I'd never seen, like accidentally catching your parents having sex. Eric was finished BOOMing. Hannah wouldn't be left alone. If I hurried, I could catch the second half of *90210*.

But just after Eric rejoined us and I was about to run for the door, I felt a change in the air. Something was happening. People in the audience—people I trusted, people who looked like they'd been sitting through these concerts for centuries—were beginning to stir. All along, I'd assumed they were just polite and immune to the awfulness, waiting to congratulate their grandson, hand him a wadded five and a warm butterscotch candy, and go home to bed. But now, they were sitting up in their seats. They were waking up their husbands. They were unscrolling their programs and switching from reading glasses to bifocals.

"Who's up next?" I elbowed Hannah.

She opened her program—the logical move—and read: "Stage band."

As she spoke, a handful of boys reemerged on stage. I felt a fluttering in my chest. Just moments before, they had been concert band boys; now, they were stage band men. They had abandoned their starchy shirts for maroon polos, loose at the neck. They tuned up leisurely, confidently, emptying their spit valves, running through scales and throwing in snatches of "Hawaii Five-O" and "R-r-rock me." At 8:15, when Mr. Franklin came back onstage, he had transformed, too. The sweaty suit jacket was gone. The shirtsleeves were rolled up to his elbows. His message was clear: now, we would be getting down to business.

Mr. Franklin held both arms aloft. The stage band raised their instruments to their mouths. Then Mr. Franklin tapped his foot, sharp against the waxy stage floor. "One! Two! Three! Fo'!" he yelled, and the stage band sprang to life.

They were nothing like the concert band had been. They were good. Genuinely good. They dug into their first song, "Hang On Sloopy," with all their heart and soul. Unlike the concert band—who'd sat frozen to their folding chairs—the stage band moved and swayed, feeling the beat. The crowd started getting into it. I heard a few hands clapping, a few orthopedic shoes tapping, one old man who shouted "Right on!"

With "Sloopy" firmly underway, Mr. Franklin busted the move he'd been waiting for all night. As if to prove his confidence in his boys (I'm sure, in private, he called them "my boys") he simply stopped conducting and sauntered away. Absently mopping his brow, contemplating his wing tips, he jived along as if he were alone on a city street and lost in thought. It was the happiest I had ever seen him. Now and then, he'd groove back over and cue one of the guys with a subtle point of the finger, like tapping ash off a cigarette. Then he would boogie off again, not even bothering to glance over his shoulder as the soloist rose from his seat.

There were different approaches to stage-band soloing. Some of the soloists tapped their feet. Some hunched their shoulders and wailed. One trumpeter reared his head back like a wild elephant, and a red-faced tuba player did an alarming, wiggly thing with his hips. It wasn't until the band's third number, "Old Time Rock 'n Roll," that the sax soloist took his cue from Mr. Franklin.

I think the first thing I fell in love with was his head. His hair was so blond it was almost white, shining in a buttery glaze of spotlight. Light glinted off the keys of his sax, skipping around like lightning bugs. His eyes squeezed shut. His brow creased into complicated furrows of feeling. He never opened his eyes, not once, but his light eyebrows raced up and down and up and down, in counterpoint to the breathy low notes and racing runs and final, piercing, high note that left him, and me, and several grandparents, gasping for breath.

He was a rock star.

"Eric!" I hissed, when the song was over and the crowd rallied to give their loudest cheer of the night.

He leaned over Hannah's lap and raised one eyebrow.

"Who was that guy?"

"Which guy?" Leave it to Eric.

"The one who just had the solo. The saxophone."

"Oh." He sat back, fingers tapping the bridge of his nose. At times like this it would have been helpful if Eric Sommes had been aware of any humans beyond his girlfriend. "I'm not sure. I think it starts with a J."

I grabbed my program off the floor and scanned the "Stage Band":

SAXOPHONES
Brian Russo
Jordan Prince

Jordan Prince. Not only did it have to be the guy, it had to be the most romantic name ever named. As the stage band launched into "Fly Like An Eagle," Mr. Franklin so proud he wandered practically into the caf, I gazed at Jordan Prince's furrowed face, my mind swimming with possibilities—Eliza Prince, Jordan and Eliza Prince, *Merry Christmas from the Princes!*—until the song ended with the shimmer of a cymbal and the curtain fell.

*   *   *

I didn't have to go so far as joining an extracurricular activity to access Jordan Prince. This was fortunate, since being in band would have meant giving up all my Wednesday afternoons, performing in public, and learning to play a musical instrument, something I hadn't done since blasting my way through "Big Fat Hen" on the recorder in third grade. I had other methods. A secret weapon: Eric Sommes.

"You've got to get Eric to introduce me," I told Hannah.

We were sprawled on the Devines's sunporch on a Monday afternoon, a bowl of grapes and a Scrabble board between us. Since my mother had started dating Harv, I'd taken to hovering around Hannah's like a moth, slipping in whenever Eric was at one of his after-school science/math/ecology clubs.

"Before Eric can introduce you to Jordan," Hannah said, sensibly, lining up UMULUS next to a C, "you need someone to introduce Jordan to Eric."

This, so far, was the only glitch in my plan: my secret weapon was the most cerebral student in York High. He could name the genus of every plant and animal, but didn't know the captain of the football team.

"They don't even know each other," Hannah added, totaling up her word score.

"What do you mean?" I tossed down B and S to make BUS. Normally I was awesome at Scrabble, but I had bigger things on my mind. "They played in band together."

"Eric's not really in band."

"But they played together."

"So?"

"So they know each other. Playing in the band is like belonging to the same church." I had no idea what I was saying, and stuffed four grapes in my mouth.

But with Hannah, there is no such thing as a fly-by comment. She blew her curly bangs off her forehead so she could look at me and narrow her eyes. "Why do you like this guy so much, anyway?"

At this point in my life, I was beginning to realize that this was one of the central differences between my friends and myself. They couldn't understand these unspoken connections. They couldn't imagine liking someone they hadn't met. These were the kinds of things that separated me from the majority of the population and linked me to people like Jordan Prince, Z Tedesco, and, potentially, Bono and Sting.

"We'd like each other. I can just tell," I countered. "It's a feeling I have. Fate, maybe."

"Maybe." Hannah has a gift for saying what she means without saying what she means. She uncrossed her legs and peered down at her tiles, swapped a few, then laid out AME next to L.

"Oh, thanks."

"What? I didn't mean you."

"Whatever." I didn't want to argue with her. More importantly, I was nervous that we were drifting too far from my mission. "I just have to meet him, okay?" I said, sounding a little more desperate than I intended. "I don't know why. I just do."

Hannah looked at me evenly. "Okay, okay. Hang on. Let me think." She sat back in her chair and scratched distractedly at a bug bite on her ankle. Then she nibbled on a grape, twisting the spiky stem around her fingertip until it turned pink.

I waited patiently, sneaking a T onto the end of BUS.

"Okay, listen," she finally said, sitting forward again. She loosened the grape stem from her finger and I watched as blood rushed back to the tip. "There's this . . . thing. In a few weeks."

Now we were getting somewhere. "What thing?" I pounced. "What? Where?"

Hannah hesitated. I could tell she regretted telling me already. Years later, she would term it *enabling*. "It's kind of a band . . . function."

At the word "function," my excitement dimmed. "What kind of function? Like performing in public? Washing cars? Selling hoagies?"

"More like a gathering." She was getting more cryptic by the word. "Sort of an end-of-the-year . . . like . . . bash."

Whoa, there. If "function" was unnerving, "bash" was a downright blazing red flag. Obviously, the term "bash" must have come via Eric, which meant it orginally came via the invitation itself, which I was suddenly sure was designed on a home computer and had little musical notes all over it and said something like "Let's 'Band' Together!"

But the romantic in me knew this might be my only shot at meeting Jordan Prince. Bash, function, bake sale, whatever. I had to go for it.

"Okay," I agreed. "But how am I supposed to get in the door? Should I pretend I sit way in the back? Act like I play the triangle or something?"

Hannah smiled, her first real smile of the afternoon. "Eliza, you can't pretend to be in band."

*   *   *

This statement, as it turned out, was truer than I could have known. The minute I was in the door of the all-band bash/function—at the house of a clarinetist named Judy, whose parents were in the Poconos and liked chintz—I was marked as a nonband member. All across the miles of painfully patterned living room, band members were trading band jokes, humming band songs, swapping photos from their band trip to Niagara Falls. The real "Rock Me Amadeus" was playing on the stereo. In front of the fireplace, a tall, pimply boy was doing his well-honed impression of Mr. Franklin, complete with walkie-talkie.

Some kids were wearing cummerbunds, for kicks.

"Are you sure I'm allowed to be here?" I whispered to Hannah.

"Nothing you can do about it now." This was true, but didn't exactly inspire confidence. Attached to Eric's hand, Hannah was legitimate. I, on the other hand, was a band bash crasher.

"Hey!" shouted a guy by the umbrella stand. He was waving inexplicably in our direction, and wearing jeans, a complicated Escher print T-shirt and a plumed hat. "Yo!" he called. "Boomer!" It took me a minute to realize he was talking to Eric, whose "1812" stint had apparently earned him an official band nickname.

"Hey, it's The Boom!" another guy shouted, and suddenly people were crowding us from all sides. For a guy who didn't know any band members, Eric was a popular man. The three of us were handed plastic cups of pee-yellow beer, half of which I gulped down on the spot. I was starting to have second thoughts about this whole scheme, and having visions of Jordan Prince wearing a chin strap.

As Hannah was getting introduced to Boomer's new friends, I slunk away. I couldn't bear the awkward moment when "The Boom" tried to explain who I was and what I was doing there. I headed for the kitchen, where four girls were blending bright pink daiquiris. They were also wearing straw hats a la "Sailor's Hornpipe," which felt meanly reassuring. If these were the girls I was up against, my chances were looking good with Jordan Prince.

I aimed for the back door, hiding behind my beer. On my way, I scanned the chintzy dining room on my right, the chintzy den on my left. Maybe, I reasoned, Jordan Prince was too cool to be here. Maybe, like me, he'd rather be somewhere (anywhere) else. But when I stepped too confidently onto the patio, there he was, sitting on the edge of the pool.

He was shirtless, of course. He was also deeply tanned, which made his light hair even lighter and his eyebrows practically invisible. Fortunately, he wasn't wearing any band paraphernalia. Unfortunately, the girl beside him wasn't, either. She'd opted for an orange-striped bikini as big as a Band-Aid.

Damn.

My heart sank as I watched Bikini operate. For the record, there was no earthly way this girl was in band. First she pulled the splash-her-feet move, just enough to get Jordan Prince wet and make him splash her in return (tramp). Then she pulled the feel-my-muscle-I've-been-doing-Cindy-Crawford's-workout-tape-and-does-it-show? move, which required he touch her arm (wench!). When she felt his bicep in exhange, I started feeling nauseous.

I was about to admit defeat, go home, and drown in some Fruit Roll-Ups and slow Sting when the girl's friend came running over. I watched the two of them confer, then Bikini turn and whisper something in Jordan's ear—a sultry "don't forget me when I'm gone," I'm sure—and scamper off with her friend, probably heading to the chintzy bathroom to discuss boys or tampons or swimming with their periods or whether you can get pregnant just by touching it. If I hadn't been in public, I might have cackled as I moved in for the kill.

Note: this was the boldest move in my rock-star repertoire to date. I had no excuse to hide behind this time. No poem reading. No fake drowning. I had only half a beer in my veins, but was feeling desperate enough to keep on moving. When I was about two feet from where Jordan Prince sat basking in his multicolored Jams, I lowered myself to the edge of the pool, wishing all at once that I had a) shaved my legs, and b) painted my toenails, and c) shown just a little more skin. As I felt water seeping through my cut-offs, I resigned myself to the fact that I might be too embarrassed to ever stand again. I had a vision of Judy the clarinetist and her family waving to me from their den, tossing me spare chicken nuggets, blankets, and last week's *TV Guide*s while I sat rooted to the edge of their pool, growing old.

I stared into the water, praying hard that Jordan Prince would say hi.

"Hi."

Unfortunately, it wasn't him who said it. But at least the ball was rolling.

Jordan Prince surveyed me through his silvery mirrored shades. This is one of the hazards of dating rock stars; they're often hidden behind their sunglasses, whether black or silver, indoor or outdoor, day or (in the words of Corey Hart) night.

"Hi," he replied.

Good, good. But where to next? "Great party!" Too fake. "So are you in the marching band?" Too nosy. "Did you know that once I was the drowning victim in my camp lifesaving class?" Too utterly lame. "You were really good in the spring concert?"

"You were really good in the spring concert," I said, and swallowed some beer. At least I had said it. If things went as well as they had with Z Tedesco, we'd be kissing inside forty-five minutes.

"Oh yeah?" Jordan Prince's eyebrows—they were, in fact, still there—furrowed into an adorably confused V. "Are you in the band?"

I almost scoffed at the idea—*are you fucking kidding me?* came to mind—but caught myself in time. "No," I swallowed. "I'm just . . . a fan."

A fan? A *fan?* Now who seemed pathetic? I sounded like some kind of psychotic band stalker. Which was only a tiny bit true.

Jordan Prince concealed a smile. Just to clarify: it wasn't an "I'm-falling-in-love-with-this-endearingly-eccentric-woman" smile, it was a "this-chick-is-insane" smile. "Wow," he said, his tone thick with mocking. I am intimately familiar with the thick-with-mocking tone. If I hadn't been the mock-ee, I would have complimented him on his delivery. "A fan, huh?" Jordan Prince said. "A band fan."

This was not good at all. Not only did Jordan Prince think I was a psychotic stalker, he now thought I was a dork. He was blatantly making fun of me. He had rhymed.

"Well, no, I'm not a *fan*, exactly," I stumbled. I was starting to sweat in my black T-shirt. "I mean, I was at the spring concert, but only kind of by accident. My friend's boyfriend was, um, in it."

"Who's your friend's boyfriend?"

I wasn't looking to go down this road, but it was better than anyplace we'd been before. "Eric," I said, raising my plastic cup and mumbling to the rim. "Eric Sommes."

Jordan's eyebrows furrowed again, now wondering if I was not only a dork and a stalker but a pathological liar, too. "There's no guy named Sommes in band."

I glanced toward the house, praying to God that Eric might materialize right then to rescue me. He didn't, of course. God knew better.

I gritted my teeth and offered, "You might know him better as . . . Boomer?"

"Oh!" Jordan Prince actually seemed to brighten a little. "The 1812 dude!"

"Dude" was an overstatement, but at least we were getting somewhere. I felt my chest unclench. Jordan Prince was smiling. I was smiling. We had survived the "band fan" setback (maybe we'd joke about it later, maybe it would become my pet name someday, when we were forty and married and he was grabbing at my hand as he reached for the Country Crock and murmured, "Good morning, my little band fan")—but, right now, I just needed to get away from this Boomer connection. I needed to tap into the sensitive side of Jordan Prince, the eyes-closed side, the side that felt "Old Time Rock 'n Roll" in the soles of his feet.

"Plus," I leaped in, "I just really like music. You know, in general."

There it was: the spark of interest. Jordan Prince's mocking smile faded. He pushed a shock of blond hair out of his face with the heel of one hand. "Oh yeah?" he said. Then, as if in slow motion, he posed the all-important: **"What kind of music do you like?"**

At that point in my dating career, I hadn't yet learned the significance of this question. For a rock star, claiming allegiance to any one "kind of music" was the equivalent of committing to a marriage or a child or, at the least, a large pet. Fielding the question took skill and finesse. An eye for detail, an ear for nuance. Until you knew a rock star's specific preferences, it was best to stay general. Speak in terms of genre only. Never mention a specific band, a specific artist, a specific album or—God help you—a specific song.

Despite all of this, it was **"I like Jack Wagner"** that came marching out of my mouth that spring day, brazen as a hooker. I capped it off with: **"Do you know the song 'All I Need'? "**

I've since spent many hours of my life trying to understand what possessed me in that moment. It's not that I hadn't moved on from my crush on Jack Wagner, or didn't have a respectable CD collection—U2, Sting, R.E.M., etc.—plus Z Tedesco's coolly brooding mix tapes. I just spoke without thinking; it was something like blurting out "your skin on mine" the first time I talked to Z. Maybe I was so overwhelmed with rock-star lust that Jack Wagner, who had once defined the feeling, simply flew from my gut to my lips like a reflex, like the time I saw a Rorschach blotch in one of Hannah's textbooks and yelled out "cheeseburger!"

It was a huge mistake, don't get me wrong. Potentially unrecoverable. I couldn't begin to explain my reasoning to Jordan Prince; it's taken me years to explain it to myself. There was nothing to do but flail "I mean, you know, a long time ago," while laughing much too hard and much too loudly.

But Jordan Prince had already shifted his gaze to somewhere over my left shoulder. He was probably searching for the bikini girl who, though she might still listen to Debbie Gibson's *Electric Youth,* was at least willing to get almost naked at the all-band bash/function.

I figured I had one small window of opportunity left, if I was lucky. My options, as I saw them, were: a) pretend to drown and hope Jordan jumped in to save me, or b) throw the music ball back in his court. Plan A seemed a touch too risky, relying too much on Jordan's participation. What if he opted *not* to rescue me? What if he just watched me flail? What if I climbed out of the pool alone, soaked, sour, and laughed out of the party by the Sailor's Hornpipe crowd?

I opted for the safe, verbal, and seated Plan B.

"So, Jordan." Had I more strength left, I would have tried to sound seductive, but at this point it was all I could do to keep my voice from shaking. "What kind of music do *you* like?"

If he wondered how I knew his name, Jordan Prince didn't ask. I watched as his eyes slid back to my face, peering over the tops of his silver shades. I watched as he took a long drink of beer, watched him watch me over the rim as he swallowed, watched as he swiped his glistening lip with the back of his deeply tanned hand.

"You really want to know?"

"Yes." Yesyesyesyesyes.

He gazed into the pool, at a yellow floaty bobbing forlornly in the deep end. "Jazz," he said. The word was poignant, perfect. His eyebrows, when he said it, rose and fell in one beat, like a single note.

I felt the back of my neck prickle, and gulped the warm inch of beer left in my cup. Jordan Prince was looking right at me. Suddenly, this was going better than I could have dreamed. I could practically feel the sexual tension mounting between us. And if my Jack Wagner line had been a huge misstep, my next move made up for it in brilliance:

"My dad's into jazz," I said. My tone was just right: thoughtful, wistful, a touch melancholic. I gazed into the distance—at what should have been a horizon or an ocean, but instead was four bassoonists in a chicken fight—and added, "at least . . . I think he is. It's been a while since I saw him."

Shameless, I know. But it worked. From the corner of my eye, I saw Jordan Prince slip off his shades. He stared at me for a long, slow moment, and when I turned to him, those blond brows were furrowing for me alone. "What do you mean?" he asked. "Where's your dad now?"

Once I'd discovered the potential rock-star dating power of Lou's abandonment, I couldn't believe I hadn't capitalized on it before. I didn't have to manufacture angst. I had angst. I coined angst. I owned angst. Over the years, I have perfected angst into a minor art form, one of precise timing, tone, pace. I should have been an Oscar contender for my nuanced performance one night in a damp corner of Sigma Pi, where I had a frat brother dabbing at his eyes with his toga. Yes, it might seem callous and selfish and mean, but here it is: if my father chose to abandon us, I chose to benefit from that abandonment any way I damn well could.

Saturday night, a week after the band bash/function, my mother found me in the bathroom layering on midnight black mascara. The room was strewn with damp towels, clogged with steam, throbbing with the sounds of *Licensed to Ill* from the boom box I'd propped on the fluffy toilet seat cover.

"Where are you going?" Mom asked. In high school, most of my interactions with my mother revolved around these questions: "Where are you going?", "How are you getting there?", "What will you do for dinner?" and "Won't that get infected?"

"Out," I said. This was one of my standard replies, along with: "Don't know" and "Maybe. What's it to you?"

In the patch of mirror I'd wiped clean with my fist, I could read my mother's face exactly: one part interested in my plans for the evening, one part worried about my plans, two parts appalled by my sloppy technique with a Wet 'n Wild wand.

"I was hoping you would eat with us tonight," she said, folding her arms across her chest. "Harv's here, you know. For dinner."

This was not news. Harv was always there for dinner. I hated eating dinner with Mom and Harv for several reasons, including Mom, Harv, and dinner. Mom, because she was always too eager for Harv and me to make friends. Harv, because I was convinced he had some kind of rare digestive-auditory problem that made his intestinal functions much too loud. Dinner, because the menu was always something along the lines of: slab of meat with meat sauce on a bed of meat.

"I can't," I said, penciling a thick black line under each eye. "I have a date."

Mom stiffened. "With whom?"

Normally I resisted giving any personal information to my mother, especially after she used good grammar. But for the past week, I'd grabbed any excuse to say Jordan Prince out loud.

"Jordan Prince."

Mom took a step into the bathroom. "Isn't he going to come around to the house?" Her crossed arms quickly disentangled and she began wringing her hands. Literally: the woman wrung her hands. Whereas she used to plant them on her hips, now the hands crashed into each other in midair, clung and fumbled. "Aren't you going to introduce him to me? And Harv?"

"Why would I introduce him to Harv?" I said, yanking open the medicine cabinet. I wanted to avoid looking at Mom's reflection, which was starting to make me edgy. As I scoured the shelves for something useful, I found myself staring instead at a short history of my family: Cherry Chapstick and Stridex (me). Lilac-scented body wash and body splash (Camilla). Oil of Olay (Mom, now). Sleeping aids (Mom, then). Maalox and Tums and a generic-brand stool softener (Harv?). I grabbed a pair of tweezers and slammed the mirrored door.

Behind me, Mom was picking up my towels from the floor. She centered each one on a towel rack, making sure each edge was equidistant from each rod. "Who is this boy?" she asked, as if Jordan was a vagrant who had just wandered into our lives off the Pennsylvania Turnpike. "What do we know about him?"

"What do we want to know about him?" I rubbed at my eyeliner with a fingertip, watching in the mirror as Mom winced. If I hadn't been running late, I would have penciled on some moles, just for kicks.

"I just want to hear about him. I want to meet him. Is that so wrong? Camilla always used to bring her friends around to the house for me to meet."

I should have known. "In other words," I said, capping the eyeliner, "you want to know if he's acceptable. If he gets straight As. If he shovels snow for the elderly. If he runs for president of the student council." I felt bad dragging Ivan into it, but sometimes you gotta do what you gotta do. "Actually, Mom, he's a pimp from outer space."

"Eliza." She was going for motherly exasperation, though I know part of her was terrified this was in some way true. "Please."

I leaned into the mirror, smearing on dark red lipstick. "He goes to my school," I conceded. "He's a musician. He plays the sax in the stage band." In the mirror, my mother's face seemed closer now, like a moon hovering over my shoulder, clenched and pink. I could practically feel her breath on my neck. In that moment, all I wanted was for her to get away from me, my life, my friends, my thoughts. Everything she touched seemed to get screwed up or disappear completely.

"And," I said, snapping the lipstick shut, "he loves jazz. Just like Dad."

I hadn't planned to say it. I instantly wished I hadn't said it. In the mirror, I saw my mother about-face and walk from the room without a word, her steps quick, rigid, as if stepping on hot coals. A guilty sweat crept up the back of my neck and crawled under my hair. I kept my eyes fixed on my pale reflection as I listened to her padding downstairs. My heartbeat echoed the sound of her footsteps, faster and more frantic as she neared the bottom of the staircase.

But when I heard the footsteps stop, followed by the low, consoling rumble of Harv's voice or Harv's large intestine or both, I stopped feeling so guilty. Why should Mom care if I was dating a guy who liked jazz? She wasn't lonely. She wasn't unhappy. She had Carnivore Harv for company. Besides, it was her fault Dad left us in the first place. I turned up the Beasties, picked up the tweezers, grabbed an eyebrow hair and yanked.

Jordan Prince would, in fact, meet my mother. I would, in fact, meet Jordan Prince's mother. Mrs. Prince would, in fact, turn out to be one of the few mothers in rock star history not to pull something grossly embarrassing. I chalk this up to the fact that, in high school, rock stars are still young enough that mothers aren't so nostalgic. Mothers are still playing tennis and joining book groups, picking up their rock star's banana peels and gym socks. And girlfriends are still relatively harmless, a pretty face in a prom photo.

Had we made it that far, I wouldn't have been surprised if Jordan Prince and I had gone to "prom" (a lack of article I refuse to accept, and #2 on my list of words to outlaw if I were president). We probably would have done the whole mainstream, color-coordinated corsage-and-boutonniere thing. Because, unlike Z Tedesco, Jordan didn't have a lot of angst. He "went with the flow" (and was actually known to use the phrase "I go with the flow"). It wasn't that he was particularly attached to proms and corsages, he was just mellow about things. His voice was mellow. His gait was mellow. Even his kissing style—dry and slow, unlike Z's propeller tongue—was mellow. He seemed biologically incapable of things like tension, reflection, moral/spiritual self-examination, or holding opinions in general. The only consternation in his body was in his furrowing forehead—the inspiration for my summer opus, "Sweet Brow 'O Mine."

On occasion, Jordan's "flow" could make me uneasy. Jealous, actually, much as I hated to admit it. For example: a July day at the Jersey shore. Jordan is turned on his stomach, carefully tanning. (I would later learn there is a certain breed of male for whom tanning is a sacred, timed event, and realize that Jordan Prince was one of them.) I'm propped on my elbows, getting a haphazard sunburn, flipping through *People* and listening to

Sinéad on my Walkman. All is well when yet another girl in a
bathing suit comes along to threaten our relationship: this time,
a red-white-and-blue bikini with the (swear to God) Budweiser
logo plastered across the butt. She kicks sand onto Jordan's feet.

"Oops!" she giggles, pausing at the foot of his towel.

I let my Walkman drop around my neck. Jordan rolls over.

"Sorry," she says. "Didn't mean it."

Like hell you didn't, I spit with my eyes.

"No problem," Jordan smiles beneath his shades.

"It was an accident," the girl smiles back, flipping her hair
over one shoulder. I might as well have been a beach umbrella.
"So I'll see ya around?"

"Sure."

And that was that. She pranced away, all beer and patrio-
tism. Jordan rolled back over. There was no comment, no
reflection, no reaction. Jordan glanced at his Swatch, probably
worried he'd missed valuable seconds of back-tanning time.

I stared at the blond back of his head, willing him to turn
around. He did not.

"She *likes* you, you know," I informed him, through
clenched teeth.

"Yeah," he said. "I know."

Oh.

From then on, instead of getting jealous, I tried to match
Jordan's laid-back 'tude. This is easier in the summer, of course,
when you don't have to deal with all the school stuff: where to
sit in the caf, whether to hold hands in the hall, how to cope if
you have the misfortune of ending up in the same gym section.

Instead, most of what we did was music—or done *to* music. Jordan talked about jazz bands, we listened to jazz bands, I listened to him talk about listening to jazz bands. We went to third base on his bed with a black-and-white poster of sweat-drenched Miles Davis inspiring us from above.

There was only one musical topic we avoided and that was The Big C: Concert Band. The few times the subject came up—once on a mini-golf double-date with Hannah and The Boom, once over milkshakes in McDonald's when "Nadia's Theme" trickled over the Muzak—it was unnerving. I'd always assumed c-band was just something Jordan tolerated, another opportunity to play the sax (or, as he unfortunately called it, the "'phone"). But when he talked about it—using words like "awesome," "righteous," once calling the bassoonists "dudes"— you'd think he belonged to some super-cool frat house. It seemed he was actually oblivious to the band's low rung on the York High social ladder. I began to suspect that being in band was a form of being brainwashed. Existing in a world unto itself. Like the chess club, or the Amish.

I tried to ignore Jordan's concert band comments and banish any association between my boyfriend and "Rock Me Amadeus" from my mind. By August, I had almost managed to convince myself he wasn't in band at all. Until it came time for camp.

"What do you mean, camp?"

We were in the food court at the Blue Horn Mall, eating gluey cheese fries from Cheesesteaks, Etc. "You know," Jordan said, prying two fries apart like a wishbone. His tone had the same kind of cheerful but terrible quality I recalled from being told I needed braces. "Band camp."

"Oh," I said. Oh no.

"We go away for a week."

Oh no. Oh no.

"To the Poconos."

Make it stop.

"To practice songs and . . ."

For the love of God!

". . . drills."

I felt something burst inside me then. Hope, maybe. Faith. Trust. The innocence of youth.

"Right," I intoned. "Drills."

"It starts on Monday," Jordan explained, stuffing a clot of fries in his mouth. His brow furrowed over his shiny shades, both of which were starting to look much less cute. "I thought you knew."

"Must have forgotten," I shrugged, and noted the traces of Velveeta gathering in the corners of his mouth.

And that was all the band camp info I asked to know. Maybe it was because I'd finally absorbed Jordan's live-and-let-live attitude. Maybe it was because I trusted his judgment so completely. Or maybe it was because, on some level, I wasn't ready to acknowledge what I already knew was true.

On Monday morning, when I went to his house to say goodbye, I couldn't deny the truth any longer. I walked upstairs, opened his bedroom door, and there was living, breathing confirmation of my deepest fear: Jordan Prince in polyester.

This person was no rock star. This person was preening in front of his full-length closet mirror, humming some kind of awful show tune/band march hybrid. He was adjusting the cuffs and buttons of his marching band uniform as if getting ready for a society dinner. He was wearing sunglasses and a plumed hat. All I could do was stare, numb, as he secured the hat on his head and fastened the chin strap. In that moment, I believe I knew how women must feel who suddenly discover their husbands are polygamists or running from the law.

Jordan walked over to where I was clutching at the bedroom wall. He cupped my face in both hands, gazing through his shades and into my eyes. He might have been going off to war.

"I'll see you soon," he said, softly. His eyebrows rose on the "see" and the "soon," which struck me as idiotic. "I'll be back on Saturday."

Saturday! I heard inside my head, a combination of screams and laughter. *Ha! By Saturday I'll be gone! Long gone! Ha ha ha ha ha!*

On the outside, I said: "Okay then."

As Jordan leaned forward to kiss me, a feather from his plumed hat tickled my cheek. I gave him a quick peck and grabbed for the door.

"Wait," Jordan said. "Just a second." I looked back over my shoulder and, too late, saw something dangling from his hand. Something soft. Long. Horribly yellow. "Before you go, do you think you could help me with this cummerbund?"

7

securities analysts

SIDE A
"The World Has Turned and Left Me Here" — Weezer
"Kamikaze" — PJ Harvey
"Seether" — Veruca Salt
"Fuck and Run" — Liz Phair
"Kiss Off" — Violent Femmes

It's rare that I have multiple weekend plans. By plans, I mean concrete. Social. Arranged in advance. Sitting in a corner of The Blue Room doesn't count, nor does watching an episode of *Boy Meets World*. Not that there's anything wrong with weekend TV. There was a time when the Saturday night lineup of *Diff'rent Strokes* and *Silver Spoons* was the highlight of my week. Shortly after, of course, the prospect of not going out on a weekend became the most painful social death I could possibly imagine. Friday and Saturday nights were booked weeks in advance with malls, movies, late-night IHOP runs. Then, by the time I made it to college, plan making became ironically obsolete. Plans hunt you in college, surround you, torment you with keg beer and strobe-lit charity balls and endless tracks of Dave Matthews.

These days, I feel no urgency about filling up my weekends. I consider this a sign of maturity. It just so happens that this Friday, Hannah and Alan have invited me over for dinner; Saturday, I am going on the long-feared, long-awaited date with Donny. Donny and I talked on the phone exactly once. His voice was sufficiently deep, free of bad accents or speech impediments. The date night had already been set (via Beryl) so our conversation went just long enough to choose a restaurant (Anthony's Italiano) and a time (8:00), trade job titles (copywriter, securities analyst), then drown in an awkward silence, chirp something like "can't wait," and hang up.

But whatever lack of connection I felt talking to Donny has been overshadowed by my new celebrity status at Dreams Come True, Inc. All week, the place has been abuzz. The Travel Agents spend hours debating my outfit. Beryl beams at me approximately two hundred times a day. Amy the Agent recommended her eyebrowist. Kelly the Agent prescribed magenta (apparently I'm a "winter" person). Jenny ripped a paper perfume sample from a magazine, picked up my wrist, and swiped it across like groceries at a checkout counter.

At several points, I found myself double-fisting Diet Coke and cake.

By Friday afternoon, there is not even a pretense of work at the office. The beginnings of "Perfectly Paris!" drift idly on my computer screen. The Agents have surrounded my chair like runners-up around the throne at the Miss America pageant. A ring of Diet Coke cans perch on the lip of my desk. Only Beryl sits alone, answering the phone—"Happy Friday afternoon!" she sings—like the naive mother relaxing upstairs while the slumber party turns intense.

After a week of friendly chatter, the Agents are getting down to the nitty-gritty. They are tapping their long fingernails on my desktop, plucking at the metal tabs on their soda cans, glancing sharply at their thin gold watches. The word "Agent" is starting to sound vaguely militaristic.

Jenny: "So where are you two going?"

Kelly: "So what does he do for a living?"

Tricia: "What kind of car does he drive?"

Aileen: "Does he cook? Does he lift? Does he jog?"

Thanks to Beryl, almost every question I can answer truthfully, even confidently, rather than my usual evasions about "art," "angst," and "finding himself." It feels strangely good, being able to do this. As if my social life is being legitimized somehow, bearing up under professional scrutiny. At the same time, I have the guilty sensation of getting away with something I shouldn't.

"We're going out to dinner," I report.

They nod.

"To Anthony's Italiano."

"Oh," says Jenny. Her tone is ominous. "Italian."

The others shake their heads, as if recognizing the symptom of an illness.

"Is that bad?"

"Not if you're careful," Kelly sighs. She puts her soda down, brushes off her palms, and raises one finger in the air, shiny and sharp as a letter opener. "Rule number one," she quips. "No long pasta."

"Long pasta?"

"Spaghetti. Linguine. Fettucine," Maggie elaborates. "Bowties or spirals are fine. But nothing that's going to fall out of your mouth."

"Or get all over your chin," says Jenny.

"Right." Kelly nods. She raises a second finger. "Number two: nothing saucy."

"Marinara," chimes Maggie. "Alfredo. Bolognese."

"Pesto," Tricia adds, as the group collectively shudders.

"Three." Kelly holds up her ring finger, the one with the big fat diamond on it. It winks in the light, as if to assert her expertise. "Under no terms do you ever eat garlic."

"No breadsticks," says Maggie. "No scampi."

"Definitely no scampi," from Aileen.

"Nothing that's going to make for a bad first kiss," Amy explains.

"No matter what you do, Eliza." Kelly leans forward, gripping my desk edge with her ringed, lacquered, knife-sharp hand. "Always anticipate the kiss."

When I pack up to leave at 5:30, I feel a combination of excitement and terror. I am cutting the cord, leaving the nest, venturing alone into a world of sculpted eyebrows and dainty pastas and clichés about cords and nests. The Agents exchange somber looks as I turn off "Perfectly Paris!" and head for the door.

"Don't forget," Kelly hisses. "Magenta!"

Jenny grips my wrist. "Avoid cheese at all costs!"

In an alarming sleight of hand, Maggie slips me a condom. It is neon pink. I stuff it in the bottom of my bookbag, feeling my face burn as I wave good-bye to Beryl, who beams back and says, "You kids have fun now!"

Outside, I walk two muggy blocks to the bus stop. All the things that regularly annoy me about this walk—the honking drivers, the Hare Krishnas, the apostrophe in House of Shoe's—roll right off me. I am in too good a mood. I am actually jittery. The kind of jittery I felt as a teenage girl sitting on the grass after the *Transformations* meeting, or perched by the pool at Judy the clarinetist's band bash/function. This, I realize, is what first dates are supposed to feel like. This is how they are meant to evolve: the awkward phone call, the plan, then the meeting. In the past, mine have gone in reverse: the meeting, the plan, then the awkward phone call. Maybe sequence has been my problem all along.

I reach the corner just in time to catch the lurching arrival of the bus and the finale of a drunk guy singing "La Bamba" and drumming on an empty KFC bucket. As the doors hiss open, I quickly calculate the section with the most women, most elderly, and fewest singing drunk guys. I slip into a plastic seat by a window, clasp my bag in my lap, and fold my hands on top of it.

The bus lumbers forward. I scan the people sitting around me, pretending to be absorbed in their newspapers or shoes. I try to guess their weekend plans—a baby shower? an office party? a round of Scattergories?—and, as the bus picks up speed, feel more determined about my date. I am ready for a real relationship. Ready to be a grown-up. To have Beryl for an in-law. To start my own collection of pins. To honeymoon in the tropics and appear in the Dreams newsletter with the caption "Typist Ties the Knot!" To buy a house with a man who whispers "I love you" in the dark on his cell phone, who replies "definitely, honey" when I offer him dinner, who supports my lower back as I slip into the backseat of his shiny, compact, Japanese car.

The woman beside me speaks. "Do you have the time?"

I check my watch. Feeling bold, I turn and make direct eye contact. She is wearing a paper bag on her head.

"Five forty-five," I say. "Cool hat."

Hannah is barefoot when she answers the door. Shoes are banned at Hannah and Alan's apartment, along with meat, fish, caffeine, transfats, and accessorizing with leather. It is a spare apartment. "Essentialist," Hannah calls it. "Life boiled down to the basics." In theory, I appreciate this concept: me, Leroy, a TV. In practice, however, I still have every birthday card I've ever received stuffed in a Tretorn shoebox in my closet.

"Eliza." Hannah looks relaxed, as usual. She is wearing an orange-and-red batik skirt that looks hand wrung. Silver beaded earrings nearly graze her shoulders. Her wild hair is secured in a pin at the back of her head. A couple of tendrils sprout around her face, vegetablelike.

"Is this Chez Hannah?" I say.

"More like Chez Alain," she says, giving me a hug. As we step back, she squints into my face, probably trying to gauge where I am in Karl recovery. I suspect this was the reason behind this dinner invite in the first place.

"Karl? Karl who?" I reassure her, stepping inside.

Hannah and Alan's is not a college apartment. It is a grown-up apartment. There are no plastic crates, tapestries, pennants, or photo montages. Nothing from the beanbag or halogen families. No black-and-white posters, secured with blue tack, of half-bared men cradling babies. Instead, they have vases. Mirrors. African violets. A goldfish named Herb, their vegetarian mascot.

Sure enough, Alan is manning the kitchen. He is in full cooking regalia tonight: oven mitts, chef's hat, full-length apron covered with lemons that says "Squeeze the Chef!" He is also wearing bedroom slippers. I nervously recall what Hannah said about the endearing "thing Alan does with his toes."

"Cheers, Eliza." Alan salutes me with a jar of cumin.

"Yo, Alan."

Hannah says, "You look like you could use some wine," and skips off to get the glasses.

I leave my shoes by the door and wander into their living room. I love this living room almost as much as I loved the sunporch at the Devines's. The windows are hung with curly ivies. The floors are hardwood, with fringy Mexican rugs. The walls are like a documentary of the last six years of Hannah's life: masks from her junior semester in Africa, Italian-sconces-French-art-and-Spanish-maracas from her three-week spin on the Eurail, photographs from her year in London, and, finally, a photo of her and Alan.

It is a picture of their faces only, poking out from the top of a sleeping bag. Both of them wear knit caps pulled down to their eyebrows. Hannah is smiling up at the camera, Alan is planting a kiss on her cheek. Much as I mock Alan's tweedy Britishisms, I can understand why Hannah loves him. Alan is safe. He is smart. He is kind to animals. Alan isn't going anywhere.

As if to prove me right, Alan peers into the rice cooker. (I note, with amazement, that Hannah is at a stage in her life when she owns a rice cooker.) "Sweetheart," he says, "do you think the rice is ready?"

She peers into the cooker. He kisses her forehead.

"What's cookin'?" I ask.

Alan steps aside and uncorks the wine as Hannah beckons me to a pot. "Ta da!" she says, lifting the lid.

I squint into the bubbling water. "Albino hot dogs?"

"Lean links." She pops the lid back on, smothering the steam. "Meatless meat. For you."

"Gee."

Alan hands us each a glass of red, giving Hannah another kiss with hers. Hannah and I sit at the table. In the center is a plate piled with healthy beige: pita, hummus, tofu, tahini. A few renegade carrots stalk the rim.

"So," Hannah says. "What's new with you?"

I start to say "not a thing"—a reflex from years of living predictably—before I realize that this time, something is. Two things, actually: 1) Camilla's pregnancy, and 2) my date with Donny. Part of me is dying to tell Hannah about the Donny-date. Another part likes that the date is still mine, not yet out there to be diced up and discussed.

"Camilla's pregnant."

"Really!" Hannah's green eyes get wider. Then they get greener, filming over with tears. "That's so wonderful."

"Brilliant news," brogues Alan.

"When is she due?" Hannah asks.

"Nine months minus seven weeks."

"January," supplies Alan.

"Boy or girl?"

"They want to be surprised."

"Oh, I would, too."

"Same," says Alan.

They exchange a compatible smile, which turns into a gaze, which turns into another kiss. I slather a pita with hummus.

"Don't forget, you guys," I remind them, as Alan returns to the stove, "if you know the gender ahead of time, you can get a head start on the name."

"Here we go." Hannah is familiar with my naming hang-ups.

"What do you mean?" Alan says.

"Naming your kid is critical, Alan," I explain. "It's like naming a character in a book. It determines everything."

"Go on." He drains the links, his glasses fogging up from the steam.

"First, you need to ask yourself: what kind of name can my kid handle? For example." I pop a cube of tofu. I have given this subject a lot of thought. "Say you're thinking of a name that's funky. A Cody. A Rory. A Dylan. A name like Dylan is a lot to live up to. You have to ask yourself: will my kid be able to pull off Dylan?"

"How can you tell?" Alan looks vaguely concerned.

"A husband and wife need to honestly assess themselves. Ask: are we cool enough, genetically, to produce a Dylan?

Because if you have an uncool Dylan, he's doomed. An uncool Dylan has a lot more to overcome, socially, than an uncool Johnny or Joey, know what I mean?" I take a gulp of wine. "The missed potential is so obvious."

Alan rubs his lenses on his apron hem. "So you're saying that *coolness*"—he verbally italicizes the word, as if to exonerate himself from my theory—"is genetic."

"Maybe." I am not after a nature-nurture debate with Alan. "To an extent."

"An extent?" He frowns, but plays along, pushing his glasses up on his nose. "Well, consider this, Eliza. Maybe there is no such thing as a name that's a bad fit. Maybe every person just grows into his or her name, naturally, so every name and person become a perfect match."

I am all prepared to cite a guy who went to Wissahickon— he was five-foot, one-inch, wore bowties, and his name was Biff—when Alan cuts me off.

"Maybe any child can rise to the occasion of a *cool* name," Alan says. He is starting to get excited. "It could be similar to nontracked classrooms. Children rising to meet their academic potential."

"Randys rising to meet their Dylan potential," Hannah murmurs.

I realize that this may not have been the wisest theory to broach with two psychiatrists-in-training. I also decide it's probably not the best time to introduce my companion theory: people honestly assessing whether or not they can pull off "You go, girl!"

Alan approaches the table, cradling two foggy dishes in his

mitted hands. Maybe this would be a good time to change the subject. I cover my lap with a napkin as Alan sets the bowl of lean links in front of me with great ceremony. The links look pale, foreign, phallic. I remember Donny.

"So," I say. "I have a date tomorrow night."

Hannah dips into the brown rice. "Karl?"

"No."

"That harmonica player you were telling me about?"

"Actually, he's not a musician."

"What is he?"

I pause a moment, for effect. "He's a securities analyst."

It is a sad, twisted day in this world when my date with a Securities Analyst evokes a more dramatic response than Camilla experiencing the miracle of life, but there it is. Hannah and Alan freeze. She with a spoonful of rice in midair. He with an oven mitt dangling from his hand.

"He's the grandson of this woman I work with," I explain.

Alan begins absently stroking his chin.

"He has an MBA. He makes six figures." I have to admit, I am enjoying this. "He drives one of those little sports cars, the ones with no tops."

"A convertible?" from Alan.

"Yeah. A convertible. And his name is Donny. Like the Osmond." I am feeling slightly mad with power. "You know, like *Donny Osmond.*"

"Wait a second." Hannah releases the spoonful of rice on her plate. "Let me clarify this. For as long as I have known you, you've gone out with musicians. Exclusively. No other guy has held any interest for you at all. And suddenly, you're dating a securities analyst—named Donny Osmond?"

"It's not actually Donny Osmond. Just Donny."

"Still."

"Still what?" I know what she means, of course; I just want to hear her say it.

"Still . . . it's like changing religions."

"It's not like there's anything wrong with it, honey," Alan reminds her.

"I'm not saying there's anything wrong with it," Hannah argues, gently. "I think it's wonderful." She glances at me. "Not that you're dating a businessman, specifically, Eliza . . . just that you're . . . expanding your options."

My feeling of power is quickly eroding. I feel myself becoming a case study, caption and page reference appearing under my chin.

"The real question is," Alan says, sitting down, stroking his chin up to his ears. "Why now? There must be a reason you suddenly find this kind of relationship appealing."

Alan is right, of course. This is the real question. Luckily, I've had a whole bus ride to prepare for it. "Well, guys," I answer, with a dramatic pause. "I guess I'm just feeling ready to settle down."

Then I sit back and wait for their responses. Hannah and Alan glance at each other—will there be tears? textbooks? a gold star on my forehead?—but after ten seconds, their glance has not let up. The glance becomes a look, look becomes a gaze, and gaze lingers, gooey and sticky and slightly pornographic. It is no longer a glance about me. It was not even, I realize, a dinner about me. I feel my entire cranium start to tense.

"Settling down must be in the air these days," Hannah says, turning to me. Alan wraps her hand in his.

10:23 A.M. My head is pounding. I've hardly slept. I might still be drunk. I've hardly eaten, except for half a lean link I choked down last night after the "announcement." From the link on, the evening is a blur of wine . . . wedding . . . summer . . . nondenominational . . . tent . . . flowers . . . three-bean salads . . . citronella candles . . . harpists . . . nondairy desserts . . .

10:42. I relocate to the couch, taking the bed with me. I submerge myself in blankets and pillows, a bottle of Advil, a college T-shirt, college warm-up pants, college baseball cap. Obviously I am regressing to hungover college weekend-morning mode, but I find it's not as comforting without the company of four to ten other college students also popping Advil and wearing baseball caps. Plus, wedding announcements were not something we dealt with back in college. No one got engaged in college. Except for Anna Maria Flora, virgin from Chattanooga, Tennessee.

10:44. Consulting VH1.

10:45. If there is anything more depressing than watching *Where Are They Now?*, it's watching reruns of *Where Are They Now?* It's the show that takes you behind the scenes into rock stars' lives, post-stardom. The first time around, watching where they are now is fun. Amusing. Even self-affirming. You can snicker at the former celebrities and how far they've fallen. But the second time around, you start feeling bad about your-

self. It is as if, by watching them twice, you are somehow impli-
cated in the patheticness.

11:20. I wallow in my patheticness. I celebrate it. I loll in it.
I embrace it, remembering all the saleswomen from Young Miss
departments over the years who told me to "Embrace your
height!" I consider calling Andrew just to hear him cringe at the
word "patheticness."

11:46. Are there different stages of dealing with your best
friend's engagement? 1) Shock. 2) Hangover. 3) Metaphor.
Example: feeling like you're in a tiny glass elevator. Example:
feeling like you're on a giant treadmill while everyone's life is
moving forward but yours.

11:55. It occurs to me that Hannah asked me to be the maid of
honor. At this point, the "honor" part is lost on me. All I can think
of are all the responsibilities that are suddenly, horribly mine: buying a dress, throwing a shower, coordinating forty to fifty kitchen
appliances, making sure the great-aunts are distracted while
Hannah opens the negligees. For Camilla's wedding, I opted to be
a bridesmaid instead of the honored maid and let Camilla give the
title to her best friend Miriam, who was a) dying for it, b) good at
it, and c) gave us all tiny, scented, underwear-drawer pillows to
keep our "delicates smelling like daisies!"

12:10 P.M. I think again about calling Andrew. Then I think
about the moment in the car the other night and feel too awkward to go through with it. Besides, Kimberley might be listening again. She might think I'm stalking her boyfriend. She
might be naked and giggling as my message drones on. Or
Andrew might pick up and, God forbid, say he has an

"announcement" (currently #1 on my list of Words to Outlaw
If I Were President).

12:28. My machine picks up. "Hi, Eliza, it's me. Just wanted
to make sure you're okay. You seemed a little distracted last
night . . . I'm sure this news is a little weird for you. Let's talk
about it. Soon. Okay? Alan and I are heading out, but call me.
And have a great date!"

12:45. I toy with canceling the date. I realize that socializing
is the last thing I am in the mood for. Being in public, getting
dressed up, eating Italian food while actively avoiding every
ingredient in Italian food. Who needs that kind of pressure? I
don't. I don't need a boyfriend. I am perfectly content the way I
am: curled on a couch with a cat and a baseball cap and the
aging Pet Shop Boys.

12:55. Conclusion: I am much better off alone.

1:00. The hour turns and *Where Are They Now?* segues into
Before They Were Rock Stars. This is the show that takes you
behind the scenes into rock stars' lives, *prestardom.* This change
feels somewhat hopeful. Instead of slipping backward, these
celebrities are moving ahead. They are getting their breaks,
finding their agents, getting four stars on *Star Search.*

1:15. I'm watching old footage of Paula Cole in a high
school musical when I start to feel more lifelike. Maybe this
show is a sign. (When you're alone and were once an English
major, everything seems like a sign.) Could these "announcements"—Camilla's pregnancy, Hannah's marriage—be happening now for a reason? Maybe they are a wake-up call for me
to get my life in gear. To save myself from being thirty, forty,

fifty years old and still dating washed-up guitar pickers, living alone with some vintage Hootie, being one of those old women on the bus with the saggy tattoos people glance at with pity.

2:00. My mush of self-pity begins to harden. I get off the couch. I feed Leroy. I pick up my mail. I make a peanut butter sandwich and write a fridge poem that's not half bad. As I'm capping the Skippy, I hear The Piano Man upstairs start playing: something regal, firm, vaguely "Pomp and Circumstance." He is the pit orchestra of my life, striking up at the perfect moment to accompany my new resolve.

2:29. The Piano Man's song gets more urgent, increasing in volume and bravado and tempo. Visions of the Donny-date float uncensored through my mind: Donny with a firm kiss, Donny with a sexy smile, Donny with a perfectly dry sense of humor, a wide range of cable channels, a solid bank account and (what the hell) an ear for indie rock. And, as a bonus, a knack for knowing what I mean, think, feel, and need without my ever having to say it.

2:56. I let myself succumb to all the feelings of paperback romances: pulses, trills, thumps, shivers. At one point, loins are involved.

3:30. So this is what it means to be "driven." After The Piano Man finishes playing, I find myself doing all kinds of embarrassing, girlish things to prepare for the date. I hear an imaginary cheering section behind me at every step: Travel Agents, eyebrowists, manicurists, Nanny.

3:33. I file my nails.

3:46. I paint my nails.

3:55. Two coats.

4:15. I smear on a green face mask to tone and exfoliate.

4:34. I shave my legs, careful with the ankles.

5:14. I shower, moisturizing and deep-conditioning my split ends, hearing echoes of Kimmy, hair stylist at Fun Cuts, who has been pleading for the last eight years: "If only you would make *friends* with your roots!"

6:00. I blow-dry for a full twenty minutes.

6:30. I dress in black, but throw a scarf (red) around my neck.

6:42. I apply makeup, but go easy on the eyeliner.

6:48. I trade in my boots for black strappy shoes my mother bought me once for a funeral.

6:55. I put in my subtlest nose ring, a tiny diamond stud.

As soon as I see Donny in the lobby of Anthony's Italiano, I a) know it is him and b) know that I know him already. I don't mean I literally know him already, he just feels so familiar it seems like I do. Unfortunately, this is not the good kind of love-at-first-sight familiar. Donny is like a character I've read before, or written before, or seen on the big screen too many times.

Our IDs in the Anthony's Italiano lobby are based on probably loose and definitely biased descriptions provided by Beryl. "He's very broad around the shoulders," she told me. "He has dark hair, like his father's. Oh, you can't miss him, Eliza. He's *extremely* handsome."

As it turns out, Donny is not hard to spot, only because everyone else in the lobby is a sweating, enormous middle-aged man or a sweating, enormous middle-aged man's wife. Based on my limited experience with Anthony's Italiano—a dinner once with Andrew's family, which is now coming back to me with grease-bright clarity—"enormous" describes most of the clientele at Anthony's. It must have something to do with unlimited breadsticks.

Donny strides right over. His ID is quick, too quick. It makes me wonder how Beryl described me to him. Tall? Flat in the chest? To her credit, Beryl's grandson is not an unattractive guy. His eyes are a nice sea-green. He has good height, fair chest span, a touch of the Baldwin brothers about him. He does, however, appear to have a faint sheen all over: shiny gray suit, black gelled hair, and dark, damp sideburns that taper by the ears like fountain pens.

"Eliza," he says.

"Donny."

We shake. His grip is overly hard, a grip that says: "I lift. Got it?"

No snap judgments, I remind myself. *No typecasting. Stay open-minded.*

"Nice place," I say, extracting my hand.

"I think so," he clips.

"You come here a lot?"

"Sometimes." Donny beckons the hostess, who hurries over. "They've got good food here. Quick service. Big portions." He coughs into his fist. "Good prices."

177

Did I just hear "good prices"? I wonder what the Agents would think about Donny the Securities Analyst admitting he picked our restaurant for its "portions" and "prices." At least he didn't say "babes."

The Italiano hostess appears beside us. She's wearing a short, slim green dress. "Two?" she says, and we trail her through one, two, three enormous dining rooms, one enormous birthday party, an enormous salad bar. I can smell Donny's cologne wafting over his shoulder like a mating scent, and think nervously of the neon pink condom in the bottom of my bag.

The hostess stops at a ferny, low-lit corner by a window. On the table, a single candle flickers under a green glass globe. "Carla will be right over to serve you," she says, hands us two tall, plastic-wrapped menus, and disappears.

"Thanks," Donny says to her butt. Literally, he could be following a script that reads DONNY: STARING AT HER BUTT.

No scripts tonight, I remind myself.

"Anyway," Donny says.

It occurs to me that this is the conversation that usually happens in a bar or at a party. Usually, there are distractions. Music, crowds, spilled rum, Electric Hoagies. Usually our faces are scrambled by black light and we're buzzing slightly and have to shout to be heard. Here, our only distractions are the light Italian Muzak and the faint strains of "Happy Birthday" from Enormous Dining Room #2.

"So Donny," I plunge. It is half courtesy, half curiosity. "I have to ask. What made you recognize me?"

Donny raises his eyebrows, which I fear also have a dab of gel in them. "Recognize you?"

"In the lobby."

"Oh." He smiles. It is not a warm, fuzzy Beryl smile, however. His smile is small, sinister and too red, like a hot pepper. Donny is conjuring up some sexual fantasy right now, I am sure of it. "Nose ring."

Bingo.

I duck down behind my leathery red menu, pretending to lose myself in Beers & Wines. Once in a while, I sneak glances at Donny. Skinny black tie, heavy gold wristwatch, wiry black wrist hair. A face that looks like it's perpetually in the middle of an important conference call, agitated and interrupted. I'm willing to bet that in the '80s he dressed *Miami Vice.*

I cast an eye over the entrees, looking for something safe to order. All of the food appears greasy and garlicky and somehow appropriate. Like everything else I'm beginning to suspect about the Donster, there's something businesslike about his choice of restaurant. Profitable mass production. Dressings by the gallon. Thawed tiramisu that arrived in flatbed trucks. Prices that all end with ".95."

Donny looks up from his menu. I look down at mine.

"See something you like?" he asks, with what may or may not be sexual innuendo. It's hard to tell with an Italian. Ziti, sex, marinara sauce—all of it seems to derive from the same sensual impulse.

"Sure," I reply.

"Good." He gives me a quick nod and slaps his menu shut.

I'm beginning to understand what Beryl means by "driven." There's a distinct energy about this guy. Money energy. Corporate energy. The energy of a man who watched too many cartoons as a child, drank too much Kool-Aid, and had no attention span at all. As if in agreement, Donny's eyes flicker around the room, noting all the meals, portions, waitresses, butts.

"So what'll you have?" he quips.

This is the critical question. According to the women's magazines and Travel Agents, at this point I should play it low-fat. I should think calories and carbs. Avoid pasta with sauce, pasta with length. *Shun cheese at all costs!*

"Chicken parmigiana," I say, as Donny's mouth twitches. I slap my menu shut and place it on top of his. "And a Bud. You?"

Before he can answer, Carla the waitress appears. She could be Anthony Italiano's daughter, she so looks the part. Thick black hair tangled down her back. Full lips. Huge chest waving its arms from beneath her slim, short Italiano-green dress.

"Ciao," she says, with a hint of an accent I am positive is fake.

Donny grins and "ciao"s her back. Good God.

"What can I do for you tonight?" Carla smiles at him. This time, there's no question about the sexual innuendo.

To his credit, Donny lets me order first (cheese, chicken, alcohol) but on his turn, he takes his time. First, he chats about the wine selection. Then, he discusses a few of the entrees. He spends

180

a full five minutes trying to pronounce one of the veal specials. Carla helps, of course, all curling tongues and heaving breasts.

Finally, Donny settles on something a la red meat. I could have predicted this. I could also predict that later, he will consult a tip card. He will use a toothpick, possibly mint-flavored. *Stop it, Eliza! Get to know him first!*

"Very good," says Carla. She plucks up our menus and lambadas away.

DONNY: STARING AT HER BUTT.

This is hell. This is, I now understand, exactly why I go to The Blue Room. This is why I go on dates in reverse. To see him first, to scope him out. To know exactly what I'm getting into.

"So." Donny picks up his green cloth napkin, flicks it open like a toreador, and fires: "What do you do for a living, exactly?"

This is grossly unfair. This was supposed to be my question. When you're a Securities Analyst, you deserve to be asked what you do for a living. I am a copywriter. What the hell does he *think* a copywriter does?

You spent twenty minutes blow-drying your hair. You haven't even had a drink yet.

"I write copy," I tell him.

Donny frowns and starts drumming one finger on the table, his gold ring rapping against the glass.

"For brochures," I explain, forcing a smile. "Newsletters. PR. For Dreams Come True. You know, the place where . . . Beryl . . . works."

"Right." Thankfully, he does know who Beryl is and where she works. "Travel place."

"Right. And what do you do?"

Unlike me, Donny thrives on the question. His reply is an onslaught of dividends and bonds and cross trades so quick and cryptic I need subtitles to translate it. I grit my teeth as financial jargon pelts me like a BB gun.

When it's over, I feel stunned. "I see."

"Great job," Donny says. "Good bennies. Stock options. Company gym."

Rudeness builds in me like a sneeze. I have to physically resist the impulse to a) start compulsively lying about myself, b) tell my one good "businessman walks into a bar" joke, or c) start humming "Deep Purple." I latch onto any moral fiber I can. Sunday School. *Brady Bunch.* Beryl.

Beryl.

"Your grandmother's great," I say, exhaling.

"Grammy's a good one."

"Especially on the phone. Wow."

"Right."

At least we are agreeing on something. I am quickly realizing, however, that Beryl might be our only tiny ledge of common ground. I wonder if we can squeeze a full two hours out of her. Grammy's favorite meals? Grammy's favorite music? Grammy's younger years: the Depression? the Nixon administration?

"Yeah," I say, "and I love her pins."

Donny's finger drumming stops. "What?"

"Her pins."

"Pins?"

"You know." I feel myself getting defensive on Beryl's behalf. "How she wears a different pin? Every day? She wears a different pin?"

Donny says, "Hadn't noticed," and glances at the enormous dessert cart rolling by us, everything on it huge and thawed and cherry topped.

Suddenly I miss Carla. We haven't eaten, we have exhausted Beryl, and I can't think of a single other thing to talk about. What would the Agents talk about now? How he likes his meat cooked? How many pounds he can bench-press? What varsity sports he played in high school?

"Seen any movies lately?" I ask. Pop culture is always safe. Universal, impersonal. An endless stretch of hospital dramas, Tom Hanks movies, and '80s sitcoms. We could get lost in Six Degrees of Kevin Bacon for hours.

Donny shrugs. "I rent, mostly."

This does not surprise me. Low prices. Big selection. Babes on film.

"Really?" I ask him. "Anything good?"

"Something with Pacino." He raps his ring, once, twice. "I can't think of the name."

"Scarface?"

"Nope."

"Scent of a Woman?"

"Nah." (Actually a fine choice in the Movies That Smell genre, but I decide that now is not the time.)

"The Godfather?"

"That's the one."

"*The Godfather* was based on a book, you know."

"I didn't."

"Do you read?"

He looks offended.

"I mean, I assume you *can* read. But do you read . . . for pleasure?"

"Don't have much time for that," Donny says, chuckling, as if I couldn't possibly understand the rigors of being a Securities Analyst. "On business trips. Flights. Business flights."

I am too frightened to ask for literary specifics. Instead I pipe up and volunteer: "I'm writing a book myself."

Why I say this, I have no idea. Maybe I have some unhealthy, subconscious need to impress Donny the Securities Analyst. Maybe, on some level, I want to throw something his way that's as foreign to him as cross trades and dividends are to me.

But Donny seems genuinely interested. He folds his hands and rests his chin on his fat gold ring. "Yeah? What's your book about?"

And the amazing thing is, I am unprepared for this question. I have prepared for all the impossible questions, the ones I will never have to answer: where I would sail on the Love Boat, what I would say if I met Bryan Adams, what Jack Wagner and I would name our kids. But I have absolutely no idea how to sum up the book to which I've devoted the bulk of my reality. It's not as simple as describing teenage antics in Sweet Valley, or Horton's business with the Who. Besides, any description I think of—girl tries to date musicians? girl tries not to date businessmen?—sounds a little too close to home.

"It's about relationships." Best to stay vague. "About connecting. Or, not connecting. With, um, people."

Donny is smiling at me, but I know he isn't listening. It's the same smile he wore while fantasizing about girls with nose rings. Right now he's probably imagining torn bodices, heaving breasts, gilt-edged covers, Carla packaged into twelve chapters. Awkward as this date has been, it occurs to me that sex might still be on the table here. In theory, I feel a slight bit flattered; in practice, I want to puke.

Donny leans toward me, his shiny tie drifting dangerously near the lit candle. "So," he says, "does this mean you're going to be the next Danielle Steels?"

Coming from someone else, I might have been insulted. Coming from Donny, I realize that this may have been a compliment. As I open my mouth to reply, Carla materializes, sensing sex in the air. She plunks my beer on the table. Donny smiles at her and makes a three-minute show of sniffing and sipping his Merlot.

"Ciao," Carla says, walking away.

"Ciao," says DONNY: STARING AT HER BUTT.

He turns back to me, still wearing the little smile. I take a deep swallow of Bud. I wonder if it would be possible to just end this now. Split the bill, raise the lights, cast off the props and go home. But because I am desperate, and because I am hungry, and because the only other possible topics seem to be global politics or a quick round of "I Spy," I go for it: "So Donny. **What kind of music do you like?**"

Possible options, as I see them:

Richard Marx.

Michael Bolton.

Maybe, just maybe, Donny Osmond.

Donny doesn't answer immediately. I think he might be mulling it over, which is a good sign at least. Then he coughs into his fist. "You know," he says, looking somewhere else. His fat gold watch glints in the candlelight. "Whatever's on."

Whatever's *on?* I feel my fingernails digging into my palms. The only thing worse than having bad musical preferences is having no musical preferences. How can a human being not care what kind of music they listen to? How can they answer the critical musical-preferences question with *Whatever's on?*

My left temple starts to pound. Faintly, I hear "So, what do you do to stay in shape?" buzzing somewhere near my left ear. If Hannah were in my head right now, she would want me to acknowledge my feelings, to discuss my anger, and she would be proud. I am enraged. I want to kick the table, rip my hair out, rip Donny's hair out by its slippery roots. I feel gypped, scammed, tricked, had. Deep down, I know it's not Donny I'm furious with. It's myself, of course. For letting myself put so much hope into this, for thinking I would be different or he would be different or something, anything, would be different from what I had expected.

Where do you go, I want to know, to find the things you weren't expecting?

Carla appears with the unlimited portion of our evening: an enormous basket of phallic garlic breadsticks. Donny winks at her and rips into one with his teeth. I feel the last of my Donny-fantasy collapsing—breadsticks, hair gel, exfoliating face mask, neon pink condom, Merlot—all of it running together in a snickering mess around my appropriately funereal black shoes. As he starts chomping the breadstick, I realize why it is I feel like I know him already: Donny is the guy I've always warned Andrew against becoming.

Through a haze of headache, I hear a cell phone begin to ring and realize it's attached to Donny. He reaches into his shiny suit pocket, happy to attract the attention of all the enormous middle-aged diners nearby. Unlike with Andrew, the phone itself doesn't surprise me. Nor does Donny's preoccupied stare as he answers. Then he lowers his voice and mutters: "Yeah, man. It's going all right."

To spare us both, I pretend not to have heard. I focus on the breadsticks. I down the rest of my beer. When Donny bleeps off the phone—"Sorry," he fibs, "sometimes I can't leave work behind"—something inside me snaps like a twig. All sense of social decency, of public humility, of proper dating/dining/pasta-eating etiquette vanishes as I am seized with an overwhelming sense of frustration, of futility, and before I know it I hear myself yelling: "My best friend got engaged!"

The enormous man at the next table frowns at me over an unlimited trough of minestrone. Donny drops his nub of breadstick like a piece of incriminating evidence. "Whoa, whoa, whoa," he bellows, for the benefit of the onlookers. He raises both his palms in mock surrender. "What are you getting at? I've only known you an hour."

As I was saying: I am much better off alone.

8

pianists, electric guitarists, and lead vocalists

SIDE B
"Bouncing Around the Room" — Phish
"Loser" — Beck
"Wicked Garden" — Stone Temple Pilots
"Fell on Black Days" — Soundgarden
"A Common Disaster" — Cowboy Junkies

Arriving at Wissahickon College at the height of the Seattle grunge craze gave me all kinds of hope. I had paid my dues with high school rock stars, and learned from my mistakes. That summer, I'd trashed all of Z Tedesco's mixes and buried every pre-1985 tape in the bottom of my closet. I pierced my upper ear (despite Mom's warnings about nerve damage) and my arrival on a college campus with a duffel bag full of black-and-denim was roughly coinciding with Pearl Jam's *Ten*.

My rock star was so close I could taste him.

Unfortunately, I had chosen a college in western

Pennsylvania where, I soon discovered, the predominant color was khaki and the predominant song, Jimmy Buffett's "Margaritaville." My first semester I remember only in fragments of foods and songs and social missteps: keg beer, chicken-flavored ramen, damp fraternity basements, Naughty by Nature, 2:00 A.M. phone calls to Hannah at Oberlin, one disastrous dance party at the student activity center. Late-night talks with my beautiful blond roommate, who was dating a beautiful blond soccer player who greeted me, "Hey, bud!"

"I don't get why you want musicians," my roommate was fond of saying. Her name was Ashley, she was from Connecticut, and had once brushed against Ricky Schroder's elbow in a CVS. "They're too skinny. But I bet they have big dicks."

This, I was learning, was not uncommon talk for beautiful blond girls from Connecticut. They liked to shock, and were often secretly raunchy. Ashley kept a sex diary with explicit lists of "Things I Want to Try" and "Things I've Tried" (with ratings). We were ideal roommates, actually, and would be for nearly three years: different enough that we didn't fight, similar enough that we could share every detail of our sex lives.

"I'm right, aren't I?" she asked me. "Bigger than the norm."

"I can't really say," I said. Which was true. I didn't have much basis for comparison. "But I can tell you that being with a musician is intense." I crunched some ramen. "Ever tried it?"

"Not yet," Ashley said.

Unfortunately, the boys I was kissing my first year of college didn't exactly qualify as intense. There was Andrew, for a whopping six semi-platonic weeks. A guy in my English seminar who briefly impressed me with his theory that Frankenstein and the monster were gay lovers. A Sigma Nu with a tongue like a sausage. A guy in men's chorus who sang phallic alma maters about trees, glens, dames and lassies. A theater major who I fell madly in love with until I spied him wearing lavender tights in *Kiss Me, Kate*.

When it came time for fall registration, I took matters into my own hands.

fall semester

The moment I stepped inside Goodman-Sawyer Music Building, I knew I'd found my niche. After two semesters spent in boring brown lecture halls accumulating required 101s, everything about this building struck me as the aftermath of some violent bout of passion: the mussed, finger-wracked heads of hair, broken chalk, untucked shirts, the mild scent of sweat in the air. As I took a seat, I surveyed the other students in Music Theory. They were not your typical Wissahickon variety. All of them were scribbling distractedly in wire-bound note-books (composing music on the page?) or gazing out the window (composing music in their heads?) or alternating between the two.

Not wanting to appear conspicuous, I busied myself scrawling the lyrics to "All I Need" over and over until the professor arrived. He was over nine feet tall, made of beard and corduroy.

"Welcome," he said. It wasn't a booming "welcome," like most professors' were. The word seemed to germinate somewhere deep inside his peppery tufts of beard and crawl grudgingly out of the corner of his mouth. "This is Music Theory. I am your professor. Call me Alvin. And this young man"—his beard nodded toward the first row—"is your T.A. Radley."

I located the guy in the front row who lifted one hand in a distracted salute. He had long dirty blond hair tucked behind his ears and was wearing a T-shirt that said "Beethoven Lives!"

"Radley is a senior. A music major. And, if I might add, quite a good clarinetist." Alvin's hand drowned in the beard for a moment, then reappeared scratching his Adam's apple. "He will provide one-on-one instruction as needed," Alvin concluded, which I decided I needed right away.

Radley's one-on-one instruction was dispensed in the basement of the music building, in a tiny room stuffed with a chunky black piano, a stereo circa 1910, and a rack of classical albums. The walls were covered with millions of tiny dots: a four-sided migraine headache. "Soundproofing," Radley explained, the night of our first session. He had very pale skin that flushed damply when he got excited. "So we can be as loud as we want."

That said, hooking up with Radley the T.A. by the month's end did not prove too much of a challenge. We were alone, after all, at night, soundproofed, and squashed on a piano bench hip to hip. All it took was one botched étude for him to take my hands in his (you know, to adjust my fingering position) except that my fingers wound up readjusted somewhere around his corduroy crotch.

"Will this affect my grade?" I whispered.

Radley's upper lip sprouted four beads of sweat, mingling with the walls in a dotty haze.

Unlike in the dorms, Radley and I didn't have to scheme to be alone during T.A. sessions. There were no roommates to avoid, no soccer players to confront, no hallmates to duck while flossing. It was the easiest rock-star love I'd ever had. All I had to do was sign up: name, date, and time of session.

"Where do I sign?" Ashley said. I laughed her off, not wanting to admit that she'd tapped into my greatest fear: that I was just one member of Radley's vast Music Theory brothel. "He sounds experimental," she said, smacking her lips.

And he was. Unfortunately, this was not because Radley was wildly creative, but because of the difficult logistics in the music room. I had already spent considerable time bragging to Ashley about our exploits:

a) on the windowsill

b) on the piano bench

c) on top of the piano (a la *Pretty Woman*).

Unfortunately, in the interest of my passing the course, part of our T.A. sessions actually did consist of me playing horrible études about farm animals and singing off-key scales. I tried to view it as foreplay. While I *la-la-la*ed my way through my triads, Radley listened intently, kissing me when I hit the right notes. Sometimes, he whispered his secret tricks for remembering the triads (the NBC theme song, the commercial jingle for CVS).

One Wednesday night, we found ourselves on a red leather sofa in the faculty lounge (thanks to Radley's official staff keys).

A Vaughan Williams CD was playing on the stereo. A Beethoven bust scowled behind my left shoulder. Suddenly Radley said: "D flat."

"What?" I opened my eyes.

"Your sex noise," he panted. "It's a D flat."

The next morning, I switched my major to English.

spring semester

Cold. Snow. Disillusionment. By January of my sophomore year, everything at Wissahickon College was beginning to look exactly the same. Every flannel was the identical blue-and-green plaid. Every guy on campus was Tyler or Jason or Jed. Every song was sung by Blues Traveler. Every lecture revolved around "unpacking the metaphor." It was time to check out the local bar.

My first trip to Jack's Tavern would mark the beginning of a new era in rock-star infatuation: the bar pickup. Though I wasn't twenty-one yet, I managed to get an old ID from my "Wissahickon Big Sister" Val, a rugby player whose sisterly influence consisted of teaching me how to funnel, chug, and dip tobacco. To the bouncer, I was Valerie Carroll from Mount Vernon, New York, born September 21, 1971. (The fact that I was not five-foot four-inches, blond-haired, or one hundred fifty pounds went unnoticed.)

Jack's was operated by a beefy, pink guy named Jack who wore Jack Daniels freebie T-shirts and regularly posted Jack Daniels specials. Not that anyone ever ordered them, or found his gimmicks amusing. The bulk of Jack's livelihood revolved around pitchers of Bud Light, Miller Light, Coors Light, and plastic boats of popcorn a frightening shade of salty, industrial yellow.

Jack's clientele was roughly seventy-five percent Wissahickon students, twenty-five percent locals who surrounded the bar in a tense barricade of Central Pennsylvanian flannel. Four of them were a band called Fistfight, a name that carried all kinds of unnerving Greaser/Soc undertones. On Thursdays, they performed their unique brand of Seattle-influenced-hard-core-small-town rock, a sort of John Mellencampy/Meat Puppets-ish thing. When the tunes got too hard, Jack gave the band the cutoff sign, and they reluctantly returned to the bar, while the Spin Doctors's "Two Princes" sailed happily through the speakers and seventy-five percent of the crowd relaxed.

Fistfight is where I spotted Travis.

"This here's the band," the lead singer would announce each week, while the bass player thwacked a string in accompaniment. "That's Curtis Shoemaker on the drums. Sparky Elwell on bass. And that mean electric guitar, that's Travis Young."

Travis strummed a chord in response, a blast of metal that made half the bar cringe and one guy yell: "That's no 'Free Bird,' buddy!" I, on the other hand, was quickly falling in love. After all the boyfriends I had (let's face it) convinced myself were rock-star material (e.g., sixteen-year-old in marching band) Travis Young was the real thing. He wore an authentic, pre-*Blair Witch* blue knit cap pulled down to his eyebrows. Dog tags hung in a formidable metal clump around his neck. While he played, he focused only on his fingers flying around on the strings. He was authentic. He was a musician in a real band, a paid band, with gigs and sessions and sets and their name chalked permanently on the blackboard underneath "Jack's $2 Shots of Jack!"

Soon enough, I was a Thursday-night regular. I sat near the band, but not too near, buoyed by pitchers and popcorn and whatever girls from the dorm I could coerce into coming with me. Later in life, I would sit alone watching bands. In fact, I would usually prefer it. But in college I was an amateur. Take, for example, the first time Travis and I made eye contact and I nearly choked on an unpopped corn. It was weeks before I would refine my pickup moves: the aggressive eye contact, confident chewing, seductive sipping and swallowing that would precede the verbal approach.

One night in March, I broke out a new lipstick: Plum Dream.

"I hate to tell you this," Ashley said, as she watched me prep in the mirror. "But I think you might be a groupie."

"Excuse me?" The Plum stopped midlip. This was not okay. Groupies were pathetic, weren't they? Groupies had no shame. No self-respect. Groupies passed out in the backs of minivans wearing half-shirts made of Lycra. "No. I'm not."

"Honestly," Ashley said, sounding apologetic. "I'm pretty sure you are."

As soon as she said this, I knew I had to make my move. I couldn't live with the possibility that I had unwittingly turned groupie. If I could just elevate my status from groupie to girl-friend, then I would have nothing to be ashamed of. I could drool over Travis Young to my heart's content.

That same night, after Jack had given Fistfight the cutoff and Travis chugged a post-gig beer, I got up the nerve to approach him. I'd rehearsed a million different openers, from complimenting his band to complimenting his voice to just complimenting his pecs and getting it over with. But when I reached the bar, I was only so bold as to ask his left shoulder: "Excuse me. Do you have the time?"

Travis Young's broad flannel back pivoted slowly away from a wall of broad flannel backs. I could feel the watch in my pocket gouging my thigh. "I was just wondering if . . ."

"Nine thirty-two," Travis said. "Wanna beer?"

And we were off.

Beer #1:

"I've seen you here before, you know," Travis said.

"Really?" I tossed my hair, all innocence. "When?"

Beer #3:

"So how old are you?" he asked, toying with my split ends.

"You tell me first."

"Twenty-five."

"Twenty."

He took the hand away.

". . . two," I added, and he put it back.

Beer #5:

"You don't have a boyfriend, do you?" Travis asked.

"Not yet," I whispered.

The magic of Bud Light, ladies and gentlemen.

Beer #8:

"Wanna make out?"

The fact that Travis Young was the first person to use the term "make out" since approximately 1985—when most guys moved on to the sex-as-hardware genre: screwing, nailing, banging, etc.—not to mention used the word "wanna," struck me as totally backwoods and, yes, totally endearing. Obviously, he was too focused on his music to care about keeping up with modern lingo. And as soon as we stepped into my dorm room, it was equally obvious he had no clue about the fundamentals of hooking up at small liberal arts colleges.

Basically, the rules go like this:

a) do not ask for too much personal information

b) do not volunteer too much personal information

c) do not attempt to make future plans

d) always, always stay aloof.

But Travis was a rebel. He inspected my dorm room with genuine interest. He looked at my CDs and pronounced them "bitchin.' " He asked questions about my pictures and posters, and frowned at my hot pot as if it were an alien life form. After kissing for about an hour, he actually didn't try to stay over. When he left, he *kissed my hand*. The next night, he called like he said he would, asked about my day, made sympathetic "awww"-like noises when I relived my killer test in Women's Studies, and showed up the following morning on his Schwinn ten-speed brandishing a single, plastic-wrapped pink rose, which I'm pretty sure he bought by the register at the local Gas

& Go but still struck me as incredibly sweet and sincere, and which I stuck, triumphantly, in a Wissahickon Dining Service mug on my windowsill.

Within my dorm, dating Travis Young rocketed me to minor cult-figure status. "She said they buy flowers," went the murmur circulating in the first-floor bathroom. "They call the next day." "They even kiss well."

"How did you get him?" asked a girl named Patrice, as we bleached our upper lips in front of the sinks.

"I don't know." I wasn't about to admit to the weeks of plotting and stressing and near-choking it took me to score Travis. "It just, kind of, happened, I guess."

I'll admit that telling people (my mother) I was dating a local and telling people (Ashley) I was having frequent, twenty-five-year-old, off-campus sex gave me a feeling of smug satisfaction. Following my lead, other girls in the dorm started eye-balling the locals down at Jack's. They chose their favorites, claimed their territories, and discussed them over butter-soaked popcorn. One night, Ashley dragged home Sparky Elwell (bass), after which she scribbled madly in her journal under "Things I've Tried." We were something like the Official Rock Star Fan Club, except with beer and actual men.

Only Andrew was unenthusiastic. "A townie?"

"Townsperson," I corrected him. We were in the dining hall poking at hamburger doused with beige gravy, a.k.a. "country steak."

"What's this guy's name?" he asked.

At this stage, Andrew and I were able to talk comfortably

about dating other people. His girlfriend-of-the-hour, for instance, was in the women's chorus and sang her answering machine message to the tune of Rupert Holmes's "Pina Colada Song."

"Travis."

Andrew snorted into his potato buds. "Travis?"

"What's wrong with Travis?"

"You mean like the cowboy-guy-on-*WKRP* Travis?"

"Not exactly, no."

"Where did you meet Travis?"

"Would you stop saying Travis?"

"I can't help it. Where did you . . . kids meet?"

"At Jack's."

"How?"

"It was after his set . . ."

"Set?"

". . . we started talking."

"Set?"

"He's in a band. Shut up."

Andrew forked up some beige burger. "Set?"

Even though Travis was fun to brag about and made an excellent grunge mix tape, the reality of our dating life was less exciting than I pretended. Most nights, he was either babysitting his sister's kids or rehearsing with the Fighters. The dates he took me on were uncomfortably fancy. ("I thought college chicks liked fancy," he said, while empowered Women's Studies lectures ran screaming through my brain.) On my turf, we stood in the corners of frat parties while Travis eyeballed Sigma Nus and Sigma

Nus eyeballed Travis and I wondered, nervously, how his band had earned the name Fistfight in the first place.

Naturally, things ended when I met his family.

"Can you help me out?" Travis asked. It was a Saturday morning and he had showed up in my doorway, not with his mother but with two small children dangling from his hands. "I told my sister I'd babysit, but I have practice."

"Huh?" Like I said, it was Saturday morning.

"Prac-tice," Travis repeated, like I was five.

"Oh."

"This is Mikey and Jodie." He disentangled the kids from his fingers. "Be back in two hours." Then he was gone.

Mikey and Jodie stared at me for about four seconds before correctly assessing that I was a wuss and commandeering my dorm room. One started jamming to my Walkman. The other was wearing my bunny slippers and snapping pictures on my camera. I caught Mikey sipping the last of a bottle of Boones Strawberry Hill.

"Andrew," I whimpered. "Help."

fall semester

By the time I found myself stoned in a weed-choked backyard falling deeply in love with Win Brewer (lead vocalist), I had earned it. After nearly three years at Wissahickon, I was finally discovering one of the few perks of attending a college in the middle of nowhere: the cheap, off-campus houses tailor-made for copless parties and student bands.

The band that night was Rocks for Jocks (a snub at Geology 50, the slackerest slacker course at Wissahickon). They were playing outdoors via fat orange extension cords snaking from the kitchen to the yard. Two living room lamps flanked the drums, casting eerie shadows on the drummer's shaved head. In front of the mic was a patch of fans holding beers and cigarettes and shuffling their feet to the beat. Dancing, I've found, is much more earnest when you're outdoors and off-campus, undiluted by spazzy strobe lights and the strains of "Never Gonna Get It." I tried to move my body as inconspicuously as possible as I fixated on Win.

After a few years' rock-star dating experience, there are several criteria I'd learned to look for: instruments, musical styles, kissing styles, clothing styles, jewelry, sunglasses, piercings (number), piercings (location). And, inevitably, the hair. It's not as much of a factor in high school, when facial growth is hormonally limited. Adult rock stars, however, will run the gamut from baldness to Fu Manchus and every hairy permutation in between. To this day, the dreadlock/goatee combo on lead vocalist Win Brewer is the all-time winner in the hair category. It was his thick blond locks that I bumped into (literally) during intermission.

"Excuse me," I said.

The dreadlocks pivoted to look at me. Up close, Win's green eyes were even greener than they'd looked behind the mic. His shirt was unbuttoned to the middle of his chest. Around his neck, a tooth dangled from a piece of leather.

"Sorry," I said. "Didn't mean to bump you."

Win glanced down at my plastic cup. Its rim was gnawed to a pulp. "Hang on." He took the cup and dropped it into a bin marked "Remember to Recycle!" Then he loped barefoot into the house and reappeared minutes later with a MEAN PEO-PLE SUCK mug filled with beer the color of mead.

"Here."

"Thanks."

We clinked. Drank. Refilled. Drank some more.

Then: "Feel like walking a dog?"

There appeared to be about thirty dogs at this party, all of them roaming around collarless and probably rabid. "Sure," I replied, praying "the dog" in question was the nonbiting variety. Win whistled to a flat-faced rottweiler who came lumbering over, face sucking the ground.

"This," Win said, thumping the dog's back, "is Tony. And this is . . . ?"

"Eliza."

"Eliza, Tony. Tony, Eliza."

"Hello," I said as I shook Win's hand, impressed by our cleverness. "And this is . . . ?" I asked, though of course I'd already eavesdropped to find out.

"Win," he said. "Like win, lose, or draw."

"Or win, win, and win," I plunged, feeling my face burn hot, and wondering who the hell had spiked the mead.

I could feel Win watching me closely as the three of us wandered into the yard behind the house. We passed a giant barbecue pit and a huge, gnarled climbing tree. "This place is amazing," I said. "Do you live here?"

"Sure."

"With who?"

"Friends. Friends of friends."

It was good enough for me.

"When I was a sophomore . . ." Win's voice was mellow, unrushed, drifting like a sigh, and I could feel the whole world decelerating as I listened, tension leaking from my joints. "All I wanted was to get away from campus. That scene, man." He stopped walking and I stopped, too, shaking off the momentary disorientation of being called "man." "It's not me."

"Me, either," I agreed, meaning it.

Win sat down in a bald spot in the grass. Tony and I did the same. I followed Win's finger as he pointed to our right, to a scattering of popsicle-stick stakes labeled "Let" and "Broc" and "Rad."

"Veggies," he explained, and I nodded. Above us, a maze of clotheslines was draped with tapestries and Indian-print blankets and prairie skirts with jingle bells at their hems.

"Laundry," he said.

I nodded again. I knew, without a doubt, Win was the rock star I'd been searching for. For a moment, I let myself pretend Win and I lived alone in the country, eating homegrown salads, co-parenting Tony, being not really married but the equivalent-of-married (because who needs a piece of paper to formalize our feelings?) via a service in the woods with a lute and a flowered veil and an exchange of homemade vows.

Win produced a joint from his pocket, which seemed only appropriate. We passed it back and forth until "Rad" and "Let" and "Broc" seemed heavy with meaning. I felt like I was floating, millions of miles from the classes and hot pots and shower caddies of my other life. For hours—or what felt like hours— Win and I sat in that one spot, touching on religion . . . child-hood . . . Santa Claus . . .

At some point, someone started beating a drum in the distance. Tony started to moan.

"Beautiful," Win said. First I thought he meant the drums, then I thought he meant the dog, then I briefly allowed myself to think he meant me. Eventually, I realized he was looking at the stars. "Beautiful . . . but sad."

You can always count on the astral reference, no matter how drugged and cryptic. "Why sad?"

"Anything beautiful is fragile," Win said, pausing an approximate minute between each word. "Beauty is doomed. Don't you think?"

Did I think? Didn't I think? I suspected he was going after a metaphor or something, but I'd only been an English major for two semesters and at the moment was so stoned I could barely figure out my last name. All I cared about was when Win Brewer, lead vocalist, would finish up his second set and take me up to his room.

Rock stars' bedrooms are a very tricky area. In my experience, they are capable of destroying a relationship before it gets a foot off the ground. Most rooms try hard to look noncommittal. They want to seem sparse, distracted, ideally just a guitar case and a frayed bandanna and a black-and-white photo of a distraught ex-girlfriend from Soho or L.A. But upon closer inspection, most rock stars' bedrooms are just the opposite.

Once I spied a Snoopy sno-cone maker. A berry-scented air freshener. A stuffed Papa Smurf. (He claimed it was a returned gift, but that didn't make it okay.)

Win's room was not too bad, thank God. There were a few squatting plants, a few pimply homemade candles, a few books of poetry—Ginsberg, Ginsberg, and Ginsberg—and an army-green sleeping bag spread across the floor. I felt my heart thump as Win knelt down and, in one slow, sexy move, unzipped it.

"After you," he said.

I carefully slipped my sandals off. Win tossed his T-shirt on the floor. As I crawled inside the bag, he dropped his earth-toned corduroys. By the time I looked up, sleeping bag yanked to my chin, the man was nude.

"Skin needs to breathe," he explained. Miraculously, this did not sound like a line. From the casual way Win strolled the room, turning off lights and tying his hair back (was that a scrunchie?), not wearing clothes actually seemed to be Win Brewer's natural state.

From inside the bag, I watched Win set the mood. He lit a few lopsided patchouli candles. He filled up the ten-disc CD changer. He was skinny, skinnier than I'd realized under his baggy rock-star duds. His arms were skinny. His dreads were skinny. His penis was the width of a carrot. It was a little disconcerting, being with a guy with more hair on his head and less fat on his body than I had. But Win exuded so much natural confidence I found myself lusting for him anyway.

We were soon zipped into a space the approximate size of a bath mat: definite make-out proximity. But the minute we started kissing, it became clear that nothing altered Win Brewer's pace. Like everything else in his life, he took his sweet time. For what seemed at least an hour, in fact, we did nothing *but* kiss. A full Lemonheads CD later, he ventured below the neck. He fumbled with my bra strap during several tracks of Superchunk and Hüsker Dü. At various points, it occurred to me that maybe he'd never encountered a girl wearing a bra before.

As dawn approached, it wasn't good old-fashioned sense that found me having sex with the lead vocalist. This was not my usual timetable. This was about being a) drunk, b) stoned, and c) somewhere way off-campus where I felt strangely and stupidly removed from real life. This was about candlelight and indie rock. This was about the kind of need brought on by hours and hours of excruciatingly patient foreplay. It was what the singers sing about: "night moves," "sexual healing," "paradise by the patchouli light."

I am not belittling the fact that Win's endurance was, by all accounts, inhuman. This was the kind of tantric, Sting-like performance I was sure distinguished the true rock stars from the wannabes. I was considering taking a time-out to call Ashley and gloat when, shockingly, Win began to sing.

"Higmph . . . mmtram . . . kmhssh unhhh . . ."

This was unprecedented rock-star behavior. Win actually appeared to be in onstage performance mode, eyes closed, face dripping with sweat, contorted with emotion.

"Bhyyy . . . fighl . . . shmat . . . mmms . . ."

I couldn't make out the words exactly. They were a combination of sultry, musical moans and murmurs. At the finale, a shout that sounded a hell of a lot like "love shack," Win collapsed beside me.

"Whoa." His eyes were round and close, his voice sleepy. "That was in*tense.*"

I nodded, pretty sure this was a compliment. As if sensing the coast was clear, Tony nosed open the bedroom door and lumbered over, sniffing around our heads and setting up camp by our feet. Win kissed me on the cheek and snuggled into my shoulder. As the three of us drifted off to sleep, the last thing I remember was Win's dreadlocks on the pillow beside me. A fuzzy blond pile, like a nest.

The next morning, I woke with regret pounding firmly in my ears. In the distance, I could hear dogs barking. I could smell bitter coffee perking. And there, sitting at his desk, I could see Win: buck naked. He had his legs crossed at the knee and was scribbling in a wire-bound notebook.

I began to panic. This was nothing like waking up on campus. No unseen slip out of a strange room, no guilty sprint across the Quad, no three-year penance of mumbled "hey"s in the dining hall over trays of country steak. On campus, no one stayed naked. No one wrote in their journals naked. No one ever, ever made coffee.

When he saw I was awake, Win waved. "Regular or decaf?"

I was living in the '60s. Or, at least, the closest thing to the '60s in the '90s. As it turned out, the majority of people (and animals) at Win's party were residents of the "commune"

(Andrew's word), a constantly changing cast of dogs, cats, new-lyweds, art majors, dropouts, hammocks, and the occasional yurt. The place had a primal, physical quality about it. Men and women all had long hair and resembled one another. They braided one another, kissed one another, pierced one another with needles and boiling water. Women had unshaved legs and pits. Unneutered animals prowled around like a nature sanctu-ary. It was suburban Philly turned on its head. I loved it.

Win and I eventually filled each other in on some of the con-cretes we'd skipped in the backyard. I found out he was from North Jersey. An only child. A music major. His name (which passed the PCT test with flying colors) was short for Winston (after a grand-parent, not a cigarette) though that didn't stop Winston Ultras from becoming the commune's cigarette of choice.

"I have a mother," I volunteered. "And a sister. And a . . . Harv. He's my mother's, I guess, fiancé." My mother and Harv were getting married that summer, but still the use of the word "fiancé" in relation to my mother struck me as ludicrous.

"Where's your dad?" Win asked. "Is he around?"

Not since Judy Mitchell's band bash/function had I been handed a setup as perfect as this. It would have been simple, even artful, to launch into my heartbreaking Lou-abandonment soliloquy. But for once, I just didn't have it in me. First of all, I had the vague impression that everyone in the commune had a back story to rival mine: divorces, addictions, treks cross-country with nothing but a bag of raw sunflower seeds and a knapsack on a stick. More important, I didn't feel I needed to perform in order for Win Brewer to take me seriously. Win

Brewer, I was catching on, took just about everything seriously.

"He left," I said.

"Intense."

And that was that.

"Intense," I would soon learn, was a crucial term within the commune. Depending on the circumstances, it was capable of carrying all kinds of meaning and nuance and emotional weight. Most commune words were similarly abstract, like *energy* and *place*. It was as if the commune spoke a different language than the rest of the world. Shorter words. Fewer syllables. Hardly any verbs at all.

Curled up at night in the sleeping bag, flushed and exhausted, Win and I would touch base on the *place* we were in, e.g., a *good place*, a *fragile place*, a *complicated place*. We read each other poems from a frayed poetry anthology that was propped beside the bed, Bible style.

Sometimes, Win would get inspired and have to go off and write lyrics in the middle of the night. Hours later, he'd crawl back into the bag and sing them to me softly. A mournful love song about my hair. One about my instep. After I let him pierce my nose, he was compelled to write a lieder cycle.

"I think I'm in love," I started admitting to people out loud.

"Wow," said Hannah. "In love or in awe?"

"You mean in-sane?" said Andrew.

"Big dick, right?" from Ashley.

Despite my friends' overwhelming show of support, I knew I had never felt anything like this. With Win, the world was cast in a new light. Everything was deeper, more significant, than I'd ever recognized. Fast-food chains were Communist. Nature was metaphorical. TV was evil. GPAs were totally passé. The more time I spent at the commune, the more my life on campus seemed petty, naive.

By December, I had given up my meal plan. I had abandoned my half-formed plans of studying abroad in Ireland (primarily in the hopes of meeting Bono, who I'd heard sometimes made random cameos in pubs). Over Christmas break, I helped Hannah pack her maximum-twenty-pound bag for Africa— tampons and razor blades and ankle-length skirts. I called Vermont to say good-bye to Andrew, who was armed with tradeable baseball caps and *Let's Go, Spain!*

In January, I moved into the commune.

spring semester

Commune living required some serious sacrifices. No one there ate meat (i.e., no chicken nuggets), listened to major labels (no Sting), or watched television (no MTV). They had no heat, except for a clanking wood stove which required I wear at least two sweatshirts and three pairs of socks at all times. In the dead of winter, having sex or taking a shower was only for the truly hardy.

The commune was a lifestyle of few physical pleasures—a fitting payback, as I saw it, for twenty years of fast food, *Three's Company*, premarital sex, and Easter seasons spent pretending that giving up sit-ups or green beans for Lent actually counted as a sacrifice. In the interest of fitting in, I gave up meat. I gave up fast food. I took up Winston Ultras. This combination of intense health and intense un-health was typical of the commune: shunning red meat while engulfing smoke. I recognized the irony, but had no choice about it. Smoking seemed to be a prerequisite for chilling with the Band.

Identifying Band members was easy. All of them wore loose, earth-toned T-shirts and loose, earth-toned corduroys. Their clothing was generally wrinkled and hopefully mismatched, to convey the impression of having been plucked absently off a bedroom floor. Back pockets were stuffed with guitar picks, drumsticks, or the occasional rusted harmonica (to convey that the wearer was particularly afflicted with "the blues").

Though when I first saw the Band they were Rocks for Jocks, I found out that name was temporary. In fact, all the Band's names were temporary; this, apparently, was the explanation for why they never went public. No one seemed willing to commit to one name, and some not even the concept of a name (one guy was pushing for an ampersand). This indecision resulted in the Band's spending hours, days, weeks, trying to come up with a solution. Naming sessions went something like this (to be read slowly, with no variation in tone):

"How 'bout Natural Born Chillers."

"How 'bout Search Engine."

"How 'bout Amnesty."

"Wait. How 'bout Anarchy."

"No. Wait. How 'bout parentheses. With nothing inside them."

"How 'bout Sexual Assault."

This could go on for hours. It was an odd blend of the intense and the inert: a roomful of people full of ideas, but unmotivated as sticks. Given enough time, the sessions would evolve into debates about the Band's *mission* or *direction* or *vision*. Invariably, things got ugly from there. Any mention of *vision* was sure to result in a) one Band member threatening to kick out another Band member, b) Band members abstractly apologizing and possibly embracing, and c) the whole gang firing up an amicable bowl on the patch of "Rad."

One word summed up life in the commune: bongos.

Like "intense," "bongos" was a word with multiple purposes and meanings. It could function as a rallying cry—"Bongos!"— which produced a group of people from thin air, cradling wooden drums between their flowery, skirted knees. Or it could function as a state of being, i.e.:

"What have you been doing?"

"Not much. You know. Bongos."

By March, I couldn't tell if the steady sound of drumming was taking place outside my body or had actually crept permanently inside my head. This crisis of the inner ear coincided with the realization that I had little or nothing in common with the commune. I wanted desperately to be like them. I was even sure, on some level, I was *supposed* to be like them. But something just never clicked. I didn't contribute to the Band's naming sessions. I didn't respond to the bongo cry. My presence in the house was hardly noticed, except after I got my wisdom teeth pulled and offered my leftover Percocet for general consumption.

In my more honest moments, I admitted to myself that I was just plain bored. So bored I sometimes thought I could actually feel time passing (it has the quality of trying to walk through foam rubber). So bored I started inventing metaphors for how bored I was. So bored I started naming my toes. So bored I realized I identified most with a cat named Nancy, who had a sarcastic meow and who I once saw sprint from the kitchen with an entire veggie burger flapping from her mouth.

I started spending more and more time in Win's sleeping bag, immersed in my English homework: African-American Women Playwrights of the 1970s, Modern Feminist Poets from the Midwest. (At small liberal arts colleges, majoring in English usually meant skipping the classics and going straight for the esoteric.) Suddenly everything I saw seemed a literary symbol for something: death, hope, birth, amniotic fluid. The sleeping bag had never seemed more womblike. I suspected Win's dread-locks had something to do with original sin.

I wrote long letters to Hannah by candlelight, addressed to a tiny village in Cameroon. I sent Andrew packages of sports clip-pings, school papers, and boxes of Cracker Jacks. Occasionally, I snuck a taste of life-beyond-the-commune. On Thursday nights, I stole away to the Mrs. Suds Laundromat to watch new episodes of *Friends*. I surreptitiously shaved my armpits. I coerced Ashley into guesting me into the campus dining hall one night, where I downed two plates of country steak. Afterward, back at the ranch, I harbored the vaguely guilty feel-ing that I'd been cheating on my boyfriend (reinforced by the Band's temporarily changing their name to Carnivore Killers).

But, if I was acting differently, Win didn't seem to notice.

One night, Andrew called from a phone booth in Seville (4:30 A.M. his time, 10:30 P.M. mine). He was blabbering sluggishly, something about a flamenco dancer named Rosa.

"Eliza," I managed to decipher from a morass of "z"s. "He doesn't even watch TV."

"What?"

"Don't deny it."

"Deny what?"

"You love TV!"

"I'm not denying it."

"Say it."

"I love TV."

"Eliza," Andrew slurred and sighed, a sigh full of nostalgia and sangria. "You used to be really, really, really, really"—he burped—"funny."

fall semester

Against my better judgment, I was back in the army-green sleeping bag come September. I wasn't thrilled about returning to the commune, but was less thrilled about the alternative: returning to campus, where Ashley had (understandably) found a new roommate and (not understandably) taken up with a rugby player called Crazy Charles who swallowed goldfish whole. Over the summer, the commune had changed only slightly. The radishes were growing, sort of. Nancy the cat was pregnant. An RV spray-painted "Why Be Normal?" had materialized next to the barbecue pit. A new crop of crashers was draped around the house, looking almost identical to last year's crashers; or else, they actually were last year's crashers, and had graduated but never left.

Win and I had had minimal contact over the summer. He was in Montana, backpacking from ranch to ranch. I was at home, temping for a podiatrist, hearing about Hannah's life-changing semester in Africa, and watching my mother walk down the aisle, all three of which inexplicably made me feel like bawling. I had received just two postcards from Win, each with a peace sign dotting the "i" in his name and the return address "Somewhere, Montana."

Despite our lack of contact, picking up where we left off was easy. Too easy, it seemed. Win read me some of his new lyrics, most of them involving dust and prairies and the recurring phrase "lasso my soul." I drowned in "Heroes of Women's Literature, Post-1945." For two weeks, the Band changed their name to Win Brewer and the Range. Although Win was still passionate and offbeat and frequently nude, our life in the commune was starting to feel a little hollow. Silly. At night, I noticed his dreadlocks were spawning tiny, curly children.

Then, one Saturday morning in October, we were crawling out of the sleeping bag toward coffee when Win asked, "Feel like a road trip?"

I was too startled to come up with an answer.

"I was just thinking," he continued, slow as a dripping faucet. "We could crash with my 'rents upstate. Chill with my high school friends. Hike. Hang."

All I could come up with was "drool"—some botched combination of "dude" and "cool"—when what I actually meant to say was "Maybe we should spend some time apart" or "I'm not really in a road-tripping kind of place right now." Instead, an hour later, I found myself driving to St. Clair, New Jersey.

The five-hour ride in a borrowed RV was the longest period Win and I had ever spent together conscious. It was also the first time we'd ventured anywhere farther from the commune than Barry's Used CDs or Ronnie's Organic Foods. When we hit highway, ten miles outside Wissahickon, I could already feel the hypnotic pot-and-bongo haze of the commune beginning to lift. In the real world, the moving world, Win's routines were more pronounced and much more annoying: stopping every hour for another hit, chugging water to stay hydrated, playing me tapes of the Band and pointing out all the totally fresh (and seemingly identical) new chords and riffs.

Three joints and six tapes later, Win steered our graffitied car/boat into what looked like the entrance of a posh country club.

"Where are we?"

"Home sweet home," Win said, leaning on the horn.

My very first thought (not that I'm happy about it) was: Mom would be so proud. After years of living vicariously through *Knots Landing* and *Benson,* I had arrived at a mansion. A real-life mansion. The stuff *Entertainment Tonight* is made of.

Naturally, the RV looked completely misplaced. I felt like I was trapped inside one of those junior high games of MASH when you watch a circling pencil and suddenly find yourself living in Paris with a BMW, fourteen kids, and a shack. All I could

hear were my mother's frantic warnings about salad-fork etiquette as Win pulled up to the gold-knockered front doors.

Mrs. Win was waiting for us in the foyer, which resembled
an enormous, shiny checkerboard. She was wearing a silky purple pantsuit and high heels. Silvery eyeshadow climbed to her
brows, which were thin as nail parings.

"Winny!" the woman squealed. Somehow, I had been
expecting something more like "Winston, dahling." Win
dropped his duffel as his mother grabbed him and planted a
squishy kiss on his cheek. "Who's your friend?" she asked, heading my way with her arms flung wide.

"That's Eliza," Win said.

"Eliza!" The woman had obviously never heard of me in her
life, but wrapped me in a perfumed hug anyway. She was like an
overeager den mother, in Gucci. "What a neat name! Is it short
for Elizabeth?"

"No. It's short for Eliza. I mean, it isn't short for anything,"
I blabbered, feeling inadequate in every way.

Win's mother didn't seem to notice my idiocy, which was
kind. Maybe she was totaling up my pierces. She herself was
wearing diamond studs the size of hams.

"Well, it's just great to meet you, Eliza," she said, then
walked back to where Win was slouching by the door. To my
surprise, she reached out and grabbed two of his dreadlocks in
her fists. "Winny," she sighed, flopping the locks back and
forth. "When are you going to cut these things off?"

"Lay off, Mom."

"But you always had such *cute* haircuts . . ."

"Mom, *stop,*" Win scowled, glancing quickly at me.

But it was too late: I could feel the transformation beginning. Win Brewer was starting to morph before my very eyes. His slow, angst-ridden drawl was suddenly sounding like a whine. His drab, baggy pants simply didn't fit him right. Flopping in his mother's hands, the dreadlocks which had cemented his rock-star status at Wissahickon were starting to resemble cute, fuzzy marionettes.

By bedtime, Win's authenticity had been chipped away bit by painful bit. His father, a kielbasa of a man stuffed into a metallic suit, arrived home just in time for dinner (duck smothered in creamy French sauce). Win, of course, refused to eat meat. Out of loyalty, I avoided the duck and stuffed myself with wine and rolls. Getting drunker by the second, I listened politely to his parents' conversation, while realizing that everything I'd taken most seriously about Win Brewer was, according to his mom and dad, a hilarious family joke.

a) His vegetarianism. "You know I don't eat meat," Win objected to the duck.

"Oh, Win. Are you still on that?" his mother said, rolling her eyes. She turned to me and launched into a detailed description of Win's favorite childhood snack: beef tips.

Mr. Win merrily speared some wing meat. "Winny's first words?" he announced, and the two of them crowed in unison: "'Home of the Whoppa!'"

b) His band. "So, picked a name yet?" Win's father asked, chuckling.

"We're working on it," Win muttered.

His parents exchanged an amused smile. "How about Indecision?" suggested Mrs. Win.

"Or Academic Probation?" from Mr. Win.

If they hadn't been wrecking my love life, I could have really gotten to like these two.

Multiply the dinner conversation by four smoking jabs, nine dreadlock jabs, and one long reminiscence about the year Win believed he actually *was* a Mutant Ninja Turtle and you'll understand why, by the end of it all, I'd abandoned the commune and was shoveling in the damn duck.

"Winny always was a showman," his mom said, pressing her hand against mine so a pound of diamond ring dug into my knuckles. "Oh, Gary. Remember when he had that magic act?"

"The squirting tulip," Mr. Win moaned. "God help us."

"You've got to go roll the tape, Gar," Mrs. Win said, "Eliza needs to see this."

"No," Win said. "No way."

Though back in the commune Win's words were like gospel, here it was a different story. "Five minutes, Winny," his mother said, in the same firm tone I'm sure she once used to send him to bed without beef tips.

"Rolling tape" was a serious understatement, since "tape" was a professional-quality montage set to the *Chariots of Fire* theme, and "rolling" entailed a movie screen descending from the ceiling as if by magic. The tape was like an upper-upper-class *Wonder Years:* Win in a headdress running around the mansion naked, Win in swim goggles running around a pool club naked, Win a little too old to be running around anywhere naked.

219

Then, a montage of fashion faux pas: a flash of little Win wearing neckties and Richie Rich shoes. A fake mustache and magician's top hat. A zillion zits and an AC/DC muscle shirt.

"He's always been finding himself," Mr. Win said, with a wink tight as a dime.

I guess it was then that I knew for sure what I'd been suspecting for a while: things would be ending between Win and me. Even so, I would wait out the weekend before making it official. I would wait out the five-hour, four-joint ride home. I would even wait out the rest of the fall semester. In December, Win and I had a long talk about his *confused place* and my *restless place* which seemed, miraculously, to satisfy us both.

"Intense," Andrew said afterward, as we toasted with Big Macs.

The day I left the commune, Win and I stood on the porch with a duffel full of sweatshirts and a crate full of English textbooks, gazing down at the mound of fur sleeping on the hammock.

"Which one do you want?" he said.

At seven weeks old, the kittens were still pretty indistinguishable. They looked a lot like a giant dust ball clinging to the side of Sarcastic Nancy. I was about to randomly extract one from the fluff when I heard a scratching noise and looked up. There was the renegade: gray-furred, yellow-eyed, wiggling his butt as he prepared to hurl himself from a hanging ivy plant into an empty guitar case.

"I'll take that one," I said.

9

imaginary boyfriends

SIDE A

"Sour Times" — Portishead
"Crucify" — Tori Amos
"King of Pain," "Driven to Tears," "So Lonely" — The Police
"How to Disappear Completely" — Radiohead
"Black" — Pearl Jam

I have stopped writing the book. Not because I'm unable to write the book, but because there is nothing new or interesting to write about. Five months after I dissented from Win's commune, I graduated from college and my life became pretty much what it is today: living in a tiny apartment, raising Leroy, avoiding my mother, obsessing over vacation typos (e.g., Carribean versus Caribbean), and frequenting The Blue Room, where I've ushered in a parade of wannabe rock stars. They are edgy. They are indie. They are Karl, just with different earrings and tattoos and haircuts and mothers.

Concerns About the Book:

a) every relationship ends the same (or is that the point?)
b) the musicians/boyfriends are kind of one-dimensional
   (or is that the point?)
c) story is becoming kind of predictable (maybe that's
   the point)
d) book has no clear point.

It is not good. I am wearing sweats. I am watching *Webster*. I have abandoned the book altogether. I have recurring flashbacks of last night's date with Donny. When I hear The Piano Man playing "Chopsticks," I consider the possibility that my life has actually become a VH1 *Behind the Music* and I have arrived at the 9:30 P.M. decline.

I resort to lists.

Words to Outlaw If I Were President:
   1) "announcement"
   2) "prom" (with no article)
   3) "securities analyst"
   4) "and a bag of chips" (suffix)

Words to Reinstate If I Were President:
   1) "sike"
   2) "no duh"
   3) "gross me out the door"

Sunday night I have a recurring series of nightmares. In one, I'm being beaten over the head by a giant garlic breadstick. In another, I'm being doused with a giant bottle labeled "Hair Pomade," clutched by a super-sized, grinning Donny Osmond.

Monday morning, I call in sick to Dreams. It is 6:30 A.M., early enough that I can avoid speaking directly to Beryl and being overcome with guilt when she quizzes me about the date and clucks sympathetically over my imaginary illness. Instead, I speak to the recorded message: a snatch of "Kokomo" followed by Kelly chirping, "Hello and thanks for calling! Let us make your dreams come true!"

"Hi, everyone," I speak after the beep. I add a weak cough, for effect. "It's Eliza. I'm sick." The way I see it, this is not untrue. I *am* sick, in a way. Sick of working. Sick of dating. Sick of writing cheerful captions for celluliteless women wearing thongs. "I'll call in when I'm better. But from the look of things, it might be a while." I add an exaggerated sniffle. "Happy Monday."

Leaving my apartment to stock up on essentials requires my very last ounce of strength. I keep my head down, my eye contact minimal. At Value Video, I rent all things John Cusack. At the all-purpose drugstore, I buy tampons and entertainment magazines. I slog through the crammed food aisle, regressing to the forbidden foods of my childhood: Jolt, Pop Tarts, shredded green Big League Chew. I buy cereals and cookies with generic brand names like Crunchy Octogons, Berry Breakfast Nuggets, and Crispy Chocolate Wafers. Unlike most things in life, they tell you exactly what you are getting.

*   *   *

Back in the apartment, buoyed by cookies, I commence hibernation. I think this is the life I was cut out to live. It is easier than trying to date rock stars, and infinitely easier than trying to understand the screwed-up, oedipal-musical psychology *behind* my trying to date rock stars. As it turns out, I don't need—or want—anyone but myself.

I adjust quickly to the formlessness of never leaving my apartment. I let dishes sit unwashed. I stop wearing makeup. I lose track of what day it is, never mind what date. I stop shaving my legs, and ignore the messages glutting my answering machine. My cicadian rhythms are dictated by cans of Jolt: surge and crash, surge and crash. I sleep during the day, do crossword puzzles at dawn. Eat Chocolate Wafers for breakfast, Berry Nuggets at night. I am defying someone, I'm just not sure whom.

Message from Hannah: "Alan and I are back from the Amish country. You have to see this incredible quilt I found. How was your big date? We're dying to hear all about it!"

Message from Andrew: "I'm watching pro billiards. Call me."

Message from Camilla: "Eliza. I need to talk to you right away about the dates for a baby shower Dara's planning. Call me by Thursday. Friday, at the absolute latest. That's when she has to let the reception hall people know. Okay? Are you doing okay? Dating anyone new? Talk to you soon. Remember: Friday."

* * *

Message from Andrew: "I'm watching *Nova*. Call me."

My only human (sort of) contact is a) the cast of *The Real World*, b) Leroy, who I talk to more and more frequently ("You're in my book!" I shout at him, clapping my hands, "Leroy, did you know you're in my book?!") and c) The Piano Man upstairs. I've actually come to look forward to his daily serenades. Usually he plays at night, around six or seven, and I curl up under an afghan and close my eyes to listen. Sometimes his music is light and mellow, sometimes rich and romantic. Other times, it is atonal. Anxious.

Message from the Queen Mother: "Honey, the girls tell me you haven't been in all week. Any chance you'll be back with us tomorrow? Our travelers need their travel news! Call us, talk to us, tell us you're alive. You had a big date, I hear?"

By Friday, it occurs to me that the Agents probably think my absence from work is post-coital. God knows what Donny said to Beryl, or if he's even spoken to Beryl. I can hear the Agents now, speculating about us around the Diet Coke and angel food: Donny and I taking off to Aruba and drinking out of hairy coconut halves, Donny and I taking off to Italy and sucking down sauceless pasta, Donny and I going to Vegas and getting hitched by Barry Manilow.

Obviously, I will have to find a new line of work.

Options:

a) Cat lady. On the plus side, I wouldn't have to leave my apartment much. I could be as privately zany as I wanted. I could never shave my legs again. On the other hand, it might get expensive in the paraphernalia department, i.e., toys, treats, tiny mittens, fisherman's sweaters, holiday accessories (antlers, bunny ears). I don't think Leroy would take too well to being accessorized, or sharing his turf with any new cats (I'm pretty sure the minimum is around thirty) who would.

b) FBI agent. I've always liked the stealth of it, the muted sarcasm, the all-black wardrobe. I'm just not crazy about the danger. I do love, however, the slim possibility of kissing David Duchovny (in my book, the only man in the world who looks good carrying a cell phone).

c) Muse. Hm. Musing has potential. It's cheap, safe, unconditional love. A boost to the self-esteem. Endless amounts of free grapes. The only drawback is the constant nakedness, but maybe I can work around it.

As I'm considering the specific requirements of muse nudity, The Piano Man starts to play. The tune is something passionate, romantic—Rachmaninoff?—packed with sweat and crescendos. Come to think of it, I realize, burrowing deeper into my couch, this musing career could work out perfectly. I could be the muse, The Piano Man my musee. Maybe we could work out an arrangement where I don't ever have to leave my apartment. He'll drop grapes through the heating vent. I'll shout encouragement from below. I'm attempting to project inspiration through the ceiling (it involves a squinching of the eyes, a pursing of the lips) when the phone rings.

It rings, and rings some more. It doesn't even occur to me to answer. Finally Andrew's voice comes on, droning like a lawn-mower. "Piccccck upppppp," he motors into the machine. "Piccccck upppppp." Then he pauses and, to my horror, begins to rap. "This is Andrew . . . callin' for my homey . . . wonderin' when she's gonna pick up the . . . phoney . . ."

He leaves me no choice. I grab it, as the machine unleashes a painful whine of feedback. "Never do that again," I tell him, frantically poking buttons on the answering machine until the hideous noise cuts off.

"Hey, got you to pick up," Andrew gloats. "What up, dog?"

Now that I am on the phone and have made both the rap-ping and the feedback disappear, I realize I'm not ready to have this conversation. I am not prepared to go public with the specifics of my life right now. A bombed date. A week spent in my pajamas. Four hundred Crispy Chocolate Wafers.

"Let me rephrase," Andrew is saying, as I stuff my mouth full of Big League Chew. "What are you watching?"

I look at the TV and glimpse David Hasselhoff. "Nothing."

"Then what are you doing?"

"Nothing."

"Why haven't you returned my messages?"

"No reason."

"Eliza. Help me out here. Where the hell have you been this week?"

I need to think fast. It shouldn't be too hard, right? I work in travel, for God's sake, an industry founded on where-the-hell-have-you-been. Aruba? Jamaica? I shake my head, clearing cookies from my brain. "I've been . . . dating somebody."

"You have? Who?"

Not an unreasonable question. But the last thing I want to get into right now is the garlicky breadsticks . . . the cell phone . . . the nightmares. "You don't know him," I stall, as the ceiling shivers with a Beethoven-ish thump. Then, in the long tradition of words traipsing out of my mouth without my conscious involvement—see "your skin on mine" (Chapter 4) and "Do you know the song 'All I Need'?" (Chapter 6)—the next sentence is out before I can stop it: "He's a pianist."

"From The Blue Room? Those are synthesizers, Eliza."

"No. I mean a real pianist." I bite my lip. "Classical."

Andrew sounds skeptical. "Where did you meet a real classical pianist?"

"Upstairs." Hm. This was actually easier than I'd thought. "I mean, he lives upstairs."

"What's his name?"

This one, however, I was not prepared for. It's much too much pressure too soon. A name as important as an Imaginary Boyfriend's deserves weeks, months to decide.

"Junxdtk?" I blurt out, a knot of gum and consonants.

"Who?"

"Juchk?"

"Jack?"

"No," I amend, clearing my throat and racking my brain. "It's Jacques."

"Jacques?"

"Yes." I am surprisingly satisfied. "Jacques. It's French."

"Yeah, thanks. How old is this Jacques?"

Twenty-four? Thirty-five? "Twenty-nine."

"Does he wear a beret?"

"Um, no."

"What does he do for a living?"

"He, you know. Performs." Obviously. "He has gigs. Around the world." Okay. "Actually, he's taking me to Aruba soon for one of his shows." I have no shame. "He doesn't want it to leak to the press, though. So you can't tell anyone. It's all very . . . understated." That part, at least, is fact.

At last I have found him, the perfect rock star/boyfriend: Imaginary Jacques.

Imaginary Jacques can be anything I want him to be. He won't have an overbearing mother. He won't have reams of baby albums. He won't have nasty personal habits or offensive catch-phrases or repulsive sleeping rituals. If Imaginary Jacques ever wore cummerbunds or Whitesnake tank tops in the '80s, I will never have to know. I get all the perks, none of the disappointments. There's no reality to bring me down.

I start to mentally revise my earlier, ear-haired version of The Piano Man. Imaginary Jacques is young, thin, dark. He has a patchy goatee, a silver hoop in his left brow. He wears scuffed moccasins and worn black jeans with sporadic, rust-colored paint stains on the knees. Before, I thought his reclusiveness was weird. Now, it makes perfect sense. Unlike other musicians, who need the stage to inflate their egos, Jacques needs nothing more than his keyboard and himself. He is the kind of musician who's in it for the art, not the chicks. Who doesn't answer his phone cause he's lost in his *fortissimos*. Who staples his thumbs to feel Beethoven's pain.

Message from Hannah: "Should I be worried, or was your date so good it hasn't ended yet? Could you just please call me back? Let me know you're okay?"

Dating will be much, much simpler with Imaginary Jacques. I won't have to worry about looking good for my Imaginary Boyfriend. I won't have to berate myself for not jogging or joining a gym. I won't have to wear makeup. I won't have to worry about sauces and cheeses and when I can and cannot eat them in public. At Dreams, I can field the Agents' questions with confidence, eloquence, waxing poetic about Imaginary Jacques's advanced degrees (MFA, Composing) and favorite pastimes (poetry, painting) and gourmet dinner recipes (insert name of seafood) marinated in (insert name of wine).

I can redeem myself at Sunday dinners.

"So, Eliza," Mom will begin.

"Mother," I'll interrupt her. "I am dating a man. He is twenty-nine. His name is Jacques. He went to Juilliard, performs in venues around the world, and we're madly in love."

A stunned silence will descend on the table.

"So what does he do?" someone (Scott, probably) will want to know.

"He's a pianist."

"Eliza," Mom will say, blushing madly. "Do you have to be vulgar?"

I spend hours designing the inside of Imaginary Jacques's apartment: sprawled record albums, half-filled wineglasses, itchy brown sweaters tossed over chair backs. Mysterious abstract art hung haphazardly on the walls. Refrigerator filled with decaying lettuce, olives, exotic cheeses, ripped loaves of crusty French bread. Grease-spotted Chinese takeout menu stuck to the refrigerator door. Crumpled receipts in the trash that say "Thanks for Chopin!" and "Come Bach soon!"

Sunday afternoon, thirteen days into hibernation, I hear a knock at my door. For a wild moment, I convince myself it's Imaginary Jacques. He has come to profess his love for me, to lure me upstairs to his tortured apartment, to woo me with a night of swordfish, Chablis, and sex in D major. On second thought, D minor. But when I press my eyeball to the peephole, I see only Andrew, his face stretched long as a tongue.

My first instinct is: Andrew has an "announcement." He and Kimberley are engaged. Pregnant. Eloped. Eloping. I feel my heartbeat start to skitter, a combination of fear and caffeine. I don't think I can take another announcement, not now. I can't handle another friend getting married, getting settled, operating rice cookers and debating baby names and arranging crackers and cheese in a fatty orange moon on a serving tray.

"Andrew," I say, swinging the door open so hard it slams against the wall. "Tell me you're not engaged."

"What?"

"Oh God."

"You lunatic. I'm not engaged."

"Swear?"

"Yes."

"Swear again?"

"Eliza!" Andrew steps inside and slams the door. "You must chill."

He must have come from the gym. At this point, the combined concepts of exercising and being in public are so removed from my life they frighten me. He's wearing running shoes, a dirty Eagles cap, a gray Wissahickon Track T-shirt. His wind pants are so energetically shiny they blind me for a second.

Andrew drops his keys on my messy kitchen counter then, slowly, surveys the apartment. I follow his gaze as it crawls around the room—from the kitchen/west wing to the bedroom/east wing—feeling more and more uneasy. Living inside my head, I see, has allowed me to ignore where I actually *do* live. And now, as if an act of revenge, the apartment sells me out detail by detail. I absorb the wads of used blue tissue, strewn about like smashed blue flowers. The dust of four hundred Crispy Chocolate Wafers. I think Leroy has spelled SOS with his food.

Andrew begins to pace the room in measured steps, like a TV lawyer looking for evidence. I creep over to the couch and sit down. As he walks, his wind pants make swift, swishing sounds that make me edgy. He picks up a half-eaten banana, runs his finger through a patch of chocolate dust. He glances at the brick-and-board coffee table, which offers up a neurotic pile of lists: Words to Outlaw If I Were President. Words to Reinstate If I Were President. Minor Characters on *Charles in Charge.*

When he reaches the TV, Andrew stops. Unfortunately, the tube is tuned in to a rerun of *Full House*. He points at the screen, turns to me, and demands: "Eliza, what the hell is going on?"

My eyes slide to my lap. I have no excuse. I am suddenly aware of the fact that my socks don't match and I haven't washed my hair since, like, Wednesday.

Andrew hits the OFF button, and Bob Saget disappears in a burst of startled static. The set hasn't known OFF in days.

"Listen," Andrew says. I look up reluctantly. His arms are folded across his chest. Leroy is parked at his feet, like a junior associate. "I heard you haven't been going to work lately."

"How could you possibly know that?"

He shrugs, protecting his inside sources. "Somebody you work with told me."

"Who?"

"She said she was a travel agent."

"Yeah, I know. Which *one?*"

"I think her name was Kelly."

"Kelly?"

Hearing this sends me into an inexplicable panic, probably the result of too much TV and too little human contact.

Clearly, my life has become a full-blown conspiracy. An *X-File*. Now the Agents have Andrew in their clutches. They are trading inside information in exchange for sucking Andrew into the Dreams Come True underworld. Soon he will be attending birthday parties and booking honeymoons, and I'll be writing captions like "Andrew takes Portugal!"

"Kelly?" I repeat, reaching for the afghan lumped on the couch beside me. I start plucking nervously at the fringe. "How did you meet Kelly?"

"It turns out she's a friend of Kimberley's sister," Andrew says, sounding annoyed. Leroy rolls onto his side and starts slurping his paw. Traitor. "Not that that's the point."

"It *is* the point," I insist, my voice rising. "It is *totally* the point!"

"Listen." Andrew takes his baseball cap off, crunches the brim in his hand, then plants it back firmly on his head. "Let's not forget I'm the functional person here. The one who's actually leaving his apartment and showing up for work every day. You're the one who just got caught watching Uncle Joey and Uncle Jesse."

I pull the afghan over my head.

"I'm just here because I'm worried. So don't go giving me the third degree."

I yank the afghan off again. "So that's what this is about? Giving me the third degree? What are you, like, checking up on me or something? Casing my apartment? Looking for some kinds of clues?" Needless to say, the conspiracy theory is taking a minute to subside.

Andrew rolls his eyes. Leroy sighs. "Look. If you don't want me to stay, I'm out the door." He points at it. "In case you forgot, that's the wooden thing over there. You use it to leave the apartment."

Not funny.

"No really, it's easy. Just turn the round metal thing, open it up, and walk right through." He actually makes little walking motions with two fingers as he explains this. Leroy, reading it as an invitation for petting, starts furiously head-butting Andrew's foot. I hate them both.

"I just want to know why you haven't been to work. It's kind of extreme, even for you," Andrew says, stooping to the floor. "But, I mean, I know how it is in the beginning of a relationship."

Relationship?

"Losing track of time, getting caught up in the flow . . ." He glances up at what must be a look of bewilderment on my face. "I assume this all has something to do with that Jacques guy, right?"

Hold on. Wait just a minute. I almost completely forgot my Imaginary Boyfriend! This is fabulous, ingenious! Aside from the glaring issue of how anyone could look at me and believe I'm romantically involved with *anyone* right now, Imaginary Jacques is the perfect plan!

"Exactly," I agree, bobbing my head feverishly. "It's all because of that Jacques guy."

"So fill me in," Andrew says, straightening up. "So far so good? No meeting the parents? No weird toe fetishes?"

235

"No. Nothing. Not a thing." Which couldn't be more true. "Just the usual falling in love stuff. You know, staying up all night. Spending every minute together."

"So where is he now?"

"What do you mean, exactly?"

"Now. Where is he now."

"I don't follow."

"Eliza."

Andrew waits, grabbing a handful of Crispy Chocolate Wafers. This is not hard to do, given that from any point in the apartment you're pretty much guaranteed some are within arm's length.

"He's in San Francisco." The only possible explanation for this city falling out of my mouth is the fact that *Full House* takes place there. I am now confusing imaginary families with imaginary boyfriends, but I don't dwell on this. "Downtown San Francisco."

"How exotic."

"He's at a pianists' meeting."

"A meeting?"

"You know, a convention kind of thing. With other pianists. From all over the world."

Andrew raises one eyebrow, a genetic talent that's always made me disproportionately jealous. He is starting to have doubts, I can tell. Then, as if my worldwide convention lie weren't flimsy enough, The Piano Man chooses that moment to begin his nightly serenade. The ceiling shivers. The windows rattle. Leroy runs for cover. I hear the goddamn opening bars of goddamn Joplin's goddamn "Heart and Soul."

The ultimate betrayal.

Andrew's floating eyebrow reappears in a deep frown. Slowly, he raises one arm and uncurls his index finger toward the ceiling. From my vantage on the couch, he looks a little like a sweat-stained Statue of Liberty.

"Is that your boyfriend?" Andrew asks, each word hard and blunt as a quarter.

"Um, yes."

"Jacques?"

"Yes."

"The guy playing 'Heart and Soul'?"

"Yes."

" 'Heart and Soul,' Eliza? I can play 'Heart and Soul'!"

I shrug. "Sometimes he likes to dabble."

"So he's not at a convention."

"Not exactly."

Andrew drops his arm. "Is he even your boyfriend?"

"Badgering the witness," I protest, weakly.

"Jesus, Eliza. Tell me you've even *met* this guy!"

I don't think I've ever felt more pathetic in my whole imaginary life. I grope for a pillow, a bastard cat, anything as long as it's soft and familiar and mine.

Andrew crosses the room in three capable, lawyerly strides and sits down beside me. He plants his hands on his shiny kneecaps and looks me in the eye. "All right. I want you to tell me what's going on."

Had I had a normal father, I think I could pause here to reflect: his tone sounds just like Dad's used to. At least, I'm pretty sure it sounds the way Dad's should have. Concerned but insistent. Caring but firm. Something about the firmness makes me crack: "HannahgotengagedandCamilla'shavingababyandyou're sayingIloveyouonacellphoneanditseemslikeeveryoneismoving onandsettlingdownandknowsexactlywhattheywantfromlifesoI agreedtogoonadatewiththissecuritiesanalystbecauseIthoughtifI juststoppeddatingmusiciansthentheeverythingwouldchangeforme butthedatewasjustlikeIexpectedandworsesomaybeit'snottheguys' faultbutmyfaultforbeingtoopickyorbeingtoonarrowmindedor orderingmychickenwithmozzarellacheese."

Andrew gets every word, God love him. "What's wrong with chicken and mozzarella cheese?" he says, sinking backward on the couch.

"You're not supposed to eat cheese on a first date, Andrew."

"Says who?"

"Says Kelly," I practically spit. (Technically, she wasn't the Agent campaigning against the cheese, but the opportunity was there and I took it.) "She said it's not a good first-date image."

I am expecting a little consolation at this point, a little mutual Agent-bashing, but Andrew laughs. "That's ironic."

"What's ironic?"

"That is."

"What's that? There's nothing ironic about that. And what happened to swearing off using the word 'ironic'? Have we learned nothing from the Alanis song?"

"What's ironic," explains Andrew, not a man to be messed with when it comes to word usage, "is somebody telling *you* about image."

I purse my lips and say, "Whatchu talkin' 'bout, Andrew?" in a well-honed Arnold from *Diff'rent Strokes*, but Andrew isn't kidding around.

"I'm talking about how completely hung up you are on this image stuff."

I yank the cover up over my knees. "Andrew. Were you just hearing what I was saying? *They* were the ones telling *me* how to act on the date. And I didn't even take their stupid advice. I drank Bud. I ordered carbs. I was a women's magazine nightmare. They're the women hung up on image."

"That's not what I'm talking about."

"Then what the hell are you talking about?"

"I'm saying, you can't exactly get away with knocking people for going after a certain image, because look at you and the rock stars. You always want these guys to be so wild and crazy and out there." Andrew then rolls his eyes and waves his arms in what I can only guess is an improvisation of "out there." "But the minute they actually *do* anything remotely unusual, anything that doesn't fit this ridiculous rock-star image you have, you cut them loose."

This is starting to get less funny.

"You're always worried about how things look instead of how things really are," he says.

"Um, have you noticed my apartment lately?" It is my last stab at keeping this conversation light. "Do you really think I'm worried about how things look?"

"But nobody can see you in here. You're in the bubble. You're in TV land. You invented your boyfriend, for God's sake!"

It's hard to argue this.

"Remember in the car?" Andrew plows on. "Outside your mom's, when you said nothing ever surprises you? You want to know why?"

"Probably not."

"It's because you never *let* anything surprise you. You're so hung up on the way you think the world's supposed to be, you never even give it a chance to prove you wrong."

I don't know if it's what he's saying that is so unsettling or the way he's saying it. With such certainty. Polish. Vehemence, even. This obviously isn't the first time Andrew has thought this through.

"Like your sister getting pregnant, or Hannah getting married, or some stupid drummer picking his nose or eating salad with his hands—you can't control every tiny little thing."

"Who says I want to control every little thing?"

Andrew slaps a palm on the cluttered coffeetable, sending Leroy bounding out from underneath it. "Exhibit A: 'Words to Outlaw If I Were President.'"

"That's just a stupid list." My voice is shaky, unconvincing. I miss my imaginary life. "I don't want to control everything. I just want people to be what they appear to be."

"But nobody is. Don't you get that?"

"I am."

"Ha!" he snorts. Both of these I mean literally: the "ha" and the snort. "You're the last person who should be making that claim."

Considering I'm wearing socks that don't match, was just caught watching the Olsen twins, used the word "woo" nine pages ago, and have spent the last week pretending to be dating a neighbor I've never even met, I realize it's not the most opportune moment for the "I am what I appear to be" defense. I forge ahead anyway, with an unoriginal: "What's that supposed to mean?"

"It means you're not a groupie! You're not some angst-filled . . . cappuccino-drinking . . . Gen X . . ." Andrew's so worked up, all he can manage are adjectives. He faces me and grips my shoulders. "That's not the real you, Eliza. Face it. The real you is nothing like what you pretend to be."

This is a blow, and Andrew knows it. I stare down at my hands, curled in my lap like something fetal. It's as if the light just changed in the apartment, giving everything a different cast. My thumb rings strike me as suddenly silly. The chipped black polish is immature, embarrassing. My fingernails, I notice, are chewed to the bone.

"I mean, the real you is better," Andrew says, more gently. "If anyone should know, it's me. I met you watching the *Brady Bunch*, remember? I'm the guy who debated with you about the merits of every cereal in the Kellogg's variety pack."

I have to smile a little at this, recalling how very wrong he was about Corn Pops.

"I think I know the real you by now, and it isn't this brooding rock-star chick." Andrew's grip on my shoulders relaxes, but his hands stay where they are. "I don't get why you won't just be yourself."

Even in my chocolate fog, I know these are the most beautiful, but impossible, words I've ever heard. The apartment starts

241

to smudge around the edges. My senses are drying up. All I can feel is the weight of Andrew's hands on my shoulders and all I can think is: here is a guy who is kind and smart and funny and knows me, the real me, the behind-the-scenes me, the artificial-cereals-and-corny-sitcoms-and-neurotic-mother-and-absent-father me, and likes me anyway.

As if watching a movie, I see my face leaning in toward Andrew's. I close my eyes. I hold my breath. I feel my chest collide with his arm, my forehead with the brim of his baseball cap. It is wrong. It is right. It is *When Harry Met Sally* without the bathrobe.

Through a haze, I hear: "Eliza."

But it is not a breathy, passionate "Eliza." It is a firm but caring "Eliza." And the haze isn't steamy or smoky, but sleep-deprived. Malnourished. Lonely.

I feel the pressure of Andrew's hands disappear. I open my eyes and glance around the room, furiously blinking. The world looks gray, fuzzy, kind of like it did in the moments before I fainted in the Blue Horn Mall Food Court, right in front of The Happy Corn Dog, after getting my ears pierced for the first time. I suck some air and wait for the room to resume its normal shapes and colors. Leroy—the one thing that's actually supposed to be gray and fuzzy—is planted in a lump at my feet, shaking his head at me in a remarkable impression of my mother.

"Are you okay?" Andrew is saying. "You're not going to pass out, are you?"

"No," I manage. It's true, I'm not. I am starting to register color again. I brush at my eyes, feeling ridiculous, as blood and logic rush back to my brain. "Sorry. For a second there, I thought you were a rock star or something."

I should have known it was too soon for humor. The joke lands limp and sad, like a dropped slice of bologna.

"Forget it," Andrew says. "I'm sorry I yelled."

"You were totally right, though."

"Still. I didn't have to yell."

"Either way," I say. "It's time for me to face the music."

I wait then, staring at my lap, wading in the tension of almost-having-kissed Andrew. What if I've ruined our friendship? What if Andrew feels embarrassed around me forever? What if honor compels him to tell Kimberley what I did and she bans him from speaking to me ever again?

Fortunately, Andrew is far too left-brained for any of that. Out of the corner of my eye, I see his dirty sneakers prop themselves on the coffeetable. "Face the music?" he says. The feet cross smugly at the ankle. "Well, that really all depends on which music. Black Sabbath? Oingo Boingo? Mr. Mister? Because if you ask me"—I can hear the grin appear on his face—"it's always time to face a little Mr. Mister."

In a feat of inept gratitude, I simultaneously burst into laughter and swipe a hand across my runny nose. And when I manage to look at my friend, full-face, Andrew is just Andrew again. Thank God. Andrew of the squeaky wind pants. Andrew of the L.L. Bean blond hair. Andrew of the knowing, and reassuringly platonic, smirk.

"I think it's time I dump Jacques and go back to work," I decide.

"No duh."

I pick up "Words to Reinstate" and blow my nose on it.

If my book were a TV movie, it would end with a scene that goes something like this:

a) Lou shows up at Dreams Come True, washed-up and balding, and as soon as I see him I realize my real father is nothing like the ideal father I've been comparing my boyfriends to for fifteen years;

b) I dial Lou from a highway pay phone, armed with nothing but a knapsack full of Tastykakes and loose change, only to find he is whiny and unfunny and nothing like the ideal father I've been comparing my boyfriends to for fifteen years;

c) Lou and I arrange to meet for breakfast in a highway diner (which, if this were one of my Movies That Smell, would have a tinge of bacon fat and burnt coffee) where he proceeds to drip ketchup on his chin and call the waitress "girlie" and I realize he is nothing like the ideal father I've been comparing my boyfriends to for fifteen years.

In the end, though, each of these scenarios feels like too much of a cop-out: father likes music + father leaves daughter = daughter spends entire young life searching for father-substitutes in the form of flawed rock stars. The equation is too easy.

After Andrew confiscates my remaining Crispy Chocolate Wafers and exits my apartment, I return gradually to the world of the living. Leroy. My dinner. Leroy's dinner. I pay bills and eat spaghetti and locate clothes for work in the morning. As I start working on the tower of dishes in the sink, I can hear Andrew's words hovering in the air around me, annoying and obvious, like fake snow settling over the inside of a cheesy plastic snow globe.

With a little food and distance, I can recognize that at least part of what he said didn't come as a total shock (though he did manage to misuse "ironic"). I know I am inflexible. Picky. Difficult to please. I'd always traced it to Nanny, called it "selective," and considered it one of my better traits. Still, Andrew's words rattled me. Andrew Callahan is the one person in my life who never yells, never psychoanalyzes, never nitpicks. For seven years, our friendship has been based largely on the assumption that we are always, always kidding. The fact that he, of all people, would see me as rigid and unrealistic—and go so far as to tell me so—makes me think I might be worse off than I thought.

Maybe he's right: my pickiness isn't just picky, it's hypocritical. I say I want rock stars for their unpredictability, but really, I want the kind of unpredictability I can count on. I want the impulsive lyrics, the ripped jeans, the deep talk, the scribbled songs on greasy napkins in highway diners at 4:00 A.M. What I don't want is the unpredictability I usually wind up with—*true* unpredictability, the kind that wears polyester uniforms or stars in community productions of *Oklahoma!* I want the rock star I wrote letters to when I was ten years old, whose face plastered my bedroom walls and watched me while I slept. Who let me love him '80s style: purely, unabashedly, without holding back.

By the time I finish scrubbing the final dish, it's almost nine o'clock. A VH1 *Behind the Music* is probably starting, but I am too caught up in my own world to wallow in Sting's or Gloria Estefan's. I make my way to my laptop, buried under stacks of magazines and coupon flyers, flip it open and, for the first time in two weeks, turn it on.

The screen comes to life warily, as if unsure whether or not to trust me again. On the fuzzy menu, I click the file titled "Book?" and there they are: one hundred two pages of me and rock stars, laid bare in twelve-point Times. I start at the beginning and proceed to scroll through the last fifteen plus years of my life, reliving each familiar sequence: a) see band, b) kiss, c) connect, d) find flaw, and e) release.

This time, the story feels different. Instead of honing in on the rock stars, I focus on the narrator. I watch her as if she were a stranger, a person I've seen reading on a ratty couch in The Blue Room or riding on the train. In public, she is aloof, brooding, dressed in black, wearing her silver pierces like a coat of hypoallergenic armor. But in private, she is someone else completely. A worrier, an envier, a burger-eater and TV-watcher, a skeptic, a control freak, a sap, a secret lover of Foreigner's "Survivor's."

"That's not the real you, Eliza," I can hear Andrew saying. "Face it: the real you is nothing like what you pretend to be."

He's right. Not once have I let my true self show to any of my nonrock-star boyfriends. The way I see it, if I had—and had been dating myself—I would have dumped me a million times over for a) talking out loud to my cat, b) not showering for over two days, c) once wearing a T-shirt emblazoned with Jack Wagner's face, and d) on and on and on. Though the rock stars might be the ones up on the makeshift stage, it's always been me performing.

Concerns About the Book (Revised):
  a) the more serious the story, the harder it is to be funny
  b) the "performing" metaphors could start to get corny
  c) the point is starting to reflect worse on the narrator than the rock stars
  d) the point is more personal than expected
  e) pretty soon, the book will need an ending.

10

mothers

By the time I hit twenty-six, I was facing the fact that my dating life wasn't working. While all the people I loved were fearlessly growing up—my sister getting pregnant, Hannah getting engaged, Andrew whispering "I love you, too" in the dark on a cell phone—I was facing the rest of my life alone. I was beginning to envision my grown-up dinner parties: Hannah and Alan analyzing each other, Andrew and Kimberley cross-examining each other. Me, somewhere in the middle, serving tuna casserole.

I had spent the last few weeks reassessing my dating strategy. In a panic, I'd agreed to go out with a securities analyst named Donny, convinced it would be the launching pad for the stabil-

248

ity and normalcy and financial/emotional security any woman my age would—should—want. All it got me was two weeks of hibernation, a relentless sugar headache, and an inferiority complex about my butt.

But now, after two weeks in my apartment, I felt invigorated. Refocused. I was ready to face the world again: heat, smog, the commuter rail, the mountain of catch-up work I knew awaited me at Dreams Come True, the battalion of Travel Agents who would want to hear every detail of my date with Donny, and Beryl the cheerful receptionist/grandmother of the Donster. Most importantly, I was determined to find an ending for my book.

The original concept was this: the book would be a guide to dating rock stars. It would be part fiction, part nonfiction. It would be part humor, part personal health. It would qualify as sociology, how-to, reference, and the performing arts. Each chapter would focus on a different kind of musician—an ambassador from the instrumental genre, if you will—and what to expect (and not expect) if you date them.

Unfortunately, I hadn't planned the ending. In my mind, the chapters had cycled along beautifully, musically, vocalists and saxophonists and electric guitarists crescendoing to a fever pitch. Maybe they would eventually form a band. At the very least, I'd figured some final words would come to me somehow, sometime—preferably in a burst of passion on a bar napkin, or scribbled on a sweaty palm—some gem of advice for readers to carry with them into the world of black-lit coffee bars and goatees and communes. Or, better yet, the act of writing the book would reward me with a real-life finale that I could conveniently transcribe.

The ideal scenario (and let's be honest, the one with the most mass-market appeal) would be: NARRATOR MEETS HER IDEAL ROCK STAR and they FALL IN LOVE and LIVE HAPPILY EVER AFTER, symbolically juxtaposed with NARRATOR'S SISTER GIVES BIRTH.

This was all totally unlikely. Not only was my sister's baby not due for another six months, there were only two males in my life at this point: The Piano Man and Andrew. I had never met The Piano Man, yet had already lied about dating The Piano Man which, in terms of endings, made him both humiliating and contrived. And Andrew (most likely the popular favorite all along) I'd recently, firmly established for the second time in my life was just my friend and not my "friend."

Besides, I didn't want an ending that was predictable. It would be easy to fictionalize Z Tedesco showing up at The Blue Room with a regular drum gig and minty fresh breath, or Jordan Prince resurfacing with perfect fashion sense and tamed eyebrows. The entire book—and, by some unsettling implication, my entire life—had been predictable. Predictability, as it turned out, was one of its unifying themes. On Monday morning, as I headed back to work, I was determined to find an ending that would "light my fire," "turn on my heart light," and generally rock my world.

But first, the familiar: breakfast with Hannah. It had been two weeks since I'd seen her, the night she and Alan told me they were getting engaged and I'd responded by downing two carafes of wine and a meatless hot dog. Since then, she'd left several nervous messages on my answering machine. When I finally called her back, last night, she said: "Oh, thank God! I was so worried!"

I'd had a guilty headache, like a peanut lodged between my eyes, ever since.

The place we met, Bagelmania, was a compromise: a cross between franchised pancakes and chamomile tea, at a spot halfway between Dreams and Penn. Bagelmania was no different from any other bagel joint except that everything was bagel shaped: windows, light fixtures, floor tiles. Even the tables had charmingly inconvenient holes in the middles. I bought my coffee and cream-cheesed poppy and found Hannah sitting by a window, picking at a green bagel and nursing a cup of tea. Only she would manage to find a bagel made of vegetables.

"Hey," I said, collapsing into a chair.

"Hi," she answered evenly.

Something was wrong. Instead of the anticipated Hannah-esque flood of warmth and relief and affection, she was a knot. Her eyes were fixed on a paper cup of pale tea. Her hair was stuffed under a straw hat, and her freckled hands were folded so tightly they had turned pink at the fingertips. Her engagement ring was perched in the middle of her clenched hands, like a third person sitting at the table between us.

"How are you?" I attempted, operating on the theory that if you ignore problems they just disappear.

"Fine."

"Oh." I racked my brain for more words. "Good."

This was physically painful. Conversations with Hannah weren't supposed to feel this way. They were easy, unpressured. They were one of the few things in my life that didn't require effort and forethought. Apparently she was angrier than I'd thought about the phone calls.

"Look," I said. "I'm really sorry I didn't call you back sooner. I meant to. I just didn't get a chance."

"It's okay," she said, without looking up.

Obviously I never should have left my apartment. There was no tension there, no awkward silences. There were no emotions at all really, just a dull sugar haze punctuated by sappy, happy, sitcom endings. I occupied the silence between us by stuffing my face with cream cheese and eavesdropping on the table/bagel next to us, where two teenage girls were gossiping about tampons, blow jobs, and their respective boyfriends, Joey and Jason. Apparently, Joey was a sloppy kisser. Jason kissed well, but liked to use the term "boobies."

"So," I said, groping for the most gossipy topic I could think of. "I survived my date. With the businessman."

"Oh?" Hannah said to her tea. "How was it?"

I had already prepared my three prerequisite sarcastic answers: "One, he talked a lot of business jargon. Two, he practically had sex with our waitress on the table." When Hannah didn't look up, didn't even flinch, I sobered. "Three, it was nothing like I expected it would be."

Hannah finally raised her head, and when she did I noticed how tired she looked. Her eyes were dry, as if worn out from crying. "What had you expected?"

Having met Donny the Securities Analyst, it was humiliating to recall everything I'd hoped he would one day become. A husband. A father. A lawn mower and barbecuer. The kind of man who called going to bed "saying na-nights." But I sensed Hannah was looking for something more than this.

"I guess I thought dating him would change things somehow," I admitted. "Put an end to this whole rock star thing."

"Did it?"

"I don't know. So far all it did was make me sort of, shut down."

Hannah's forehead wrinkled into a scattering of little lines. "What do you mean?"

"I mean that this, here, today"—I waved a hand at Bagelmania at large —"is the first time I've left my apartment in about two weeks."

At once, Hannah's tension seemed to give. She unclasped her hands, reaching across the table for one of mine. "Two weeks?" she whispered. "What were you doing alone in your apartment for two weeks?"

"You know, eating Cocoa Puffs. Watching *Dawson's Creek*," I rattled off, then paused. Sometimes being sarcastic could be more tiring than being real. "I had some things I needed to work out, I guess."

"Why didn't you call me? I would have come over."

"I know. I don't know." I shrugged into my coffee. "I guess I needed to take some time. For myself." In retrospect, my hibernation was sounding a hell of a lot healthier than it actually had been. "I had some projects to take care of."

"What projects?"

I repeat: I never should have left my apartment. I hadn't intended to tell Hannah about my book, at least not until it was finished, and now I was trapped. I knew, of course, that I could quickly invent some other project if I had to. As a kid, I was queen of the short-lived but well-potentialed creative project. A Shrinky Dink gallery. The rock star membership cards. An interpretive piece with Loom Loopers.

But this moment seemed to call for honesty. "I've kind of been writing a book."

Hannah sat back abruptly. Like an afterthought, she snatched her hand back with her. "What kind of book?"

"It's sort of a . . . I don't know how to describe it. Sort of a rock-star exposé. A dating retrospective kind of a thing."

At that, Hannah's eyes instantly filled with tears, as if they had been lurking just below the surface looking for a window of opportunity. It wasn't the most positive first review I could have hoped for: mention book, evoke weeping.

"Not exactly a vote of confidence," I informed her.

"Oh, Eliza, it's not that." She grabbed at a pink Bagelmania napkin, dabbed at her eyes, and gave her nose a messy blow. At the next table, Joey's Girl and Jason's Girl (but sadly, no "Jessie's Girl") turned to watch us, as unapologetic as if we were an afternoon soap. "It's wonderful for you," Hannah said. "Really."

It seemed rhetorical, but I went for it anyway: "Then why are you crying, exactly?"

"I just feel *sad,*" Hannah said with unusual vehemence. Joey's Girl gave Jason's Girl a "this is getting good" poke in the arm. "I feel sad that we haven't spoken in two weeks. I feel sad that you didn't call me when you needed someone. And I feel sad that you've been writing this, this rock-star exposé"—she waved her hands in a pink paper flourish, sending her napkin fluttering off the table to land on the toe of Jason's Girl's red Skecher—"that I didn't know anything about."

"Well, you shouldn't." I spoke carefully. Rarely was I in the position of consoling Hannah, and the times I had been, it wasn't about our friendship. It was about the rest of the world: a documentary she'd seen about the desecration of the rainforest, or roadkill she'd looked in the face ("he was smiling right at me!" she wailed). Personal problems she usually seemed able to process somewhere deep inside her, in a mystical, enviable network of Enya and gingko. "I mean, you shouldn't feel bad. I didn't tell anyone. It wasn't just you."

This wasn't exactly true; I had told Donny the Securities Analyst (but only to impress him) and Karl the Bass Guitarist (only to get out of spending time with him). I hadn't told anyone important.

"Not even Andrew," I added, which was true, and seemed to calm her down a little. Sniffling, she fished a tissue out of her tapestry bag. "I just didn't want any outside opinions, you know?"

This proved to be my fatal mistake. Hannah's splotchy, pink face sprung tears again. "Oh God," she said, chomping down on her lower lip. "You think I psychoanalyze you."

"No. I don't. I didn't say that."

"You didn't tell me about your book because you didn't want me interfering. You think I give you too much advice."

"I *want* your advice. I'm the one who asks for it, remember?"

"You don't have to say that." She tossed her head back and forth, so some hair escaped the straw hat and frizzed around her face. "You don't have to confide in me about anything unless you want to. Of course not. I'm being unreasonable." She drew a snuffled breath. "This isn't about you. And it isn't about your book."

"Then what's it about?"

Hannah looked at me plainly. "Me."

Oddly enough, this possibility hadn't even occurred to me. For so many years, we'd been Hannah the Capable and Eliza the Mess that to think of Hannah as the one with the problem seemed inherently wrong.

Hannah dabbed at her nose with her tissue, then put the crumpled wad next to her plate. "It's just that lately, I've been feeling like we're not as close as we used to be."

Now it was my turn to feel alarmed. "What are you talking about?"

"Well, we'll go days without talking to each other. We never used to do that. I've been planning my wedding, and you haven't been a part of it. Not just the food and the dresses, but . . . you don't even know how Alan proposed. Or how I'm even *feeling* about getting married." Her lips began to quiver. "And now I find out you've been going through this trauma, and writing a book . . ." "Trauma" seemed extreme, but I skipped it. Hannah's hands fluttered helplessly and landed in her lap. "I just miss you."

I ducked behind my bagel. This kind of naked emotion

made me squirm in any setting, but especially in a crowded Bagelmania in Center City. I shot Jason's Girl and Joey's Girl what I hoped was my piercing, don't-mess-with-me look.

"But you have Alan," I reminded Hannah, an attempt to keep us above ground.

"I know. And I love Alan. But it's not the same as having a female friend."

This distinction might sound obvious, but it came as news to me. From what I'd observed so far of Alan Pinkerton, it appeared he could serve every possible function. Boyfriend. Therapist. Personal chef. Even female friend, if called upon. Apparently there were things I did not know, and probably should have.

"Can I admit something?" Hannah said.

I nodded.

"Sometimes I feel, really, I don't know. Confused." She laughed, a kind of startled hiccup, as if amused she'd admitted this out loud.

"About marrying Alan?"

She shook her head. "It's not Alan. When I think about being with Alan for the rest of my life, I feel lucky. Like I've been given this, this incredible gift." She tucked her loose hair behind her ears. "But then other times, I feel like I'm giving something up. Know what I mean?"

I had no idea. "Giving what up? Getting hit on in bars? Getting called 'momma'? Finding out the guy you thought was hot wears headgear? It ain't all it's cracked up to be, sister."

Hannah shook her head, more vehemently. A few curls

popped loose from behind her ears. "It's not about meeting other men. I couldn't care less about other men. It's like I'm giving up some part of *me.*"

Suddenly I felt young, much younger than Hannah, as if we were discussing some cryptic adult subject—taxes, mortgages, whiskey sours—I couldn't hope to understand. "I don't get it."

"I mean . . ." She started fingering the tassel of her tea bag. "For instance. You know how important it's always been for me to work with people, and volunteer, and things like that? Well, I think about things like that now, and I know I can still do them, but they just don't feel as . . . *necessary.*" She paused. "Alan is the center of my world now, and I want that. It's just that sometimes it feels like the rest of my world can get along fine without me."

She looked down, as if consulting her tea for explanation. I took a nervous swallow of coffee. I knew what I needed to tell my friend, and knew that I meant it, as corny and sitcom-written as it would sound. "If it helps, I still need you."

Hannah's gaze shifted from her tea to me. I tensed, hoping she wouldn't cry again. Instead, all I got was a mildly curious: "Why?"

It wasn't exactly the response you're looking for after one of the more sincere and vulnerable moments of your life. Such moments shouldn't require supporting examples.

"Why?" I repeated, a touch defensive. "I don't know, let's see. Because you introduced me to meatless hot dogs. You meet me in Denny's in the middle of the night. You explain why I dump rock stars all over the tristate area." But Hannah looked so intent, so invested in my every word, that I let the humor go. "Actually, I could use your help right now. With an ending. For my book."

It was as if I'd invited her on a mission to space: Hannah began composing herself with total seriousness. She breathed a series of inhales and exhales, each approximately one whole minute. She closed her eyes, a visualization technique I'd seen her try before when looking for her car keys or consoling her spleen. Then she nodded. "Okay. Tell me the story."

Problem was, Hannah was bound to notice the "story" almost exactly resembled the last fifteen years of my life. Not only would she recognize me, but a) herself, b) her family, and c) an unfortunate mention of her going to third base with Eric Sommes. "Just so you know, some of this might sound a little familiar."

"Am I in it?" From the eagerness in her voice, it sounded like this might actually be a good thing.

"Well, kind of. But not just you. Those Saturday night dinners on your sunporch. Your dad's record albums. Your mom. Your brothers. The Official Rock Star Fan Club." The more I confessed, the more I wondered how and when I should be contacting a lawyer. "Boomer," I mumbled.

"Eric Sommes?" she squealed. Honest to God, a squeal: loud, painful, pitched nearly out of human range. I flashed a smug look at Joey's Girl and Jason's Girl; we could still give them a run for their money.

"God, I haven't thought of him in years!" Hannah gnawed on a renegade curl. "He was so sweet."

"He was obsessed with you."

"He was just devoted."

"Anyway. As I was saying." I was eager to change the subject. God knows Eric Sommes had already taken up far more than his rightful share of my book. "The way the book goes, the narrator dates all these different musicians." Hannah closed her eyes again, a smile playing on her lips. "A drummer. A singer. A sax player. You get the picture."

She nodded. The picture wasn't hard to get, for obvious reasons.

"But none of them could steal her heart," I went on, deepening my voice like a movie trailer. "The question is: will she find true love? Will she and Jack Wagner live happily ever after? Or is she doomed to a life of pickiness and loneliness forever?" At this point, I had the J Girls enraptured; they were practically ready to buy the hardback. "Basically," I concluded, "she's waiting for something big to happen."

"Okay. Tell me where she is. Describe the scene."

I glanced around, trying not to look conspicuous. "Well, for starters, there's coffee. One lone cup of herbal tea. Mass-produced bagels. Pink windows. Two nosy teenage girls. A woman who might have been our Home Ec teacher from York. You know, the one with the lisp?"

"Eliza," Hannah interrupted. "Are we living in your ending?"

"Maybe. If it's good enough."

It was supposed to be funny, but Hannah wasn't taking her assignment lightly. Meanwhile, Jason's Girl and Joey's Girl, freaked out by the postmodern turn this little show had taken, exchanged a panicky "this never happens on *Felicity*" look, gathered up their tiny, strappy backpacks and tottered off on their foot-high sandals. For several minutes, Hannah kept her eyes closed. I imagined her conjuring up offbeat scenarios in which the narrator a) renounces meat or b) embraces her inner goddess or c) both.

When she opened them, I was expecting the worst. "Do you want my opinion?"

I nodded. "Yes."

"I think you should just let the ending happen."

Of course. Naturally, this would be Hannah's solution: the just-add-herbs school of writing. Naturally this would be what happened if you let your special, secret project loose in a crowded Bagelmania in downtown Philadelphia: it came back to you chewed up, unrecognizable.

"You can't just let it *happen*," I told her. "It's not like the ending is going to write itself."

"I know," Hannah said, calmly. "I'm just saying, maybe you shouldn't look for it so hard."

In theory, Hannah's advice sounded good. In practice, though, I was fairly sure no good ending was going to present itself unless I stepped in to coerce it, bribe it, or smother it in adjectives. On my six-block walk to Dreams Come True, I kept my eyes peeled for symbols, metaphors, or attractively angst-filled men carrying rusted harmonicas or scarred guitar cases. The only potentially interesting thing I saw was a homeless man waving a Mexican flag and yelling "Free Hawaii!"

The minute I arrived at Dreams, any progress on my book was put on temporary hold. In the space of five minutes, I was bombarded with a) Beryl the receptionist, wanting to know all about my date with her grandson, b) the Travel Agents, wanting to know all about my date with Beryl's grandson, and c) the avalanche of bikini-clad brochures smirking on my desktop.

"It was nice," I answered Beryl. I racked my brain for words that were vague, noncommittal, words that could apply to anything from a good night kiss to a bruschetta appetizer. *"Really nice."* Damn Donny for not debriefing his grandmother himself. "He had nice . . . hair."

It was weak, but seemed to work. Beryl's face burst into smiles, cheeks inflating like twin nectarines. "He does have nice hair, doesn't he? So healthy and thick."

"Yes. Thick," I intoned, feeling ill, and headed for my desk. "See you later, Beryl."

"Happy Monday!" she replied, reaching for her pin of the day: a plastic frog with a string dangling between its webbed feet. *"R-r-r-ribit!"* the pin croaked when she pulled the string. *"Have a toad-ally great day!"*

As I neared my workstation, I realized the Donny interrogation was only just beginning. Travel Agents were hovering around my cluttered desk like an army of anxious bees. They were soundlessly sipping their Diet Cokes, tapping their high heels, drumming their French-manicured pinky fingers on their aluminum cans. After my two-week post-date absence, the Agents had to know the verdict would be extreme: either very good or very, very bad.

"Happy Monday," I offered, waving a casual hello.

In an unprecedented move, the Agents skipped the pleasantries. No one waved. No one spoke. No one "Happy" anythinged. Some couldn't even look me in the eye. Then, from somewhere in the depths of the crowd, a lone voice commanded: "Eliza!"

With something like reverence—or was it terror?—the sea of Agents parted, and I found myself face-to-face with none other than the Queen Mother herself. As she stepped forward, it dawned on me that I just might be in major trouble for cutting work for two weeks. Maybe QM was going to fire me, make a public example of me to send a warning to the rest of the staff. She took a menacing step toward my desk, her face tight-lipped and tanned to almost black.

"So," she said, leaning forward and gouging her fuchsia fingertips into my desktop planner. I felt my heartbeat leap into my ears. QM looked me up and down, searching my face with her hawklike eyes, which were caked in purplish-black mascara and narrowed to the width of pennies. "Don't keep us in suspense, honey," she rasped. "How was the date?"

Apparently, even in the dog-eat-dog world of the upscale travel business, two weeks of unwritten ad copy pales in comparison to a date with a Securities Analyst. Surveying the rapt crowd, I knew I had to be honest. These women had invested a lot in the predate planning effort; they deserved the truth. I sat down heavily, glancing over my shoulder to make sure Beryl was out of earshot, then addressed the group.

"Everyone, I am sorry to have to tell you this," I sighed.

"The date with Donny the Securities Analyst was a disaster. It sucked."

On second thought, maybe there is such a thing as too much honesty. The Agents and QM looked so chagrined that the date went badly and/or offended by the word "sucked" that I spent the next several minutes madly stammering in an effort to justify myself. I catalogued all the inexcusable things Donny had done, i.e., admitting he was cheap, staring at other women's butts. (I conveniently managed to omit all of my own faux pas, i.e., shouting in the restaurant, ordering mozzarella, accidentally implying Donny couldn't read.)

When I had assured them all I'd given the date a fair shot— yes, I *did* wear a bra; no, I did *not* drag him to a rave—they began returning to their respective workstations, dejected but sympathetic. One or two Agents rattled off some vital stats about the few unmarried men they were still aware of—an electrician in Yardley, a third cousin somewhere in the Pacific Northwest—and QM offered a terse "Practice makes perfect," which had no apparent relevance at all.

Once they had all drifted off, I tried my best to refocus. (By that I mean, of course, refocus on the work of finishing my book, while pretending to refocus on "Skiing Stowaways!") I cleared an islet on my desktop and turned on my computer. I had just begun sifting through the tornado of brochures, wondering if any might provide a good setting for my final chapter, when Beryl sang out: "Eliza! You have a call on line two!"

Understand: I never get phone calls in the office. I happen to prefer it that way. It is part of the reason I write for a living;

to remain behind the scenes, cynical and left to my own devices. "Did they say who it was?"

"Just a minute!" Beryl said, then called back: "It's your mother!"

My instincts, in order of appearance: a) Beryl had begun losing her mind during my two-week absence, b) Donny and his grandmother had orchestrated a bitter, unfunny practical joke at my expense, or c) the caller was actually Andrew, doing his impression of my mother. The last one was most likely.

"Got it," I said, dug out my phone, and pushed the blinking button. I was ready to play hardball with a half-decent impression I'd worked up of Andrew's Uncle Ned. "Hello?"

"Hello? Eliza?"

It wasn't Andrew. It actually was my mother.

"Mom?"

"I'm sorry to bother you at work, but it's kind of important, honey. There's something I need to talk to you about."

Correction: this was *not* my mother. This woman was an imposter, and not a good one. She spoke too calmly, she called me "honey," and she hadn't yet made me feel guilty or unmarried at all.

"What is it? Is something wrong?"

"No, no, nothing's wrong. But I'd rather talk in person." I heard her draw in a long breath, then exhale it. (Since when did my mother exhale? Ever?) "Can you come over for dinner?"

"When?"

"Tonight."

"Why? Is Camilla coming?"

"No."

"What about Harv?"

"He's working late. It'll be just the two of us."

Was the woman nuts? I think the last time we'd done anything "just the two of us," I was fifteen and she was taking me to Dr. Greenblatt's for a tetanus shot.

"I'm in the city now," Mom said, "but I should be home by four—"

This was the final straw. My mother never came into the city. Downtown Philly made her anxious. The crowds. The noise. The public bathrooms. The sausage-and-egg sandwiches sold on street corners. Whenever she and Harv stopped by my apartment—because they "happened to be in the neighborhood"—she brought her own hand sanitizer and checked that all my doors and windows were tightly locked.

"I could have dinner ready by six," Mom was saying. "Can you come right after work?"

On the inside, I was coming up with all kinds of clever, witty excuses, but somehow "Yeah, I guess" tripped out of my mouth. "Six," I repeated, and before Mom could shock me with something else, dropped the phone back in its cradle.

The red light on line two went dark. For minutes, I stared at the silent phone pad, willing it to get up and explain itself. When I felt Maggie looking at me, I forced my gaze to the computer. I mustered the illusion of doing work by repeatedly, neurotically tapping the letter "a" while running through every possible explanation for my mother's invitation:

a) she was getting divorced (not likely)

b) she was having an affair (less likely)

c) she was having a baby (gross me out)

d) she was disowning me once and for all and wanted to be on her own turf, eating homemade meat in meat sauce, while she did it.

Although "d" had a certain charm, none of them seemed right. For the next two hours, I worried my way through a blur of ski resort jargon (i.e., "cozy," "exhilarating," and the unfortunately necessary "winter wonderland") but by noon, had no better idea what my mother was planning. All I had was a more palpable feeling of dread.

As I was tapping "h" and considering cake, I felt a hand drop on my left shoulder. "Are you okay?" Maggie asked.

"Me?" I stopped tapping. "Fine. Why?"

"We heard you got a phone call before."

So I wasn't the only one shocked when I got phone calls. "It wasn't Donny, if that's what you're wondering."

"That's not what we're wondering."

At the "we," my glance skittered around the office. "Oh."

"Everything okay?" she asked again.

"Everything's fine."

Maggie just kept standing there until I heard a familiar pop and fizz behind my left ear. I saw a pink-nailed hand reach across my screen and set a can of Diet Coke on my mouse pad. "You look like you could use one," Maggie said.

*　　*　　*

I managed to find an empty seat on the 5:24 Glendale Local. This in itself was no small feat. Even more impressive was the fact that I looked scary enough to prevent anyone from sitting beside me. Under normal circumstances, this would have given me immense satisfaction. I'd logged hours of public transportation perfecting my "don't even think about it" look when strangers hesitated near me in the aisle. But today, strangers were wise to stay out of my way. I felt increasingly unstable as the train hurtled toward my mother and my meaty dinner and the news I'd finally deduced must be waiting for me when I got there:

Lou was back.

This theory was unconfirmed, of course, but it would explain everything. It would explain why Mom had been in the city (obviously Lou wouldn't come to the suburbs, but would meet her in a swank jazz club or trendy coffee bar). It would explain why she sounded so calm on the phone (shock, thinly disguised as serenity). It would explain why she called me "honey" (to delude Lou into thinking we had a healthy relationship and she'd done a good job parenting on her own for the last fifteen years).

I gnawed my cuticles off one by one as the train barreled on toward Glendale, seeming much faster and more single-minded than ever before. Outside the window, the city became less gritty and more charming the farther we got from downtown. Buildings shortened, streets widened. Trees sprang from the asphalt. At the train stations, brick walls smothered with bleeding spray paint gradually morphed into cute little coffee shops with names like "The Choo Choo Café."

"Glendale next," the conductor announced, poking his head inside our car. "Glendale, next and final stop," he added, which sounded ominous and probably symbolic of something I couldn't afford to contemplate.

The other remaining passengers started standing and crowding into the aisle, fishing in their briefcases and leather shoulder bags. Most of them were classic urban professionals: the kind of men who read the business section on elevators, the kind of women who wore Keds with skirts in the '80s.

"Tyler! It's Mommy!" one woman yelled into a cell phone the width of a slice of cheese. Usually, I had a mental field day with people like her; invariably they talked much too loudly, spoke about nothing that couldn't wait five minutes, and had at least one child named Tyler. "Did the maid come? Did Daddy call? I'll be there soon, sweetie. Take the manicotti out of the freezer. Then sit still and watch TV."

As she hung up, preparing to go home to her husband and her Tyler and her manicotti, something leaped in my chest: maybe Lou was waiting at my mother's. It hadn't occurred to me before, but wasn't out of the question. Maybe that's why Harv had to "work late." (Come to think of it, had Harv ever had to work late before?) Maybe Lou was asking us to forgive him and let him back into our lives. Maybe he wanted to make amends for ditching us for a life of chaise longues and suntanned women and delinquent cats. Maybe life wasn't so different from a TV movie after all.

The train lurched to a sickening stop, making everyone jostle and stick out a foot for support. When the metal door slammed open—"Glendale," the conductor intoned—we started single-filing out like a fire drill on a school bus. My legs felt watery as I stepped into the muggy August evening. The air was like a locker room: damp, warm, too close. As the business-people headed for their respective SUVs, the parking lot a chorus of bleeps, chirps, and spastic, flashing headlights, I commenced the three-block walk to 118 Greenlaw Avenue.

The neighborhood was strangely empty. It had the fixed quality of a movie set, everything bright and still, as if caught in time. As I walked, I had the eerie sensation of my life in the present unraveling, peeling back, giving rise to the echoes of other ages and other walks. It was like my own home movie, in reverse. First: summer. I am seventeen, earrings grazing the tops of my shoulders, hair gelled flat to my skull. I'm dressed in some senseless combination of long underwear and men's boxer shorts, clinging damply to the hand of Jordan Prince as he drones on about the " 'phone" and the "timpani dudes," his blond eyebrows popping up every few seconds over the tops of his *Top Gun*-style shades.

Then it's fall. I am fifteen, angry, and entitled, pounding these same sidewalks with Z Tedesco as we choke down Marlboro Reds. We sigh and spit and vent bitterly about our home lives, Z's forehead swathed in an Axl-esque bandanna that droops down his back like a human tail. He is railing against his overbearing mother and father while I half pay attention, thinking of my own mother camped frozen in front of *Fantasy Island* and my father drifting vaguely around the West Coast, and nodding at Z, blood galloping through my veins, skin thickening by the minute.

Or I am ten. Heading home from school with my brand-new best friend Hannah. Our lunchboxes (hers Strawberry Shortcake, mine Miss Piggy on a Harley) bang against our knees, backpacks droop around our waists, sneakers sag under the collective weight of a year's worth of friendship pins. "So what's going on with your mom and dad?" Hannah asks me, kindly, as I tag along behind her, sugar-dazed and dry-mouthed from sucking Fun Dips. I always manage to avoid her questions somehow, hiding behind a mounting repertoire of razor-sharp impressions and sarcastic knock-knock jokes.

Now, as I reached Greenlaw, my pace slowed instinctively. I had the urge to hook a sharp left and hightail it to the Devines's house, where Hannah's parents were probably still curled up on the porch grooving to Bob and Carly and drinking chai. Instead, I took Greenlaw's sidewalk square by square, careful not to step on the cracks. It was the way I'd walked as a kid. Even then, my mother had the uncanny ability to fill me with extreme anxiety; in that particular instance, over the possibility of losing my step and inadvertently breaking her back.

By the time I reached the bluebird-topped mailbox, I was practically on tiptoe. I scanned the yard. So far, everything was par for the course. The lawn was mowed, the bushes pruned, the flowers arranged in orderly rows, like tiny pink teeth. I climbed the porch steps and hesitated. For at least a minute I stared at the brass knocker, inscribed with a looping *M*, wondering for the first time in my life if I should knock first. I decided against it; best not to give up any shred of control I had left.

"Hello?" I called, pushing the door open.

No answer. No sign of Lou either, and no evidence of anything out of the ordinary. The living room was characteristically neurotic. End tables glossy with lemon-scented polish. Magazines arranged in a scallop, waiting-room style. The family photos were all evenly spaced on the mantel; in my mother's universe, each frame being of equal size and prominence meant everyone in them was equally loved.

"Eliza?" Mom's voice floated in from the kitchen. It was definitely unsteady. "Is that you?"

"Me," I think I said.

I waded across what seemed like miles of thick, sea-green carpet zigzagged with fresh vacuum tracks. I could hear voices coming from the kitchen, multiple voices, a cacophony of voices. My mother was not alone. Already I could see the moment that would change my life forever: my father at the kitchen table with a grizzled gray beard, a web of wrinkles around his eyes, a coffee mug in his hand, and a look on his face that was worn and tired and so sorry.

When I stepped into the kitchen, the scene I found was so ordinary it was hilarious. My mother was alone. Not only that, she was hollowing a cantaloupe. She was wearing slippers and a nubbly pink bathrobe, her face was slathered in what appeared to be sour cream, UB40's "Red Red Wine" (a.k.a. the cacophony) was pseudorapping on the stovetop radio and the kitchen table was not just empty, but aggressively empty, blank except for a salt shaker and two rubber placemats shaped like watermelons.

I don't know what surprised me more: the fact that Lou wasn't waiting for me, or the way my heart hurt to admit it.

"What is it?" Mom asked. She had turned away from the counter, hands oozing cantaloupe guts. How my father would have despised this picture: a melon baller, wrinkle concealer, a processed tune from the late '80s. It screamed so much suburbia. "You look like you just saw a ghost."

I felt a surge of anger at her. For seeing through the look on my face. For introducing the terribly perfect word "ghost" into this moment. For letting me get my hopes so far up by inviting me to dinner in the first place.

"Maybe it was just your face," I snapped.

As soon as I said it, I felt badly. I just couldn't stop myself. In this house I was sixteen again. I was fourteen. Thirteen. Eight. I was piercing my ears and locking myself in my room and blasting Twisted Sister's "We're Not Gonna Take It" and inscribing my name on every pure, unmarked surface I could find—foggy bathroom mirrors, the smooth tops of new I Can't Believe It's Not Butter!s—just to make her mad. I was angry that Lou wasn't there to see me, angry at myself for believing he would be. And, somehow, it seemed natural to hold my mother responsible for all of it.

I did feel bad about snapping at her, though. I prepared for Mom to fire back—this is what she and I did best, after all—but she just gestured mildly to the stove and said: "Keep an eye on the casserole, will you?"

If she'd retorted, I could have felt less guilty. I could have volleyed back with, "What kind of casserole? Moose?" and the evening's sparring would have been underway. Instead I said, "What kind?"

"Tuna," my mother replied, and left the room.

It might seem odd that a life-changing moment could hinge on a tuna fish casserole. By all accounts, the gesture should be something grand, something sentimental, something along the lines of reuniting on a ship deck or singing gaily while wearing plaid and hiking the Alps. But the fact that my mother had made this dinner, my dinner, the same bland, boring, beige dinner I'd been torturing her with for three years of Sunday dinners, was comparable to another mother forking over a kidney or a family heirloom.

I cracked open the oven, peered through the blast of heat. Sure enough, a tuna casserole was browning nicely at the edges. Shutting the door gently, I peeked into the saucepan, gave some peas an apologetic stir, then scooped up the empty melon rinds and dumped them in the trash can. When Mom returned, she was wearing jeans and a pale blue sweatshirt that said HELLO FROM ORLANDO! Her face was scrubbed pink.

"I think it might be ready," I chirped.

Mom said nothing. She stuffed her hands into a pair of oven mitts thick and shiny as boxing gloves and slid the casserole onto the stove to cool. Then she busied herself at the counter: checking pots, pouring drinks, slicing the cantaloupe into tidy half-moons.

"Can I help or something?"

"I've got it," Mom said. "Why don't you just go relax."

Relaxing was the last thing I was capable of, but I grabbed

the opportunity to slink away and hide. In the dining room, I perched in a high-backed wooden chair, grateful to be alone. I soon realized, though, that without the rest of the Sunday dinner crew the dining room was immense. The ceiling was too high, the windows too small, the table about eight miles too long. Two places were set directly across from each other, face-off style.

I started to panic. How would we ever make it through this dinner? How would we fill so much space with so little to say? Suddenly I longed for Camilla modeling her napkin animals (they really were clever, if you thought about it) or Scott telling his fraternity stories (that crazy whippersnapper!) or thick, kind, hairy Harv sitting at the head of the table—he wouldn't even have to speak—just sharing the burden of all this empty air.

Mom came in with the casserole in her mitted hands, saying, "You can bring in the salad if you wa—" as I went leaping from my chair. We managed to stir up a brief commotion involving creamed corn—even shared a tense joke about salad versus dessert forks, heh heh—but inside of three minutes, we were seated. Silent. Served. The cantaloupe grinned up at us, smirking orange mouths.

Usually, this was the part when everybody started complimenting everything. Camilla would be gushing, Scott kissing butt, Harv mumbling something indistinguishable and punctuated with "dear" or "darling," and my mother blushing like a teenager through the whole event. Tonight, the only sound was Sue slurping at her paws. When Mom bit a carrot, it echoed.

I tasted a bite of casserole and, almost against my will, admitted, "This is really good." And I wasn't just feeling obligated. As a tuna connoisseur, I could say this with a fair amount of expertise. "What's that funny flavor?"

"Maybe the roasted cashews?"

"Cashews?" This was shocking. My recipe never mentioned cashews.

"Or else the mandarin oranges . . ."

"Oranges?"

"Chow mein noodles?"

"Chow? Maine? Noodles?" I blinked. After so many years of making casseroles, accepting the concept of combining tuna and oranges was like rejecting my entire belief system. I took another bite, feeling a pang of guilt when I thought of my own recipe sitting naively at home, featuring ingredients more along the lines of: potato chips (crushed).

Chewing, I said, "I've never heard of chow mein noodles in a tuna casserole."

And instead of correcting my tuna ignorance and/or table manners, Mom said: "If you want, I can give you the recipe."

It was surreal. An hour ago, I was the "don't even think about sitting with me" chick in black clothes with no cuticles scowling on the outbound train. Now I was a woman who came to visit with her mother, who swapped casserole recipes and kindnesses.

Then Mom set her fork down, too carefully: obviously a prelude to the "talk." I felt myself tense up all over again. In the midst of the scandalous tuna-and-fruit episode, I'd almost managed to forget the lingering possibility of Lou being back in our lives. Thirty minutes ago, I'd been ready for this news. I had wanted it, depended on it. Now, I wasn't so sure. I needed just a few minutes more of not knowing. Maybe a little more recipe swapping. We were doing strangely well with the recipe swapping.

Give me meatloaf!

Pork chops!

Shepherd's pie!

"Well," Mom began, over the shouts of poultry clamoring in my ears, "you already know there's something I wanted to talk to you about." Her voice was strangely toneless, as if she'd rehearsed this speech before. I fixed my eyes on the soupy vat of creamed corn.

"This isn't easy for me to say, so I'm just going to say it." I glanced up to see her mouth silently open, close, and open again, like a fish gulping for water. "I've been seeing a therapist."

Like a cartoon, her lips clamped shut and her eyes bulged wide, as if recoiling from the impact of letting the words loose. I didn't know what to say. Honestly, for the last two hours, I'd been so prepared for the Lou announcement that this news struck me as relatively harmless.

"That's it?" I blurted.

This was not the wisest move. When Mom looked hurt, I quickly amended: "I mean, who is he? This therapist?"

"It's a she," Mom replied, toying with the edges of her linen napkin. "Her name is Lola."

By some act of God, I managed to keep my mouth shut as Kinks lyrics threatened to eat me alive.

"She has an office downtown, near Broad and Walnut . . . you know, where we used to see *The Nutcracker?*" She brushed a hand in front of her face, flicking the thought away like a hair that had strayed out of line. "What am I saying, of course you know—that's your neck of the woods now, isn't it?" She laughed a loud, shaky laugh, then abruptly sobered up. "Anyway. That's where Lola's office is. I've been seeing her for about ten years."

Whoa there. Ten years? This information was more unsettling. Not the concept of therapy itself. Therapy itself I could handle—this was the year 2000, the age of *Frasier* and *Good Will Hunting*, besides which I'd been considering myself Hannah's unofficial patient for about fifteen years—it was the combination of therapy and my mother. There just couldn't be a therapist in my mother's life. I *knew* my mother's life. I had her down to a science. She was the woman who got her roots done by a girl named Lorelei the first Wednesday of every month. She fretted over Harv's cholesterol levels. She got excited about things like self-cleaning ovens and save-a-step lasagnas. This was not a woman who had been seeing a Center City therapist for the past ten years. Besides, ten years ago, I was living in this house. I spent every summer here during college. The possibility that my mother had been carrying on any sort of private life under my nose—much less seeing a therapist, much less in Center City, much less for *ten years*—was simply not realistic.

Mom cleared her throat. "Lola thinks it would be a good idea if we talked about this."

"We?"

"She thinks it might be good for us."

"What does Lola know about us?"

"Well, I talk to her, Eliza. That's why people go to therapists. I tell her things."

"What things?"

Mom raised her shoulders, then froze them midshrug. "Things going on in my life." The shoulders huddled by her head like earmuffs. "Things that are important to me. And you, believe it or not, are one of them."

"Believe it or not"? Who was this woman? Since when did she do sarcasm? My heart started thudding in my temples. I wanted my old mom back. The one who snapped and ridiculed and nitpicked. The one who never failed to demand where I was going and who I was going with and what I was piercing when I got there. Hearing her talk about her relationship with this Lola person made me feel, not for the first time in my life, abandoned.

"I know this must be a lot to take in at once," Mom said, a line surely prepped in advance by the all-knowing Lola. "So if there's anything you want to ask me . . ."

Yeah, there might be a thing or two. Like: why did you see this Lola behind my back? Does "she look like a woman and talk like a man"? What kinds of things did you tell her about me? Where's the part where you say my father's back in town and can't wait to see me? And who the hell ever heard of putting mandarin oranges in a tuna casserole?

But all that came out was: "Why did you start going?"

Mom pushed her plate forward and knotted her hands on the table. They were clenched so tightly the knuckles looked like they were about to leap through her skin. "It was when I first met Harv. He's the one who encouraged me to see someone."

First the concept of citrus tuna, then the therapist named for a Kinks song. Now I was supposed to believe Harv was a sensitive, quiche-eating '90s guy? The only subjects I'd ever heard transpire between Mom and Harv were concrete things, household things, things that needed either fixing or eating: the leaking radiator, clogging sink drain, leftover chop suey in the fridge. Was no one in my life who they seemed to be?

"Things were difficult for me then," Mom admitted. At this, her hands sprang apart and began fussing needlessly with the sweating casserole lid. "After your father left, raising you girls alone"—her hands flitted to the serving spoon quietly drowning in the corn—"and talking to Harv let me open up about some things." She rescued the spoon and deposited it, dripping, on a trivet shaped like a cow. "Things I didn't even know I was feeling."

"Things about me?"

"Some of them." She glanced at me and I looked quickly away, my eyes landing on one of those smug cantaloupe bastards. I wanted to punch him in the jaw. "I was always worried I was a bad mother. Nothing I ever did seemed right. I didn't feel like I was doing a good job with you two. Especially you."

At this point my ears had started ringing, like I was trapped inside a giant seashell. My mouth was dry. My fingertips were inexplicably numb. This wasn't the ending I had planned on. It was never supposed to be about *my* mother. It was supposed to be about the other mothers, the rock stars' mothers, the ones who fussed and ferreted and crashed soph hops. The ones who demystified their sons with a pinch on the cheek or a plate of cheese or an embarrassing old home video. The ones who never failed to expose their children for what they really were.

"Why are you telling me this now?"

Mom looked at her plate, picked up her fork, tidily speared a pea, then quipped: "I heard you haven't been going to work."

All at once my timid voice was buoyed by a wave of outrage. "Is there anyone out there who *doesn't* know every detail of my private life?"

Mom gave me a sorry shrug, as if to say, probably not.

"Who told you?"

"It doesn't matter who—"

"It does matter! It matters to me!"

Mom sighed, but it wasn't her usual exasperated-mother-from-a-'50s-sitcom sigh. This sigh was thin, tired. Real. She laid her forked pea on the rim of her plate. "Andrew called," she said, and by the preteen blush climbing her cheeks I knew it had to be true. "Last night, after he got back from your apartment. He's just worried about you, that's all."

I guess I couldn't blame him for that. Nothing Andrew had seen at my apartment—my unwashed clothes, my all-cookie diet, my declining taste in TV, not to mention my unprovoked sexual assault—was particularly confidence inspiring.

"And so am I," Mom added. "All I could think of last

281

night, all night long, was the time in my life when I started to—"

I cringed.

"—'shut down,' was how Andrew put it. Years ago, after your father left, I could barely leave the house. You must remember that."

"Kind of," I murmured, though I remembered every glazed look and canned sitcom and thawed dinner care of Chef Boyardee, every night I crept down the hall to peek into my mother's room and make sure she was still there.

"When I think about those years . . ." Mom drew a shaky breath, but her voice remained amazingly steady. "There are lots of things I regret. But my biggest regret is that I never taught you girls how to face reality. Not to avoid it, like I did."

It was probably the most painfully honest and emotionally healthy moment that had ever passed between us. Naturally, I panicked and regressed: sibling rivalry.

"So does Camilla know?" I pounced. "About Lola?"

Mom shook her head. For some reason, being the first to know—in effect, the first to be worrisome enough to *require* knowing—gave me a twisted sense of pride. "I'll tell her soon, though," Mom said. "To be honest, I wish I'd done it long ago."

I felt a prickle of envy. There was only room for one worrisome daughter in this family and, historically, it had been me.

"Sometimes I think Camilla takes after me, that she doesn't face her life either." As she spoke, Mom folded her napkin into smaller and smaller triangles. "Not that she doesn't stay active. I know she throws herself into her job and her marriage and her classes . . . what are they? Origami?" Apparently, the technical term for her neurotic napkin folding had managed to escape her. "She's always kept busy like that. I just wonder if she ever stops to ask herself if she's happy doing it."

She let the napkin go limp on the table and stared at it, as if expecting the linen to stand and speak.

"But Eliza, on the other hand." Her voice sounded suddenly light, detached, as if musing out loud to an empty room. She began to smile a little, and looked nostalgic, as if remembering someone we both used to know. "Eliza always knew just what she wanted. Even when she was a little girl. She was always so independent . . . more like her father."

I didn't speak. I barely breathed, afraid if I made any sudden moves she would snap out of it and start spewing tips for broiling chicken or keeping lipstick from bleeding out of the lines. Even though, somehow, right now, I knew she wouldn't.

"Lola thinks it's part of the reason I was always harder on her," Mom went on, looking at a spot somewhere over my shoulder, as I floated in the third person. "I never had what she did, that ability to think for myself. And I think being around it made me insecure."

She looked at me. "You're different from me, Eliza," she said. "You're strong."

I'm not strong, I felt like crying. *I'm nervous. I'm critical. I kill relationships before they begin. I'm picky and unrealistic and frightened of feeling pain, of feeling love, of feeling anything.* "I'm not," I whispered, but I'm not sure she heard.

Mom sniffled, pressed a corner of her napkin to each eye,

and blinked rapidly, as if to realign her face. When she stopped, her expression was soft and vaguely amused. "Remember the mothers on the TV shows we used to watch, Eliza? The ones who always had the perfect advice to give their kids in the last five minutes?"

I nodded. I remembered.

"I guess all I can tell you is what I wish I'd done different." She smiled a faint, apologetic smile. "Don't be like I was. Don't spend your life afraid of living it."

After dinner, while Mom scrubbed down the kitchen (because some things will never change) I went upstairs to my old room. I hadn't been in my room—much less called it "my room"—for nearly three years, ever since Mom had decided to use it to store Harv's exercise equipment. At the time, I was convinced the room would become immediately and irrevocably Harved: brown, warm, smelling of sweat and beef. As it turned out, except for the Lifecycle tucked almost endearingly in the far corner, my room looked unchanged.

My old dresser was still there, my old bed. The ceiling remained the angst-ridden gray-black color I'd insisted on painting it during my Morrissey period. I spotted a few torn poster corners and yellowed bits of Scotch tape still clinging to the walls, from the long-ago night I'd purged my life of Jack Wagner. When I opened the closet, I found a stack of cardboard boxes. Luckily, my mother can't throw anything away, either.

I dug into the first dust-filmed box and pawed through a legacy of humiliation. Old diaries. *Teen Beats.* Yearbooks.

Transformations magazines. My sticker book. A mix tape I'd regrettably labeled "Red Hot High School Hits!" Unfinished letters that began "Dear Z . . ." I made a mental note to label that box "Do Not Open Even After I'm Dead" and tore into the next one, a musty clump of jeans in various shades of black, with strategic patches and rips and fades.

It was in the third box that I found what I was hunting for: the T-shirts. Most were either black or tie-dyed. I spotted one Coca-Cola rugby and one "Junior Science Champs 1988" courtesy of Eric Sommes (and that is absolutely his final mention). Crumpled at the bottom of the box, probably tossed there in the heat of heartbreak, I spotted him: Jack Wagner.

It was hard to believe, but the T-shirt was even more absurd than I remembered. After more than a decade apart, I could see it for what it really was: an acrylic blond man with a bare triangle of chest, a sultry smile, and a name in glitter. The fact that I was once a person who could have a) looked this cheesy, b) left the house looking this cheesy, and c) still thought I was the coolest person alive made me feel simultaneously appalled, fascinated, and a little wistful.

I dug down to the bottom of the box, pulled the T-shirt out, and tossed my tank top on the bed. I squeezed Jack over my head, forcing my arms into the tight armholes, and confronted the mirror on the back of my closet door. The shirt was much too small. The decal was flaking off. The haircut on it was hilariously outdated. No part of the ensemble had seen a washing machine since 1984.

And yet, seeing my reflection, I found something I'd lost.

Not the shirt itself, or the rock star on it, or any of the musicians I'd dumped for their haircuts or cummerbunds or childhoods. It wasn't the men I could have been dating instead. It wasn't my father. I had lost the kind of love that once let me wear a T-shirt this absurd in the first place. The kind of love that was unashamed, honest. The kind that knew no fear. The kind of love that would kiss a mother, thank her, and wear this glittery rockin' cotton blend all the way back home.

getting over jack wagner

SIDE A

"Cool Rock Boy"
— Juliana Hatfield
"Everyday I Write the
Book" — Elvis Costello
"Sick of Myself"
— Matthew Sweet
"Kiss Off"
— Violent Femmes
"How to Disappear
Completely" — Radiohead

SIDE B

"All I Need"
— Jack Wagner
"I Love Rock-n-Roll"
— Joan Jett & the
Blackhearts
"Slave to Love"
— Bryan Ferry
"Common Disaster"
— Cowboy Junkies
"Here's Where the Story
Ends" — The Sundays

up close and personal
with the author

TRUTH: HAVE YOU DATED LOTS OF "ROCK STARS"?

I was always inexplicably drawn to musicians, ever since an early infatuation with REO Speedwagon's "Can't Fight this Feeling." (My cousin was the serious Jack Wagner fan; she has his autograph in a frame.) I wasn't as committed or as exclusive as Eliza, but I have to admit—and I have no excuse for this—I was a sucker for earrings, stubble, black T-shirts. After college, I had a mild run of the prerequisite, early-twentysomething rock-star boyfriends: a drummer, a guitarist, a "townie" in a band, a guy with a brow ring who blasted a lot of Fugees. Lately, though, there's been no common thread among the people I've dated, unless you count a vague concern about ending up in the next book.

DATING HISTORY ASIDE, HOW AUTOBIOGRAPHICAL IS ELIZA?

Despite our names being only two letters different (which, oddly, I only noticed after the book was finished) I see us as similar but not the same. Various details of my life show up, reshaped, in hers: my stint in the high school band (concert, not marching), a job ghost-writing exotic travel articles, my cat Leroy. We possess some of the same personal qualities, but—like many things in fiction, including the rock stars—they have their roots in real life and are then exaggerated, intensified, taken to the extreme.

HOW DID THE IDEA FOR THE BOOK COME ABOUT?

In graduate school I wrote a story called "Deep" about a young woman who flip-flopped between dating "bankers" (i.e., safe and boring) and "rock stars" (i.e., passionate and deep). I was twenty-three, and pretty sure that all "legitimate" fiction should be heavy and serious and full of angst. Having fun with the story felt a little bit like cheating; I was worried about how my class would react. The response to the story was heated, hilarious, and surprising. Women identified with it; some men were offended. It became a small-scale gender war—a line about a "banker" who "cut bagels before he freezes them" had people literally yelling.

WHAT IN PARTICULAR SURPRISED YOU ABOUT THE CLASS'S RESPONSE?

Some people reacted to the stereotypes, which didn't surprise me much. The characters *were* stereotypes. They were supposed to be stereotypes. Eliza lives in a world of TV characters and song lyrics. What surprised me more was how many women identified personally with the angst-filled, brooding musician thing. Now, though, I've come to expect it. It's amazing how many women—women with husbands and mortgages and four kids—have a "rock star" kicking around in their past. At first, when they hear "rock star," they don't relate. But when they hear the amended definition—"By 'rock star,' I mean a guy in a local band who practices drums in his mother's basement"?—they say, "Oh, I have one of those."

WHAT MADE YOU DECIDE TO TURN THE STORY INTO A NOVEL?

More than two years after I wrote the story, it was still lingering. I found myself jotting down notes like: "Rocker v. musician" and "Milli Vanilli?" and "Older rock stars—facial hair." Meanwhile, certain ideas and characters kept surfacing in other writings: women with short-lived relationships, commitment issues, perfection issues, reality/fantasy issues, herbal best friends, weaknesses for men with guitars. I felt like I needed to give these issues more room or they might stalk my fiction forever. Around that same time, the original story was published in *Salmagundi* magazine, and revisiting it reminded me how much fun it was to write. Most of my writing, then and now, is more "serious" fiction, but I realized I was wrong in thinking fiction is less legitimate if it makes you laugh.

WAS IT EASIER TO WRITE SOMETHING FUNNY?

Not easier. Along the way, there were moments of amusement and fun nostalgia—recalling obscure Wham! songs or grilling friends about the fluorescent shorts they wore in junior high—that aren't usually a part of the writing process. They felt like unexpected job perks. On the other hand, I think what's hard about funny is that you don't want the story to be just funny. You want there to be substance to it, a layer of seriousness underneath, and it was hard to find and maintain that seriousness without losing the humor.

WERE YOU INFLUENCED BY, OR WORRIED BY, THE WAVE OF HUMOROUS FICTION PUBLISHED BY YOUNG WOMEN IN THE PAST FEW YEARS?

Obviously, there are lots of books out there about funny, twentysomething women dealing with funny, twentysomething issues. I've read and liked a lot of them, but I've also felt a little gypped. Sometimes, after spending 200 pages really identifying with the main character, the perfect guy comes strolling into the picture and the ending feels unrealistic. At first, I tried various takes on the perfect-guy-strolling-into-the-picture ending too. But they were feeling forced, and I was getting increasingly angry. I didn't want to see Eliza compromised in the end, or requiring a boyfriend to be happy. Though *she* might have thought her book was about finding a rock star, ultimately it was never really about that. I wanted her to be a character whose sense of self-worth wasn't defined by dates or boyfriends or low-carb diets, whose story doesn't end with the perfect boyfriend but leaves the reader feeling hopeful anyway.

Like what you just read? Then don't miss these other great books from Downtown Press!

IRISH GIRLS ABOUT TOWN
Maeve Binchy, Marian Keyes, Cathy Kelly, et al.
(available February 2003)

THE MAN I SHOULD HAVE MARRIED
Pamela Redmond Satran
(available March 2003)

GETTING OVER JACK WAGNER
Elise Juska
(available April 2003)

THE SONG READER
Lisa Tucker
(available May 2003)

THE HEAT SEEKERS
Zane
(available May 2003)